LAUREN GREENE

Fight for Her

Palm Cove Book 2

Autumn
Ink
Press

For Keesa, the Mia to my Kendahl. Love you bestie.

Content Warning

Dear Readers,

Fight For Her can be read as a standalone romance but I'd recommend reading Palm Cove book 1, *Fight For It* to get the full picture of our Krav family. *Fight for Her* contains consensual sexual activity and explicit language as well as depictions of panic attacks and anxiety, flashbacks to childhood abuse, and alcoholism. Please read with care.

-Lauren

Kendahl's Playlist

Question...?-Taylor Swift

Fine- Kyle Hume

Sex, Drugs, Etc.-Beach Weather

Stop Draggin' My Heart Around-Stevie Nicks

You're So Vain- Carly Simon

I Wanna Be Yours- Arctic Monkeys

Here With Me-d4vd

Bejeweled-Taylor Swift

Dog Days Are Over-Florence + The Machine

Dreams-Fleetwood Mac

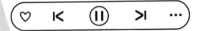

Coby's Playlist

love song-YUNGBLUD

Sweet Tooth- Cavetown

I Miss You-Incubus

I Want You To Want Me-Letters To Cleo

Love Is a Battlefield-The Amity Affliction

Just Pretend-Bad Omens

Even When I'm Not With You-Pierce The Veil

Everlong-Foo Fighters

golden hour- JVKE

Lucky People-Waterparks

Chapter 1

Kendahl

SOMEONE WISE ONCE TOLD me that men were like drinks. It took a lot of sampling to find your favorite one and getting drunk was inevitable. Once you'd find a favorite, you could never count on it to taste the same again. The deluxe frozen cocktail complete with a cherry garnish speared on a cute umbrella would get watered down over time until eventually, it tasted like Kool-Aid with a shot of vodka thrown in. And sometimes when you least expected it, your favorite drink would disappear off the menu entirely.

Did I say it was a wise person? It was actually from the mind of my eccentric alcoholic mother.

It doesn't change the fact that she was right. I'd done years of sampling in different locations and all I had to show for it was a hangover from hell.

So there I was, attempting to cure the mother of all hangovers with a little hair of the dog, otherwise known as a blind date. My left eye twitched again, which was an annoyance I tried to chalk up to too much caffeine rather than the stress induced reaction it was. Time moved entirely too slowly like some higher powered being calling the shots up in their cloud castle just had to show their sense of humor at that very moment.

Sitting across from me, my date was painstakingly telling me about his ex-wife for the third time that night. It had started as a casual name drop. By the time our drinks came, I knew everything but her blood type and social security number. Yes, I was exaggerating a teeny amount, but honestly, not that much.

He wasn't a bad looking guy with his thick head of dark hair and chiseled jawline. His front teeth were a bit crooked and his brown eyes looked as though they were pulled toward his nose with an invisible string. They were only a few millimeters too close but enough that I noticed they were off.

When my mom's friend, Sally, just had to set me up with her nephew, I should have done the logical thing and ran for the hills. But Sally was a better saleswoman than most, as she delivered her thesis with gusto on why her nephew, Billy, was the greatest man to have ever lived. By the end of the hour-long conversation, I agreed to one date despite my mother sitting at the table rolling her eyes at Sally and scoffing. My mother never believed in monogamy.

I'd be lying if I said I hadn't been somewhat eager to be asked out. The past few months had put me through the ringer emotionally, and I needed a night out, one night to help me feel alive, young, and free. But after everything I'd been through, I wasn't into random guys from dating apps even with my newly acquired Krav Maga skills. So set ups from women in their fifties, with questionable dating habits themselves, was my best option.

Billy's palm slithered between the breadbasket and our glasses of merlot, reminding me of a snake creeping toward its prey. My twitching eye followed its path straight to its intended target—my hand, which I inched closer to the edge of the white clothed table.

I wasn't quick enough. He grasped my hand, covered it with both of his, and squeezed. Oh God, his palms were sweaty. This was way too much physical contact for me. Did unwanted hand holding warrant a knee strike? Maybe a light chokehold? I'd let those ideas simmer on the back burner.

Billy cleared his throat. "I can see us going the distance, Kendahl. After everything Sally told me about you, I was already smitten. I've been so lonely since my divorce."

Smitten, what guy uses that word?

"I know I'm coming on strong." He let out an awkward chuckle while I struggled to keep my grimace at bay. "But I really want to take things to the next level. What do you think?"

Was he talking about sex? No, thank you, was what I thought. I knew a stage five clinger when I saw one, and Billy was stage one hundred. One taste of intimacy and I'd need to leave the country to escape him. Even if I was interested in dating him, he was clearly still hung up on his wife.

Nope.

No matter how much I craved attention, Billy would not be that guy. I pried my hand away from his grip and took a tentative sip of wine. There had to be a way to let him down easy. As his hands slunk back to his lap, his eyes grew ten sizes. Mia used the same look on me all the time to get her way. They reminded me of the puppies I took care of at the animal shelter when I volunteered as a teen. Those stinkers always knew how to get me into their pen with treats and toys.

I forced my gaze onto the breadbasket, then my wineglass. Finally, I searched the area for our server.

Please, someone, anyone, come interrupt us.

When nobody came to my rescue, I steeled myself. "Listen, Billy ... I think you're a nice guy." His wide eyes drooped like a cartoon hound-dog. "I'm not looking for anything serious right now. I'm sorry if you got the wrong idea." Not anything serious with you, was what I really meant.

What the hell had Sally told him about me?

"It's my looks, isn't it? Why would I think a bombshell like you would be interested in me?" The hound-dog eyes searched my face while his shoulders sagged.

I coughed. "No, that's not it. You're a good-looking guy, Billy. Someone out there would be lucky to have you." *Someone who didn't mind a guy who talked about his ex nonstop.*

"I should probably get going, but thank you so much for dinner. This was really nice." I forced my lips into a cheery grin. It probably came off as the type of smile you'd make when you pass someone on your way out of a public bathroom. You're going one way and they're going the other, so you kind of shimmy out of the way and smile politely. It was awkward and cringe all rolled into one.

"Well, I guess if this isn't going anywhere, and I'm not even going to get laid, then you can pay your half of the check." Billy grabbed his wineglass and downed the rest of its contents in one gulp and then signaled the server to bring the check with that obnoxious pen to paper gesture.

If I had liquid in my mouth, I would have spit it out across the room. Who was this guy? And what had he done with the Billy I sat across from for the past hour and a half?

I grabbed my purse and pushed up out of my chair. "Okay. Rude." I dug out some cash and dropped it in the middle of the table before collecting myself. I wasn't going to let him get the last word.

"That should cover my meal. And by the way, maybe if you led with wanting to get laid," I leaned in, until my face was an inch from his and pushed my tits together, "and not cried about your ex the whole night, you could have had some fun with these. Goodbye, Billy."

I turned on my heel and left, not waiting for a response. He needed some therapy, or a life coach, or advice that wasn't from his aunt Sally.

As I left the restaurant and the cool night breeze hit my face, I felt instantly better. Ocean air should be bottled and sold as an antidepressant. If anything, this date would provide me and Mia with a good laugh. I had promised I would call her as soon as I got home. She was such a mother hen. I'd bet anything she was looking at her phone every five minutes waiting for a text or call from me. Shawn was probably stuffing her with snacks and talking her down from getting in her car and driving to the restaurant.

I headed toward my car. As soon as I was seated, I shot Mia a text to let her know the date was finished. I couldn't wait to get home and into pajamas.

Mia: *Girl! Finally! I've been checking my phone every few minutes since 8. How'd it go?!*

I laughed. I knew her so well. Twirling a strand of hair around my finger, I thought about a clever response.

Me: *I wanted a cosmo and got a Boone's farm that had been left open for 2 days after a frat party.*

Mia: *Oh no...you haven't used the drink analogy in a while. Details?!*

Me: *I'll call you when I get home. Gotta get out of these heels.*

Mia: *Pleaseeee do!*

I narrowly avoided a conversation with my downstairs neighbor Mr. Fry and escaped into my apartment door. Heaving a sigh of relief, I flung my bra and heels onto the floor in three seconds flat. Sometimes the best part of going out was getting back home afterward and shucking off my outfit.

Normally socializing energized me. I was a true extrovert and thrived on interesting conversation and meeting new people. I was the kid in school who would burst with excitement when the teacher announced a group project. It gave me a break from the monotony of sitting alone at a desk, taking notes, and reading silently.

But lately, I didn't know. Something inside me had shifted. Ben cheated on me, my first time back on the dating scene ended in a near assault, then I had opened myself up to Coby. I didn't even know what to call what we were. The term dating didn't feel right.

We'd texted a bunch, and some of the conversations had had me reaching for my favorite toy afterward. There had been moments at the gym with lingering touches and heated glances. Plus so many hot make-out sessions after our couple of dates. It was a miracle I hadn't thrown him into my bed and kept him there for days. I came close but a part of me was still hurting from Ben. That pain and rejection kept me from sharing my body so easily. Coby respected my boundaries, even if he made it hard some of those nights for me to keep my resolve intact.

My skin flushed thinking about his dirty mouth and how well he'd use it. *"Fuck Kendahl, your lips taste so sweet. Imagining what your pussy tastes like is driving me wild."* He'd savor my lips, brushing his tongue over them, before licking the beauty mark above my cupid's bow.

Maybe we had been dating.

At the time, I wasn't ready to call it that. He'd set clear boundaries also. He didn't do serious. It was the perfect way for me to dip my feet back into the water. And now here I am, happy I didn't let myself get swept up in him.

As promised, I clicked on Mia's video call icon while flitting around getting comfortable. I desperately wanted to take off my makeup and apply a mask while drinking a bedtime glass of wine. Mia answered on the second ring. She looked cute lounging on her bed. Her head of curls rivaled Mufasa's mane after being released from her usual messy bun.

"Hey, Mi. I'm home and safe. You can stop holding your breath now." I teased, but there was some truth to my jest. Neither of us has been the same since my close call with that guy a few months ago. There were still moments when I closed my eyes and I could hear his voice in my ear saying, *"You're a filthy whore, aren't you?"* and still feel his fingertips biting into my thigh hard enough that I cried out. I knew Mia held on to guilt for letting me leave the bar with him.

"Haha, I'm not that bad. I was breathing without a paper bag the entire night. Thank you very much. I only stalked your location three times from my phone, and that's a personal best for me."

I shook my head as I grabbed a makeup removing wipe from my crowded bathroom countertop. "I'm glad you didn't succumb to paper bag breathing. Regardless, I'm done with dating. That guy, Billy. I don't even have words."

"I'm sorry, love. I didn't have high hopes since he was a setup from your mom."

"True." I snorted and wiped around my eyes to remove my stubborn mascara while I gave Mia the rundown of my date.

"I don't know what's going on lately. I can't connect with people like I normally do. I feel like I'm turning into you." Mia's eyes narrowed. "Not in a bad way. Just that going out and meeting people seems to drain me lately. I literally dream of coming home and putting on pjs all day. It's weird is all."

Mia chewed her lip, and I caught a peek of a furry blond head in the corner of her camera.

"Remy, come lie down." She scratched Shawn's golden retriever, and he plopped next to her. "Sorry, he's my little shadow these days. Maybe you just need to find your spark again. You've had a rough few months. Oooh! Let's have a girls' night—me, you, and Livvy. We can make vision boards, drink rosé, eat too much cheese, and watch a movie. We can talk about everything with you. It's been too long."

I propped my phone against the bathroom mirror and smeared black goo all over my face. The cooling sensation felt incredible.

Usually, I'd love that idea. Maybe not a movie. More often than not, Mia and I clashed in our movie tastes. But an involuntarily groan escaped my lips. "Sorry, I think I'm just cranky right now. That sounds fun. Let's do it soon, okay?"

Soon meant at an undisclosed time, which may or may not ever happen. Mia's face fell and her brows drew together.

"Ken, I can tell you're blowing me off. Let's talk about it. You know you can tell me anything. What would make you happy today?"

I avoided her gaze, focusing instead on tidying the random tubes of lipstick strewn on my counter. Even through the phone screen, she could see right through me.

"Honestly, I have no idea. I think that's the issue. I love going to Krav class with you guys, and work is okay, but something's missing, I guess."

I tried not to think about the obnoxiously hot elephant lingering between our silent pauses. Mia knew better than to mention him, but I could see her pursing her bottom lip contemplating voicing his name.

"Is it possible you're still crushing on Coby?"

There it was.

She spoke faster. "I know you said it was nothing, and you weren't that into him, but maybe, deep down, you wanted to see where the relationship would go? Maybe him ending it the way he did bothers you more than you want to believe?" The way she tilted her head to the side, questioning, made her look like Remy's twin.

I shrugged and studied my tube of MAC Ruby Woo like it was the most interesting object in the world.

Thinking about Coby had me feeling confusing things, feelings I flat out refused to feel about him. We didn't even sleep together, and he managed to get under my skin. I felt like someone served me an enchanted apple a la Snow White. One bite and I was a goner for Coby. But if I didn't bring him to the front of my mind, then I could keep the enchantments far away.

"I'm not *crushing* on him. I'm *pissed* at him. There's a difference."

"We have no idea why he up and left. There could have been some kind of family emergency, or maybe he was chosen to compete in a Krav competition abroad. I don't know. Stranger things have happened. Don't listen to all the bologna rumors. I'm sure he'll be back soon and then you guys can talk."

I huffed and peeled my mask off. I loved this part. My skin always felt like a baby's bottom afterward, and I got to see all the dead skin and gunk that came out of my pores.

"I don't care why he up and left. I don't care about him. But it would have been nice to have gotten an actual reason when he dumped me. That's all."

Mia sat up and took a sip out of her water bottle. "I'll never understand the minds of men. You weren't the only one that got the vague text. He only told Mark he wasn't going to be around the gym for a while. Without it they'd have formed a search party and called the cops after a few days. I know it's not the same thing, but maybe it can offer some comfort."

I left the bathroom and plopped onto my bed, tucking my legs underneath me. "Whatever. We weren't serious. He made it abundantly clear that he didn't do serious when we started talking. Honestly, after Ben and the bar guy, it was the main reason I even talked to him." That and the fact that he was six feet of hot, muscular man. Finding a man like him in Palm Cove was a rarity.

I thought about Coby's tanned skin with faint lines showing he didn't shy away from the sun. He had perfect bone structure and a smile that could make me skip a breath. He flaunted his stupid smile with his perfect white teeth whenever he could. And don't even get me started on his eyes—hazel gray, like deep pools of water or clouds before a storm. When he studied you, it felt like you were the only person in existence. Those eyes had a life of their own.

"Okay, well it was just a thought." Mia spoke so softly that she made me realize how gruff I probably sounded. "Hopefully, we'll hear from him soon, and maybe that'll put your mind at ease. In the meantime, do some journaling and think about some things that would make you feel like your old self again. Maybe talk with Claudia at work tomorrow too."

I yawned, realizing how tired I was. "Okay, Mi, I'll try. Sorry for being a grump. Love you."

She beamed. "I love you too, grumpiness and all. Get some rest. And tell your mom, the next time you talk to her, no more setups, especially from Sally."

That pulled a laugh out of me. "Number one on my to-do list. Night, Mi."

"Night." She puckered her lips for a quick camera smooch before the screen went blank.

As exhausted as I felt, I had to do my secret nightly ritual before I could settle. Ritual might be the wrong word, truthfully,

I'd only done it in the month since Coby sent me the vaguest of breakup texts and mysteriously disappeared out of Palm Cove.

I pulled up his profile on Facebook and scrolled through his photos and posts, searching for details that may allude to where he was or what he was up to. I knew I was being ridiculous doing this night after night, but seeing his face before I fell asleep made me feel peaceful even with how angry I was at him. Wherever he was, and whatever he was doing, maybe he was thinking of me too?

Chapter 2

Coby

I SWALLOWED THE LAST dregs of beer and wiped my mouth with the back of my hand. The ice-cold beer here at the Cowboy Club, was the only thing keeping me sane the past few weeks. Leaning back on my rickety wooden barstool, I signaled to Pete to bring me another. I wanted to get to the point where I almost forgot that I was back in my shithole of a hometown before sleep took me under.

Looking around this place, it hadn't changed much since I used to sneak in here and finish off my old man's whiskey while trying to cajole him back home for my mama. The entire bar was built, floor to ceiling, with wooden planks. They looked rustic and homey, but nothing held the scent of spilled beer, piss, and vomit like old, warped wood. The tongue and groove flooring was misaligned in spots after years of bar fights and cowboy boot scuffs. If you didn't watch where you were walking, you'd bust your ass on those uneven death traps. Pete couldn't care less though. This bar has been in his family since Verdant Valley was founded and named Lord only knows how many years ago. Hell would freeze over before he changed a thing in here.

I let my eyes run over the multiple stuffed bison heads hanging like prized possessions and the one lonely jukebox that only played songs from 1955. A few old, dejected miners sat around nursing their beers, counting down the minutes until they'd have to go back home to their wives.

My mama drilled into me that only unsavory women came to the Cowboy Club from the time I could listen. It was bullshit; I knew. Even so, I couldn't help but hear my mama's voice as I eyed the curvy redhead who'd been checking me out all night from across the bar. She turned to her friend beside her and laughed under her breath before running her fingers through her hair and taking a slow pull from her beer.

There was no doubt she was unsavory. But what my mama didn't know about me was, unsavory was how I needed them these days, and here in good old small town, USA, the pickings were slim. The women here were either married at eighteen and living the miner's wife lifestyle or just passing through on their way to Yellowstone or Jackson. I didn't blame them. There was absolutely nothing special or exciting about Verdant Valley, Wyoming.

I took a swig of my beer and peeked at Red every few seconds. I couldn't come off as too interested. I knew these types. They wanted the mysterious asshole guys. They were probably from California, or something, on a road trip adventure and wanted to fuck some cowboy who looked like Rip Wheeler from that stupid-ass show *Yellowstone*. That wasn't me. Although, being back up here in the mountains made me grow my beard out again.

I'd probably shave it off once I went back to Florida.

As I finished my beer, I decided it was now or never. Any more to drink and my dick might not do what I wanted it to do. I pushed off the stool, which caused a shrill squeal to cut through the chatter of the bar. Red turned and looked my way. I tipped my chin up at her from across the space and dropped a twenty on the bar for Pete.

She turned back to her friend and murmured something too low for me to hear. I knew I had her. Like a fisherman, I had cast my bait and now it was time to reel her in.

I spun on my heel and the sole of my beat-up boots stuck to the floor with each step. Deliberately keeping my gaze cast downward, I made my way to the single bathroom down the dilapidated hallway at the back of the bar.

I leaned against the ancient pedestal sink and tried to avoid focusing on the smell of stale tobacco and piss. For as nasty as the bar was, it wasn't too dirty. I'd been in more disgusting bar bathrooms over the years.

"Three." I counted down the seconds. Red would open the door, be shy at first, then pretend she had no idea I was in here.

"Two." I willed my dick to get ready. *Come on big guy. You've been here a month, and the only action you've seen is my right hand. We got this. You will not think of her.*

"One."

The door swung open, and Red stumbled in. Her eyes widened as she saw me leaning there with my hands in the pockets of my jeans. I knew the act well.

"Oh. I...I didn't realize you were in here." She cleared her throat and waited for me to reply as she slowly pushed the door closed and twisted the lock.

She sauntered closer, which gave me my first close up look at her. She had insane curves. Her waist begged me to wrap my hands around it. So much so that my palms tingled. Her tits spilled out of her tight henley, and her thighs were so thick I could picture them wrapped around my face.

But she wasn't Kendahl. She wore too much makeup. It was caked on like she was trying to hide something, her lipstick too bright for her skin, making her puffed up lips look cartoonish. Her face was perfectly symmetrical, almost too perfect. A face that only a skilled surgeon could create. I got a whiff of her perfume, floral and too strong. My head throbbed.

"Well, since we're both in here, maybe we should get to know each other better." Red raised a flawlessly shaped brow, and I only had a moment to decide what the fuck I wanted.

I had never been picky before. Hell, I'd fucked my way through the Florida coast after my divorce never learning more than a first name and keeping each hook up firmly a no strings attached deal. That's how I liked it, two bodies giving each other pleasure and blocking out any other thoughts. There was only need and desire, plain and simple.

I swallowed the lump in my throat and flashed my smile at her. This smile dropped panties like they were lubed up with oil. "What did you have in mind, beautiful?"

She brought a shot glass to her lips, tilted her head back, and swallowed it in one gulp. I hadn't even noticed she was carrying it. Her tongue darted out to lick a drip of liquor off the corner of her lip. My brain turned off as I watched the movement like it was happening in slow motion. A familiar pang of want hit me square in the chest, and I needed to taste her, to see what she just drank.

"How about I show you?"

She closed the distance between us in one step, and before I could reply, her pillowy lips were on mine. This woman wasted no time. She devoured my mouth, forcing my lips open with her tongue. She'd drank tequila, a strong one at that.

I barely breathed, let alone figured out if this was hot or not. Something was happening in my pants. It didn't take much for that to happen. But I wasn't nearly as excited as I should have been.

I closed my eyes and let my hands guide me. I ran my palms over her tits, which were very fake. No judgment. I loved a good fake set of tits. It fit Red's whole motif to the tee.

As I palmed my way down to her full ass, my thoughts drifted to Kendahl again, and the way her perfect lips moved against mine and how every time we'd break apart for a breath a small moan escaped her lips. I pictured the beauty mark above her cupid's bow and how much I loved to lick it. She'd laugh and call me weird, but her face would light up.

Fuck, fuck, fuck.

Red ground her hips against me and rubbed at my dick through my jeans. "Let's get these off you."

She gave my bottom lip a nibble before moving her head downward. This was not a slow, seductive move south. This was a zero to sixty in one second movement. My zipper was undone and my half-hard cock was yanked out of the opening in my boxer briefs. A cough sputtered out of me because she wasted no time taking my cock into her mouth and sucking... hard.

"Shit," I wheezed on an exhale. This woman had the enthusiasm of a teenager trying to get laid for the first time.

She scraped her teeth against me, and I jolted. She was so warm and wet. I closed my eyes and tried not to think, but to enjoy getting blown. She pulled her mouth off me with a pop and looked up, still gripping my cock with one hand.

"It looks like you're ready now."

Was I?

Red stood up, her full height an inch or two less than mine and unzipped her jeans. "You have a condom, cowboy?"

Her jeans fell to the floor beside us. Of course, I had a condom. I was Coby Barnes. I never left home without them. But here was my out.

I tucked my dick back in to my pants and zipped up before I could change my mind.

"Shit." I ran my hand through my hair and tried to fake a look of dismay. "No, I don't have one. I should go."

Her face fell, but she placed a hand on my chest to steady me. A plan was clearly formulating in her mind.

"I have some back in my hotel room. How about I finish what I started here and then we go back and have some real fun?"

I avoided her gaze by looking up into the flickering light and down at the overused toilet. Anywhere but her face. I had never, ever turned down a blowjob in my life. I was going to hate myself later or give myself a pat on the back. Either way, this situation wasn't easy.

"Look," I started, taking her hand off my chest and bringing it back to the side of her body. "I need—"

Someone pounded on the door, and a loud, slurring voice said, "The hell ya doin' in there? Been waitin' ten minutes already. I'm gon piss myself."

"Oh shit," Red said as she clumsily slid on her jeans and adjusted her top.

Thank you God of drunk hillbillies. I hadn't known how I was going to get out of this.

As soon as I twisted the lock, the door was wrenched open by a middle-aged white dude in a dirty mining uniform. He stumbled in, pushed us to the side, and we barely made it out the door before he started pissing.

That was my moment to escape. "Hey, why don't you go check in with your friend, and I'll meet you outside?"

Red smiled, probably thinking I was a thoughtful guy for remembering she came in with her friend. She nodded, leaned in, and planted a wet kiss on my lips. I knew if I looked in a mirror my mouth would be covered in pink. As soon as she walked toward her friend, I bolted out the door with a quick smirk and nod toward Pete.

I drove down the deserted streets in my rented SUV not knowing if I should be smacking myself or patting my back. Worst of all, I was completely sober from that encounter. My headlights illuminated wooden fences and overgrown grass along the side of the road. It was a warmer than normal fall for Verdant, and the bugs were holding out strong.

Twenty minutes later, I pulled into my childhood home, a squat stick build house built in the seventies. Parked sideways on the lawn's only patch of grass was my asshole brother Clyde's brand-new pickup truck. It was his self-declared pride and joy with a car loan that surely cost most of his monthly income.

Nothing had changed in the fifteen years since I'd left. My piece of shit father hadn't upgraded or fixed a single thing. Between the plumbing issues, boiler that's original to the house, and the leaky roof, it was a miracle the place was still habitable.

I pushed the anger into the pit of my stomach where it mixed with the looming guilt I had for leaving my mama all those years ago.

Clyde hadn't been at the house when I left for the Cowboy Club earlier, so that meant Daisy had locked his sorry drunk ass out for the night again. I hoped he went inside and passed out like he did every couple of days since I'd been back. Our mama didn't need to be woken up by him.

I checked in on her first. She was still sound asleep in her frilly nightgown, curled onto the outer corner of the bed like my father was going to come home from the bar any minute and take up the rest of the space. Old habits die hard.

As I was leaving her bedroom, I knocked my hip against her bureau. "Fuck," the cuss spilled out and I glanced back to find Mama stirring.

"Jed?" she mumbled. "I'm sorry, I fell asleep. I'll warm up your supper." She swung her thin legs to the floor but before she stood I stopped her with a gentle hand on her shoulder.

"Mama, it's Coby. I'm sorry I woke you. I wanted to check on you before I went to bed. It's alright, you can go back to sleep."

"Coby?" she scooted back into bed and covered herself. "I did it again, didn't I? I forgot."

She did and every time it happened my heart broke. "It's okay. Let's get you comfortable, Mama. It's late." I tucked her in tightly, taking in the comforting scent of her cold cream.

Sighing, she took my hand in hers. "Thank you. I thought you'd left. Gone off to find your lady friend, the pretty one from the picture."

"No, I'm here. I was only in town." She nodded and gave my hand a squeeze.

"You should go get her, Son. She's a good one. I can tell."

Why did I show Mama that picture? I smiled, it was hard not to when she looked at me with so much love, and she pressed her fingertip into my dimple. "I don't know. She won't want to see me." She was a woman you held onto, a keeper. I wasn't ready for what she needed.

"I may be old and losing my grip, but I know this. There isn't a woman out there that doesn't want their lover to fight for them. If she's the one, show her."

"Mama, I—"

"Honesty, trust, and love. Be yourself. I know you can do it, Son."

I nodded, not wanting to go deeper into this discussion. None of those things had worked for me in the past, plus I didn't know what I wanted with Kendahl. I kissed Mama's cheek and said goodnight, closing her door behind me.

Breathing a sigh of relief that I was done with our conversation, I got myself ready for another night of sleeping on a musty, lumpy, old couch. I'd have to endure Clyde's grunting snores from the couch beside me. Too bad the only time he showed up here was to crash instead of showing up to help out like a decent person, but I'd learned long ago that decent wasn't in Clyde's vocabulary.

As I rested my head against the new pillow I had bought at the Dollar General being as quiet as I could to not wake the beast, I pulled out my cellphone. If I could, I'd look through Kendahl's

Facebook page and see what she was up to. See if she'd moved on with someone else. The thought of another man's hands on her had me fisting my phone in a death grip.

Mama's speech clearly had my feelings stirring. Maybe I'd work up the nerve to text her and explain myself with something more than the cowardly message I had sent the night I left for Wyoming. But the backward town had no cell service. It was like the whole place was frozen in time. The mountains and the mining companies have continuously blocked towers being built, and Verdant was a town that actively fought technology. Spotty Wi-Fi could be found in a few spots around town, but my father would have rather eaten rusty nails than paid to install it in his home.

I opened my photo app and scrolled to find the one photo I had of Kendahl and me, a wobbly selfie taken swiftly the night I met her at Mark's Krav party. The outside lights on Mark's patio illuminated her blonde hair like it was spun gold. She was tipsy and the gleam in her blue eyes showed it. For weeks I'd studied that photo, memorizing different small details of her face like they held the answers to life's greatest mysteries. My chest ached every night I'd tormented myself, but her face was the only thing that brought me comfort.

Tomorrow would be a rough day. After burying my father, weeks of packing, and fixing the place up, I was finally moving my mother to an assisted living community in Salt Lake City. She didn't give in easily, and my prick of a brother was no help at all, but I had finally won her over when the brochure arrived in the mail. I showed her that the complex had a piano she could use anytime. Hers had broken years ago, and my father never let her get it fixed. Those fingers that taught me to play as a child had itched to tickle the ivories for far too long.

Once she was settled and secure in her new home, I could continue emptying their hovel and list it for sale. I was more than ready to get back to my real home in Palm Cove and put this awful month behind me.

Chapter 3

Kendahl

THE FOLLOWING MORNING CLAUDIA took one look at me as I walked into the office and said, "Edwards." Her all-knowing stare bore into me. She was basically the human version of the Eye of Sauron. "Let me guess. You had a date last night, and it did not go well?"

I blanched and slung my Louis bag behind my desk chair. I loved my Louis almost as much as I loved my friends and family. It was a gift from Claudia for my one-year work-a-versary. She treated me well.

"I think you went into the wrong line of work. You should have been a detective. I could see you running the CIA."

She scoffed. "My talent for reading people is a gift that has gotten me far, my dear. Now come. Let's have coffee and catch up on the weekend." Her accent coming out thick.

She ushered me forward. Her black bob swayed with each step. For a woman in her sixties, Claudia was a minx. She landed twenty somethings frequently. I don't know if it was her charisma or her smoking body, but as soon as I met her, she pulled me in like an invisible gravitational force.

I lifted my chin, trying to channel even a sliver of Claudia's prowess, followed her into her office, and plopped in the chair adjacent to her sleek modern desk.

"I don't even care about the date. It was a blip on the radar of my life. The guy was laughable. He spent the whole date talking about his ex and then as soon as I shot him down, his whole attitude changed."

Claudia shoved me an espresso in a tiny cup. She had a fancy Breville machine in her office. The woman practically lived off espresso. This was probably her third of the morning and it was only nine.

"Typical. My first husband, God rest his soul, tried to pull the 'pity me' card on our first date. I leaned across the table and told him to cut the shit. He listened. End of story."

She was a queen.

"Trust me. My date didn't have the last word," I said.

She shot her espresso like a Miami spring breaker shooting cheap tequila. "Pick your head up, Edwards. No need to pout over a bad date. You have the power of youth, beauty, and brains on your side. Remember, we bow to no man."

Nodding, I sipped my espresso and tried not to wince. I was a caramel macchiato girl. Espresso tasted like mud. "So, boss, anything new going on this week that I need to know about?" A forced smile played at the corner of my lips.

I knew we hadn't signed any new clients in months, so I highly doubted it. My week would likely consist of monitoring a few social media accounts for local businesses and maybe writing up some press releases.

"We have Berry's Vineyard Fall Festival coming up, so I'll need you to push that." She tapped her manicured fingernails on her desk while looking over her paper calendar. She was old-fashioned about using a pen and paper for her scheduling. "Don't give me that look. I know their wine is... not for everyone. But it's not our job to critique it."

Citrus and berry wine was not my thing. I kept my mouth shut and typed notes into my phone planner as she spoke.

"Then it's the dog groomers." She tapped aggressively. "Name please?"

I looked up from my screen. "You mean Spoiled to the Bone?"

Knocking her fist onto the desk like I just gave her winning lottery numbers, she looked back at me. "Yes, them. The grand opening for their second location is next month, and we need to push the rebrand for their new doggie spa and daycare center."

"Okay, I'll take care of it." Another glamorous day in my life.

Then her phone rang, which was my cue to leave. I rose from the plush chair and straightened out my skirt.

Back at my desk, I worked on scanning data and emailing a few local news sources. As I hammered off my usual email boasting about our clients, an idea came to me. Maybe we could connect the groomers' grand opening with a town wide adoption event shortly after. I made a note to talk to Claudia about it. Nothing was better for publicity than a charity event.

By lunchtime, our intern Lee had burst into the office. Their outfit choice made my eyes hurt, but I was used to that by now. Lee had been interning with us for a few months, earning on the job credit for their last year in college. They wore a coordinated outfit; the theme being neon green. It gave an eighties vibe. More power to them to be so fabulous and bold with their fashion choices. They must have done their hair over the weekend too because their choppy wolf cut was sporting some green streaks.

I stood up to stretch my legs. "Hey, Lee. Love the outfit."

They beamed. "Thanks. I was feeling alien-core vibes this morning." They pushed their hair away from their ears to show me a pair of chunky alien head earrings that dangled like pendulums.

"Psychedelic." I smiled naturally for the first time all morning.

Lee stuck their head into Claudia's door. From the corner of my eye I saw Claudia's exasperated look as she took in Lee's outfit. Claudia loved Lee as much as I did even if they drove her crazy.

I went back to my computer screen where I pulled up PRC areers.com and scrolled the listings. I did this a few times a week lately. So many of the companies were located in Los Angeles or New York with celebrities or high-profile companies as their clientele. I clicked on one of the listings at the top.

Stratestar Agency

Hollywood, CA

With over four decades in the business, Stratestar gets PR

Have you ever dreamed of working with top Hollywood celebs? Do you want to take your career to the next level?

We are searching for a PR Specialist with superb communication skills who flourishes in a fast-paced environment. Must be creative, a team player, and above all be able to think outside the box.

Stratestar was famous in the PR world. Their CEO, Victor Moss, had his own reality show a few years ago. I skimmed the rest of the qualifications all of which I had exceeded at this point in my career. For a moment, I let myself dream of that life. Me on a red carpet, palm trees swaying in the balmy California breeze. Camera flashes clicking all around me, like music to my ears. I'd usher a Kardashian sister to their marks as I gave TMZ a confident "no comment" regarding their most recent scandal.

Until Lee made a squeak and uttered, "Oh no" loud enough to pull me out of my reverie.

They had their phone centimeters from their face while their fingers scrolled lightning fast. Calmly, like I was talking someone off a ledge, I approached them.

"Lee? What's wrong?"

It wasn't unusual for Lee to squeak and squeal ten times a day for random reasons. Sometimes it was an adorable puppy video, a news headline about Timothy Chalamet, or a sale at Fringe, their favorite boutique. But the looks on their face made me think it was for none of those reasons.

"Should I get Claudia?" I asked tentatively. Their eyes flashed to mine before they shook their head.

"No, I think I can do damage control."

I didn't wait for them to explain. Prying their phone from their death grip, I scanned the screen. Instagram was open. Everything looked normal.

But, wait? Why was there a photo of their cat, Mr. Kittykins leg up high, grooming himself on Chez Famille's page with the caption: *Wine not? Today's chef's special looks droolworthy. Don't you agree? #provencale #cuisinefrench #chicken #meat*?

The post had hundreds of likes and comments. I could feel ideas ping ponging around in my skull. We had to fix this. Chef Lambert was our pickiest client. He'd get pissed for the most minute of reasons especially since last year when a Yelp reviewer blasted them for serving chicken when they were supposed to get duck. He acted like the review was a personal attack. I didn't know how he managed to keep staff at his place.

"Lee? When did you post this?" I forced my voice to be calm and steady.

"Yesterday afternoon. Claudia sent me a message from Lambert with a photo of some chicken dish. I guess I was tired and accidentally posted Mr. Kittykins instead."

Lee was pacing now. "Should we delete it? It looks like the comments aren't all bad."

I read through quickly. Lee was right, most of them thought the post was hilarious and commented how cute Mr. Kittykins was. There were others though, that said things like "DISGUSTING" or "EW" or "@sugarbaby101 I told you my chicken tasted off when we ate there."

Shit.

We had to pull Claudia in for this. She couldn't be caught off guard when Lambert saw the post. Freaking, Lee. I handed them back the phone and sent them into Claudia's office with a sympathetic look.

A headache throbbed at the base of my skull. As I sat back down, I thought about that job posting and how different an Instagram post gone awry would be in the glitzy world of Hollywood. Without another thought, I opened up the job listing again and sent my most recent resume to the contact there. It was a shot in the dark, but the thrill helped me pull through the rest of the afternoon.

I'd never been so happy to get to Krav class on a Monday evening. After hours of listening to Lambert holler in Claudia's office, the gym was like an oasis. The familiar scent of sweat and Old Spice enveloped me, and I instantly relaxed my shoulders.

I almost didn't come to class. My headache went away, thanks to multiple ibuprofens, but the day depleted my social battery. I used to thrive on solving issues with difficult clients. Claudia told me I had a knack for it. But I'd lost that enthusiasm somewhere.

My classes at Krav Maga on Main had become a well of energy for me these past few months. At first, I only went to placate Mia. But after a few classes, I could see how she got hooked so fast. There was something empowering about punching the crap out of a pad or rolling someone bigger than you.

"I heard from a level two that he has a secret family in the Midwest..." I sighed as I listened in on more Coby gossip. I moved closer to the two women. They stopped their conversation mid-sentence and grimaced at me. I didn't know what was worse, Coby leaving or the rumor mill circulating around the gym. Coby would love to know that all the students were talking about him. I could picture him smirking and saying something cocky like, *"How could I blame them."*

Mia poked her head from around the corner and beamed at me. She was assisting a few level one classes now that she was a level two. Shawn was assisting more too especially now that Coby wasn't around. The way he kept a casual palm on her low back when they stood together in the gym was as cute as it was nauseating.

After giving me a hug, Mia stepped back to appraise me. "Rough day?"

"You could say that." I sighed and rubbed my temple. I pulled my gloves out of my gym bag and slid them on, adjusting the Velcro. "I'm ready to turn off my brain for the next forty-five minutes."

Her lips turned down, and she brought one arm around my shoulders. "Want to get dinner afterward and talk?"

An internal battle formed in my mind. Tiny Kendahl's on my shoulders silently arguing for victory. On one hand, I loved Mia, and she was always great to talk to. But on the other hand, I wasn't ready to voice some of the thoughts going through my mind to her. Not yet. Like the fact that I daydreamed daily about leaving Palm Cove or that, even though it killed me, I couldn't get one particular guy out of my head.

"I think I'm just going to go home and heat up some leftovers. Maybe another night this week?"

I tried to avoid her wide eyes and raised brows. "Sure. Whatever you want, love."

Mark A.K.A. Sifu, formally, came out of his office, patting shoulders with and beaming at his students. "You ready, level one?"

Murmurs spread throughout the other students, and I searched the group for my usual partner, Mia's sister Olivia, but I guess she hadn't made it to class.

After stowing my purse and water in a cubby, I took my place in the crowded room. The crimson walls and dark concrete floors woke me instantly. Those and Mark's booming voice commanding us to do jumping jacks. We warmed up for a good ten minutes, cycling through grueling jump squats, burpees and pushups (I could do maybe three, on my knees. But at least I was trying).

Halfway through the warm-up, Olivia showed up with Alex hobbling behind her on crutches. His clunky leg cast knocked into spare pads along the side of the wall. Poor kid. Being a pre-teen was hard enough without having to lug a heavy cast around. Olivia whispered something in Alex's ear as she gave him his iPad and pointed to a chair in the waiting area.

She shuffled in beside me, catching the tail end of pushups. Mia saw her from the side of the room where she paced, waiting for the meat of the class to begin, and waved. Coby used to take up that same position except instead of pacing, he'd lounge against the wall like he owned the place.

"Glad you're here." I huffed between pushups. "I really didn't want to have to work with anyone else. How's Alex doing?"

She shook her head and pretended to pushup. "He's hanging in there." She glanced in her son's direction. "I told him if he was good during class, I'd let him get some in app purchase on his game when we got home. He's been going stir-crazy not being able to play outside or swim."

"I can imagine. He's been through a lot... a move, a new school, a broken leg. How are you holding up?"

We took a second lying flat on our stomachs and catching our breaths. Olivia sighed and stretched her arms above her head.

"It was a shit show of a day to say the least, but I'm glad I made it here."

Getting back to our feet, I smiled. "Me too. It looks like we both have some emotions to unleash on the pad tonight."

"You got that right."

Forty minutes later, breathless and sweating, Olivia and I collected our stuff and chugged from our water bottles. She checked on Alex, then helped him into the gym area. I patted his back as he went by and gave him a thumbs up but he brushed me off, went straight to his favorite dummy in the corner of the room, punched it, and laughed like a little imp.

After every class finished and the next came in, Mark loved to have everyone sit down as a group and give us some inspirational words. He also talked about any news going on in the coming weeks or ribbed on his assistants. He loved fucking with Coby most of all, but since Coby's been gone, he'd focused his attention on others.

I didn't mind those moments. They really pushed the whole Krav family sentiment. Plus, it gave me a few minutes to get my heart rate back down to a normal level before getting in the car to drive.

The fluorescent lights shone off Mark's bald, gleaming head. "Great job, everyone. I'm loving the progress you're all making on elbow and palm strikes. Remember to move around more. If someone is going to attack you in real life, they're not going to stand there and come at you like a statue. Other than that, Jill is here with some news." He motioned to Jill, who hung out against the wall near Mia. Jill was a single mom who hadn't had it easy especially after she lost everything in a house fire a few months ago. I could still smell the acrid scent of smoke from when I picked Mia up in front of the house that night. Jill looked beautiful standing in front of the room, radiant even. Her normal sallow skin held a glow and she stood up straighter than usual.

"Hey all, I know you're probably ready to get going, so I'll make this short." She motioned her hands to a big guy named Mike, who I'd only spoken to once during a group drill. He stood up, grunting with the effort of it, and cut through the other students toward the front of the room. When he reached Jill, the smile he wore overshadowed anything else about him. They joined hands, and the room quieted.

"Mike and I are getting married." Jill gushed as she held her left hand out. The glittery rock on her finger was far larger than I would have thought. *Go Mike.*

A chorus of congratulations and way to go's echoed from everyone. Mike blushed and kissed Jill's hand. He looked crazy about her. Good for them. If only my jaw would stop clenching when I attempted a smile. "Thanks, everyone. I'm the luckiest bastard in the world."

Mike's voice was deep and gruff much like his outward appearance. Jill cut in. "We're overjoyed to have met here in class. You're all like family to us. Especially because everyone came together to help me and Kayla after the fire. You don't know how much that meant to me."

"To us." Mike added with eyes on Jill and Jill alone.

"We want to invite all of you to our wedding. It's next week-end in the Keys."

I let this information take root. Damn that was soon. Mike worked fast to lock his woman down. I didn't blame them. When you knew it was right, why wait?

Jill went on. "We know it's last minute. Mike's family owns an inn down there, and they had a cancellation, so we jumped on it. We understand if you can't make it, but we hope to see as many of you there as possible."

With full watt smiles on both their faces, they sidled over toward the exit to chat with Mark. "Oh, on your way out, grab an invitation! All the info is on there as well as my email to RSVP. We need to know by Friday of this week if you'll be there."

After saying another round of goodbyes to Mia and Olivia and congratulating Jill with a stiff hug on the way out, I sat back in the seat of my car as my mind reeled. Maybe a little getaway to the Keys was exactly what I needed to recharge and figure out what I wanted to do with my life. Maybe I'd even get a certain someone out of my head completely. Being in Palm Cove with my mother calling me every five minutes and dealing with Lee's mistakes made it difficult to focus on the future. Staring out at the now dark Main Street with its most hopping location being Sal's Pizza, a frozen rum drink on the beach surrounded by awesome people sounded like heaven.

Chapter 4

Coby

MY MAMA STARED VACANTLY out the window as we drove into Salt Lake City. Thinning white hair took over where dark curls once were and lines deep as canyons spread across her forehead. Lines that were a roadmap for the years of worry and grief that she dealt with living with my father.

I almost hadn't believed that my father was dead when Daisy called me. The stubborn son of a bitch I grew up with would have seen death knocking at his doorstep and shoved his boot straight up that cloaked fucker's ass while hollering at him to get off his property.

Mama had been blank and empty ever since I came back. When I'd first walked into the house weeks ago, I had an inkling that she didn't recognize me. After a moment, her vision seemed to clear, and she embraced me, pinching my dimple like she'd always done. Maybe she was in shock? She too must have thought Jed Barnes would remain a crotchety old man until he was well over a hundred.

I stepped out of the car first, taking in the surrounding mountains some of which were already capped with snow. Green grass and full trees of varying colors stood out everywhere I looked, vibrant in a way that Verdant Valley could never be. I walked around to the passenger side and helped her out of the car. My mother's hazel eyes met mine before she looked beyond me.

"That's a lot of green, huh, Mama?" I gestured to a nearby tree with squirrels scurrying up and down, chittering. "You'll even get to enjoy fall colors here. Nice, right?"

She nodded but reached her frail hand on my arm to steady her balance. "It looks lovely."

Caroline Barnes had learned to become a woman of few words after years of marriage to my father. I always wondered if that's why I was so talkative, to make up for all the awkward silences growing up in my home.

We made our way toward the entrance of Breezy Village. Fragrant planters of golden mums and yellow pansies lined the path, fallen leaves crunched underfoot, releasing their crisp scent into the air. After so many weeks of inhaling dust while packing the house in Verdant Valley, my senses seemed to liven up again outside in the fresh air.

Mama shuffled along beside me, quiet and small. Her grip on mine was the only thing that kept me from believing she wasn't a shadow.

Inside, a slim black woman greeted us. Her graying hair was cut short. She wore a navy skirt with a matching jacket, not a wrinkle to be seen. The feature that stood out the most was her chunky macaroni necklace. I'd pin her to be in her fifties, maybe with a couple of grandkids. She had that look about her, like she'd sneak you a ginger snap under the table while your mom wasn't looking.

I reached out to shake her hand. The gentle squeeze she gave me, followed by a soft smile, let me know she was aware of how tough my situation was.

"Welcome to our village Barnes family." She reached out her knobby hand to my mother's and gently squeezed. "I'm Mrs. Thompson, the manager here. We're so very happy to have you."

With a quick glance at my mother, I saw her meeting Mrs. Thompson's eyes and the trepidation she had earlier seemed to lessen.

Mrs. Thompson took us on a brief tour of the main facility, which was aptly named the Village Square. My mother would come here for her main meals and social activities. Staff members dressed in scrubs passed us in the brightly lit hallways and waved or said hello.

With each passing minute, the tightness in my chest receded. I hadn't realized how wound up I'd gotten on the drive. I'd been going through the motions of making sure mama was comfortable, but in doing so, I hadn't stopped to consider how incredibly nerve wracking it was for me to be moving my mother out of state and away from everything she'd known for over forty years.

The sliver of doubt I was holding onto shattered the moment my mother saw the grand piano. The shining white beauty was tucked into a corner of the enormous common room next to a floor to ceiling window. She increased her pace. Her hands visibly shook until she reached it.

I stood back a few feet to watch. Tears formed in the corners of my eyes. And I didn't fucking cry easily. She caressed the smooth lid like she was reuniting with a lost lover. Mrs. Thompson glanced at me and her lips turned up in a bright smile.

"It's been a long time, hasn't it?" She clapped a hand on my shoulder, sensing that I was getting emotional.

I cleared my throat and watched as my mother sat on the gleaming bench like a pro. "Too long. At least twenty years."

I didn't want to share all the details of my childhood with this woman, no matter how motherly she came off. She didn't need to know that my father had slammed the case of our crumbling upright piano when I was thirteen or that he raged at my mother for having the audacity to ask if she could play at the Cowboy Club on the weekends for some extra money. He had always looked at her teaching me and Clyde the piano with a curled lip, spitting that we thought we were better than him with our fancy music.

There she was, Caroline Barnes, finally reunited with her first love, music. I breathed in as deep as I could, willing myself to remember the way my mother's eyes shone, how deftly she stroked those keys, and the melodic tune that came from her fingertips as they glided across the keyboard.

Stars prickled the darkening sky by the time I left Breezy Village. A lovely orderly named Jeanie helped me get Mama unpacked and settled into her studio apartment. We set up framed photos of me and Clyde as boys right near her bed and another one of Clyde and Daisy, posing next to a Christmas tree. It was from when they first moved in together and weren't as dysfunctional.

It surprised me that Mama hadn't packed any photos of my father. But as I looked over at her resting on her new plush sofa with her eyes closed and her breathing slowed, I thought maybe she wasn't as attached to Jed Barnes as she always made me believe. Maybe, deep down, she was happy he was gone.

As I requested, her new home was only a short walk from the main hub. This place was costing me a fortune, but after so many years of my mother not letting me help her, this was the least I could do for her and my own guilt-ridden brain.

A part of me wanted to explore Salt Lake City for the night. I was finally in a town where I didn't know a soul, and I could breathe easy knowing my mama was being cared for. As I drove to my hotel, I passed bars and restaurants with windows lit up and filled with people from all walks of life.

I could go into any one of these places, sit down, enjoy a real drink that wasn't a Coors on tap, and take in the sights—by sights I meant women. I shook my head as I remembered Red. If I couldn't get my shit together with her, then what the hell was I thinking I'd do here?

Instead, I plodded up to my room at the Holiday Inn and ordered a burger and fries on DoorDash. I tried not to beat myself up. Yes, I was pathetic, but I also had a tough day. Fuck, tough weeks really.

I sprawled out on the double bed after eating my grease pit meal. Of course they didn't have any king bedrooms left. My feet hung from the edges, but at least the pillows were plump and didn't smell like old cigarettes.

That was when a thought occurred to me. I was finally out of Verdant, which meant I should have cell service. It had been so many weeks without it that other than pulling it out to look at Kendahl's photo like a stalker, my phone had become no more than a paperweight.

My mother had a landline. I could have reached out to everyone in Palm Cove, but other than keeping my clinic updated and letting Mark know I would be away for a bit, I hadn't had the mental energy for much else. Maybe that made me a selfish prick. I could talk to a wall, but that didn't mean I excelled at real communication. Or so I was told many, many times by Amy before she left me.

I dug my phone out of the luggage at my feet and plugged it in. I ran my hand through my hair and noticed I was grinding my teeth so hard that my jaw ached. Why was I nervous?

Instead of staring at the screen, waiting for enough juice to power it up, I pushed myself up off the creaky bed and paced along the threadbare floral carpeting in the square box of a room.

What if I had no messages? I didn't deserve any from Kendahl, not after the shitty way I had ended things. But maybe she had messaged me? Maybe her lackluster "okay" wasn't all she had to say? Fuck, I was acting like an insecure teenager. I knew why. It was because she was one of a fucking kind, and she had my heart in a vice grip.

On my tenth lap from bed to bathroom and back again, a familiar chirp sounded. My shoulders slumped in relief. Someone cared and wondered if I was still alive. It chirped again... and again.... and again, so many times that I rushed over and clicked the button to silence my phone. It wasn't that late, but I didn't want to wake whoever was next door.

Weeks of messages popped up on my home screen with little bubbles of concern and banners of questions. I scanned them as my eyes searched for one name.

Kendahl: *I thought about your message. I know you weren't looking for anything serious. I guess what I'm saying is... it's fine. But I don't think we can stay friends. It would be too weird.*

Kendahl: *Everyone's worried about you up and leaving. Just let us know you're ok when you get to wherever it is.*

Then a week later.

Kendahl: *I know I said I didn't want to be friends and I don't. Mia's worried since we haven't heard anything from you. Maybe give her or Shawn a call. I hate to see her upset.*

I closed my eyes for a moment and rubbed my palms along the worn comforter. When had they gotten so sweaty?

The next message came about a week after the above one.

Kendahl: *I don't know why you left. It's none of my business. But can you please let someone know you're ok? Not cool to ghost us all. Pretty shitty actually.*

Kendahl: *Ugh! Just... freaking call, text, Facebook. Something.*

Oh boy. She was pissed. I don't know why I found that funny, but I did. I could picture her face getting all red and her twisting her hair around her finger while she jabbed each letter of that message harder than she needed to.

That was the last text from her, and it was sent a week ago. A sinking feeling hit my gut that had nothing to do with the massive burger I just ate. Had she given up on me?

Palm Cove was two hours ahead with the time zones. Shawn would be up. He slept so little it was a miracle he functioned. I ignored the other messages, most from clients or the second physical therapist in my office. He must have been overloaded without me there since he rarely messaged me. I hoped hiring that new PT assistant was at least lightening his workload a little.

Shawn answered on the first ring. "Am I seeing what I think I'm seeing? Coby? Bro, where the hell have you been?"

I let out a small laugh at his use of the word *bro*. Shawn had become, for lack of a better word, nicer since he started dating Mia. We were more like friendly acquaintances before she came along. He was detached like the thought of having a actual friend was too much to handle. Part of that was probably that I was talking to his girl's best friend. He was almost as protective of Kendahl and Olivia as he was of Mia. But he seemed to like me enough, at least he did before I left.

I went back to pacing the length of the room, stopping briefly to look out the window at the parking lot.

"It's me. I'm sorry I didn't tell you I was leaving, man. I knew Mark or..." I hesitated, not wanting to bring her up to him. "Kendahl would fill everyone in."

In the background, I heard Mia asking Shawn who he was talking to. She squealed and from the shuffling sounds, I assumed she'd grabbed the phone from him.

"Coby Barnes, you had me worried sick." I assumed correctly. "Not just me, all of us at the gym. All Mark said was that you couldn't come to class, but then when you weren't answering anyone and not at home or work...and then sending Kendahl that text, not cool. I thought you were better than that."

I slumped against the wall. "Okay, okay. I'm sorry. I had an emergency and had to book it. The town where I've been had no cell service whatsoever." I decided not to comment on the Kendahl part of her tirade or that I purposely didn't reach out.

Her voice softened. "Is everything alright? What's been going on?"

I wavered. I wasn't ready to tell people about my father passing away or that I had to pack up every possession that my parents owned to sell their property and get my mother into a care home. I didn't want to drag Verdant Valley Coby into the life I worked so hard to create in Florida. I let my past go a long time ago, and the more I told these people, people I saw almost every day, the more they'd see that side of me. I'd no longer be perpetual bachelor and physical therapist slash assistant Krav Maga teacher. I'd be Coby from Bumblefuck, USA who grew up with an abusive, alcoholic father, a mother who hid in her own skin, and a younger brother who was on the same path as his dickhead father. I'd get pity, and I didn't need their pity.

I had a hard enough time breaking away from my past by being the first person in my family to attend college. I scraped together pennies to get the hell out of Wyoming, and I met Amy during my residency in California. I thought she was it for me. As much as the idea of monogamy made me sick (look what marriage did for my parents), I knew Amy was the one. Until I made the mistake of bringing her back home with me to meet my family after we eloped. I didn't blame Amy for finding someone better not long after. I wouldn't want to be a Barnes either.

So I wouldn't tell anyone in Palm Cove the real reason I left. They'd forget soon enough anyway once things got back to normal, and I was home.

"Yeah, everything's fine." My stomach churned as the lie slid out of my lips. I brushed my hand through my hair again. "A friend from college had a family emergency and needed me to help out at his clinic. Been doing PT in Wyoming all this time."

Shit. Bad karma stay away. I hated lying to my friends.

Mia made a humming noise. "Oh no, is everything alright? I hope it was nothing too serious."

"Much better. He just got back to town, and I'm getting ready to head back home in a few days." *After I finished tying up loose ends with the house.*

"Hold on." The phone went silent for a second, and I plopped back down on the bed. Suddenly the call switched to FaceTime. I clicked accept and then there were Shawn and Mia's faces. They looked tired. Mia had her signature messy bun and was wearing glasses that I'd never seen, and Shawn's overgrown hair looked like he'd been racking his hands through it.

"Okay, that's better. Now we can both talk to you," she said. I flashed a smile, hoping they didn't see through it to how exhausted I was.

"When did you say you're coming home?" Mia asked, chewing the corner of her lip. I could see now that they were sitting in bed, propped up by a bunch of pillows.

I did a quick mental calculation. Today was Wednesday. If I hustled, I could finish by the weekend but most likely, it would be early next week. I told them as much.

"Do you have to get right back to work? Because Jill and Mike are getting married in the Keys next weekend and everyone is going. It would be awesome if you could come."

The way she said *awesome* with those big eyes of hers was not fair. She should work in sales, not accounting.

"Yeah," Shawn added. "It would be cool if you could come and save me from all this mushy wedding stuff that I know Mia and Kendahl will drag me to."

Kendahl was going? Was I sweating all the sudden? I cleared my throat, forcing a chuckle. "I'll see what I can do. After where I've been, a wedding in the Keys sounds like a hell of a good time."

More squeals pierced my ears along with a howl from Shawn's golden retriever, Remy.

"I'll email you all the details. And you better respond this time." Mia crooked her finger, shaking it at the screen like a schoolteacher. "Oh and..." she hesitated. "I shouldn't be telling you this, but Kendahl has been in sort of a weird mood lately. She's pissed as hell at you, understandably. So under no circumstances are you to get under her skin."

I held my hands up in mock surrender. "I'll respond. I promise."

She narrowed her brows and brought the phone closer to her face. "And Kendahl?"

I had no desire to get under her skin, whatever that meant, but I did want to make things right. Was I the reason she was in a weird mood? I hoped not. I needed to get her out of my system though. Otherwise, I could never go back to how things were before if that was even what I wanted anymore.

"I'll make things right with Kendahl," Smiling brightly at her I added, "promise."

"Good. You know I like you Coby, but Ken is my best friend. Don't make me kick your ass." She passed the phone to Shawn.

"And I won't hold her back." He smirked.

I held my hands up again. "I believe you."

I laid back after the call ended, trying to slow my racing heart. I wanted to go. Hell, I needed a break more than ever. Plus, Jill was a sweetheart. We became friends when I helped her move into her new place after the fire. I'd love to be there to support her. But a wedding? With Kendahl? A romantic, lovey-dovey, magical, beach wedding where the woman who occupied every corner of my mind would be? I knew I wanted to see her to make things right but that was riding on her wanting to talk to me again.

An email from Mia pinged in my mail app, and my heart jumped through my rib cage. I had no choice. I was going to the Florida Keys.

Chapter 5

Kendahl

Florida took my breath away. It was easy to forget how beautiful the scenery was when I spent most of my time in an office. Avoiding Mia and Shawn's love fest in the front seat, I opted to stare out the window of Shawn's truck instead. We were halfway across the seven-mile bridge toward Serenity Key, a part of Florida I'd never explored. Waves crashed against the concrete girders and splashed feet into the air. Boats of all sizes skimmed by in the distance, creating patterns in their wake that I could almost trace through the window. Puffy, pillow-like clouds seemed to reach the horizon, blocking the afternoon sun. It was all so picturesque.

"Look!" Mia pointed at her passenger window. "I think I saw a dolphin jumping."

She sounded like an excited little kid. It made my shriveled heart grow a few sizes like The Grinch when he realized the true meaning of Christmas.

"I think I saw it too." I didn't, but I wanted to see her smile.

Shawn gazed out the window before bringing his attention back to the road. "Those clouds look a little menacing. I hope we don't get shitty weather." He reached his palm out and settled it on Mia's thigh. They were so touchy feely and cute. I wished I brought a barf bag.

Avery piped up from beside me, looking up from her phone. "I checked the weather before we left, and it said something about a storm, but they weren't sure if it was going to blow out to sea." She pushed her sunglasses onto her cropped pink and brown hair and scooted closer to her window.

I stared up at the clouds again. "Let's hope so. Jill and Mike can't have a beach wedding in a storm." *And I couldn't get my poolside drink on either.*

Seabirds swooped and dove catching fish in their beaks. Who would have thought I'd have seen this much nature from a truck window? Feeling relaxed already, I willed myself to keep these images with me so I could conjure them whenever I was stressed.

"Weren't you and Coby planning a trip to the Keys at one point?" Mia asked while she twisted a loose strand of hair around her finger.

I winced at the use of his name.

"I don't know. Maybe? Why are you bringing him up?" *And breaking best friend code in the process.* She glanced at Shawn before looking back out her window.

"No reason. Just making conversation."

We went quiet again, each of us watched the waves out the window until Mia chimed in again. "I wonder how Coby's doing. You haven't heard from him have you, Avery?" Avery removed an earbud from one ear while I clenched my jaw.

"What did you say?" Avery asked. "Sorry, I'm listening to a podcast about the history of this bridge."

"Never mind. Sorry to bother you." She waved her hand and plopped her feet on the dash, tapping her toes to the music.

I knew my best friend better than I knew anyone else, so that meant I knew she only used her high squeaky voice in certain situations. She was either in customer service mode or hiding something, every single time. Mia pulled the visor down to fix her bun, but I caught her eyeing me in the mirror—suspicious as hell. I narrowed my eyes at her letting her know I was on to her. I didn't know what she was up to, but I was paying attention.

After pulling off our exit and driving through the quaint seaside town, we finally pulled up to a huge Queen Anne Victorian style home. The sign that hung above the wide set of steps read Marin Inn and Restaurant in paint worn down by years of sandy wind. The estate was a beautiful shade of Tiffany blue with white shutters and a wraparound porch on its ground floor and upper level. Tall palms stretched up toward the second story and rich green shrubbery lined the walk. It reminded me of a bed and breakfast out of a black-and-white movie.

We parked and got out of the truck, stretching our knotted-up limbs. There seemed to be quite a few vehicles already parked in the small adjacent lot. "This wind is fierce," I called out to Mia as we dragged our suitcases up the path with the ocean breeze blowing our hair in front of our faces.

She looked out past the main road and toward the shore. "Yeah, it's probably because we're so close to the beach." Nodding, I followed them up the creaking steps into the lobby.

"Wow, there's a lot of people in this place. You think they're all here for the wedding?" I asked my group of friends. There had to be at least twenty smushed around the single mahogany desk all clutching garment bags and propping their wheelie suitcases against any random wall space. Buildings this old were not meant to hold this many people in one space at one time. My eyes momentarily met the frantic faced young woman behind the desk, and I knew I had to jump in and help out.

"Mi, can you hold onto my bag?" I didn't wait for a response as I maneuvered my way through the crowd toward the stressed-out concierge.

"Excuse me," I bellowed in my best PR voice. When all eyes turned to me, I continued. "Is everyone here for Jill and Mike's wedding?"

I'd only just arrived, but I didn't see anyone from class, not yet at least. No sign of the bride or groom in this throng either.

A chorus of yeses filled my ears, some sounded more huffed than necessary. I turned toward the employee and noticed her nametag read Bethany. Up close I could see that her dark hair was most defiantly dyed black and the red dots of a missing eyebrow ring were noticeable. She looked to be in her early twenties, and as her wide eyes took me in, she adjusted her posture.

"Hi, Bethany, I'm Kendahl Edwards. Sorry to take over. It looked like you could use a hand. Are you the only one working at the moment?" The line of wedding guests continued to talk among themselves.

Bethany gulped and responded, "Yes, my parents own the inn. I live on the third floor. They were supposed to be here for check-in. Uncle Mike told them guests would be showing up."

I sighed. "Let me help you. I'm sure it can't be too hard right?" Bethany bobbed her head, her eyes still the size of saucers.

She walked me through how to check-in. While they did the majority of the processing via a computer program, the inn still used old-fashioned keys. They were large enough to peek out of a normal sized pocket and each one had a keychain attached with a hand painted sea animal.

"These are cute." I gestured to the rack of keys. At first glance it looked like this place had about thirty rooms, which was bigger than it looked.

She grimaced. "Yeah, that was my mom's idea. She's cheesy like that. Guests seem to like it though."

With Bethany manning the computer and me handing out keys and itineraries, we made quick work of the line. Most of the guests cooed over her, saying they remember when she was born and then asking eighty-five questions about her parents. I guess Mike had a big family comprised mostly of senior citizens.

I looked up from the row of keys to see Mia beaming at me, hand in hand with Shawn. "Girl, that was amazing how you took charge."

Avery stood behind them, her tall frame peeking out from behind Shawn. It looked like she was eyeing Bethany very closely. Hmmm, I sensed even more romance in the air. *Great.*

I pulled at the back of my neck. The mad rush had me feeling a bit winded. The sweat, the humidity in the air, and all the love eyes happening made me more than ready to escape to my room.

I hip bumped Bethany, who looked mortified at the gesture. "Just helping out my new buddy here." Over Bethany's shoulder, I spotted Mia and Shawn's reservation on the screen. "Let's see here. It says you have the dolphin room." I plucked the key from the rack and handed it over along with the white cardstock itinerary. "Lucky. I'm in the urchin room. Seriously, Bethany, why did your mother name a hotel room after a spiky, bottom-dwelling fish?"

Mia giggled, and Bethany spoke up, her low voice making me jump. "Actually, fun fact, urchins aren't fish. They're echinoderms. They are found in all five oceans of the world."

She turned and plucked away at the keyboard apparently done talking with us. I think Bethany and Lee would get along swimmingly. I giggled to myself at my own pun. Wow. I really needed to lay down.

"Okay, then, I think I hear my room calling for me." Finding my bag propped against the desk, I grabbed it and made my way toward the wrap around staircase. Avery followed with Mia and Shawn trailing behind, speaking quietly to each other.

As we reached the second floor, Avery slung her weekend bag over her shoulder and stopped at a door with a painted seahorse plaque on it. "It looks like we have a group dinner and cocktails in a few hours at the restaurant next door. Wanna meet downstairs at five?" That would give me some time to decompress. Yes please.

"Sure, sounds good." I turned toward Mia, adding, "Have fun, lovebirds. See you in a couple hours."

I didn't know what to expect when I approached the urchin room. Would there be taxidermied sea creatures on shelves with spikes jutting out from their lifeless bodies? Or a hideous duvet cover decorated in cartoon versions of the spiny monstrosities complete with urchin-shaped throw pillows?

Thank the big guy upstairs because there was none of that. It wasn't one hundred percent urchin free, though. A large painting of multiple brightly colored creatures on the shore hung above the queen-sized bed. They were all tucked into themselves, no spikes showing, but looking weirdly vagina like. Maybe I could take it down while I was here?

The room most definitely had a purple theme going on. There was a purple comforter, purple curtains, and a lilac accent chair in the corner. They had adorned the bathroom with yet another urchin painting, and you guessed it... purple shower curtain. I could not wait to meet Bethany's mother. I'd bet she was a character.

After wheeling my bag to the small bureau, I plopped onto the bed and curled up against the soft cushions. I felt myself deflate as a long groan escaped my lips. This wasn't like me. I never felt exhausted from being around my friends. Maybe I shouldn't have come? I needed the break, but my brain forgot to compute how much social energy I'd need to expel being here. If my battery was already this drained from a car ride and a few chaotic minutes in a hotel lobby, how would I survive a long weekend?

I grabbed my phone from my purse and tapped the screen to check my messages. As expected, Lee had texted me multiple times.

Lee: *Nothing to worry about here. Just um... if you happen to hear from Ms. Flores, can you assure her we have everything under control?*

I dragged my palm across my face. Why, Lee? No. This was my vacation. Other than a catastrophic emergency, I would switch my phone off and clear my head. Claudia was there. As much as Lee hated to bother her, they'd have to go to her for help.

Before I chucked my phone for the weekend, I had to check in with my mom. I found her number in my recent calls and dialed. She answered on the first ring. The tell-tale sounds of her inhaling a Marlboro Light hit my ears before she'd even spoke a word. "Baby doll, I didn't think you'd have time to call me, what with your 'oh so fancy' vacation weekend and all."

I scoffed. Typical Mom, thinking I lived such a glamorous life.

"Mom, it's not fancy. The way you talk, you'd think I was at the Ritz or something." I sprawled out, stretching my legs.

Her exhale came like a hiss, and I could almost smell the noxious fumes of her smoke. "Well, what do I know? I could never afford to stay in fancy hotels."

I had to steer the conversation away from whatever this was, or she'd take me down the guilt trip rabbit hole of Melanie Edwards's despair.

"Mom, you remember you have your meeting tonight, right? Is Sally going to drive you over or should I order you an Uber?"

I could picture her sitting on her ancient black leather couch, letting her cigarette burn out until the ashes dropped in her lap and she nearly burned her fingers on the filter.

"Mom, you there?"

She coughed. "I'm here, I'm here. Hold your horses."

"The meeting. How are you getting there and back?" I was getting impatient. She acted as though this was her first rodeo when, in reality, she'd been attending AA meetings in the recreational hall of Palm Cove Methodist church for the past two years. Ever since she drove wasted and nearly killed someone. Just another thing keeping me tied to Florida, my non-driving, alcoholic, hot mess of a mother.

"Richard's going to pick me up. Don't worry about me. Go enjoy yourself. Find a handsome guy to occupy your weekend."

"Richard? Who's that?" I asked.

I could never keep track of their names. My mother was and always had been a serial dater who believed that "staying in one place with one partner for too long was a fate worse than death." Those were her exact words. She never told me much about my father. Only that they'd mutually decided their fling had run its course. I'd always thought there was more to the story but she kept her lips firmly sealed on the matter.

I think she'd keel over and die if I ever got married. My entire childhood was just me and her bouncing around from shitty town to shitty town. She'd find some lowlife guy to occupy her time for a few weeks, get him to pay for our food and her booze, maybe more, before she got bored and moved on. I became an expert in executing the midnight slip away by the time I was ten.

Now that she was sober, she was more invested in my life than during the entire eighteen years of my childhood. That included trying to squeeze every detail of my dating life out of me like we're a couple of teenagers at a sleepover.

"I met him at the church. I told you about him, didn't I? Big guy, like six foot five, big feet too, if you know what I mean?" she said.

"Ew, Mom. I don't want to think about your random old man boyfriend's penis." I huffed into the phone. "If you're getting to your meetings this weekend is all I care about. Please be responsible, and don't tell Richard anything about me this time. I don't need to get a phone call from any of your hookup's sons, okay?"

Her voice grew thick with an expert-level passive-aggressive edge. "I can't help it if I love my beautiful only daughter so much that I want everyone to know it."

Was it five o'clock yet? I was past needing a nap and moved on to needing a beverage instead.

"I love you too, Mom. Be good, and I'll talk to you when I get back."

She mimicked kissy noises and told me to stop mothering her so much, she was a "grown woman for Christ's sake." Easy for her to say after I spent my entire life making sure we were fed, clothed, and healthy.

With the important business taken care of, I tossed my phone to the other side of the bed where it rolled off with a thunk. Whatever. I didn't need it anyway.

I found the itinerary in my purse and looked it over. With as last minute as this wedding was, I hadn't expected this level of organization. Jill, or someone close to her, was a wedding planning master.

Welcome to Mike and Jill's Wedding Weekend!
Kick back, relax, and enjoy your time on beautiful Serenity Key
Thursday
-**Upon arrival, Check-in**
-**5:00 p.m. Dinner and drinks at The Marin Grill**
Friday
-**9:00 a.m. Workout on the beach followed by brunch and spa day**
-**7:00 p.m. Dinner and drinks at The Marin Grill**
Saturday
-**9:00 a.m. Boat day and snorkeling**
-**6:00 p.m. Rehearsal dinner**
Sunday
-**2:00 p.m. Wedding (see invitation for details)**
When posting photos on social media be sure to use **#MarinGetsMarried**

I wasn't sure how to feel about the entire weekend being meticulously planned out for us, but in a way, it would be nice to just go with the flow and turn my brain off. Every day I was planning, problem solving, and leading. It was time to let my hair down and get my party on.

Chapter 6

Kendahl

As exhausted as I felt, hanging out in my urchin lair alone was not my idea of a good time, so I changed into going-out jeans and a black lacy cropped top, which I paired with my favorite spiked black heels. With another glance in the mirror, I smoothed out my humidity-poofed hair and slapped some gloss on my lips. It wasn't my usual level of effort for a night out, but I was going to be surrounded by couples at a small mom-and-pop restaurant, not picking up guys at a club. It would do.

The sky had darkened to a charcoal gray, and the wind whipped my hair in front of my face. So much for my attempt to look put together. Mia texted me to let me know that she and Shawn were already at the bar and saving me a seat. I wondered who else showed up in the few hours of chill time we all had in our rooms. I spit out strands that got stuck to my sticky gloss as I made my way next door.

It seemed that every guest from the inn was already there. Raucous laughter and Beach Boy tunes poured through the open wall of the bar. Hints of garlic, fried food, and salty sea air invaded my nostrils causing my stomach to growl. I hoped there was decent food since it was the only option within walking distance. Plus, it wasn't like I'd bail on our group to go eat alone like a snob.

I peered into the open bar window and spotted Shawn with his arm slung around Mia's shoulders. She noticed me and waved my way. Her curly hair was even bigger thanks to the increased humidity. I pushed my way through the wooden doors and my stomach growled again. Damn stomach, it was like I'd never smelled fried fish before.

"Looking hot, Ken. Ooh you're wearing those heels you texted me a picture of!" Mia stood up and squeezed me in a rib-crushing hug. I fingered one of her bouncy curls. She didn't know how lucky she was to have this gorgeous hair.

"Thank you, love. I'm obsessed with your hair right now. Humidity does you well. Me, not so much." I perched on the wooden bar stool and waved to Shawn, Avery, and Bethany. The bartender was a middle-aged woman who looked like she knew how to make a strong cocktail, so I ordered a margarita with a double shot before I surveyed the area.

They'd went with the same theme as the inn, nautical inspiration lined the walls. I'm talking anchors, a giant swordfish, paintings of boats, and those brown fishing nets. They'd found a theme and ran with it. It worked, though. This place was flipping adorable and gave me all the island vibes.

Avery, Bethany, and I chatted about the island. I learned many useless facts, such as the population of yearlong residents was less than a thousand people, and the rare yellow-crowned night-tipped heron only bred on this island and only in April. Bethany was like a walking encyclopedia. But I'd never seen Avery so enthralled or so animated. Her usually stoic demeanor was nowhere to be seen in Bethany's presence as she tilted her head and inched closer, hanging on her every word.

Taking my new facts and delicious margarita, I decided to leave them to their conversation and do a lap around the bar. I had spotted Mike and Jill come in a few minutes before, but a swarm of relatives quickly swallowed them up in a bustle of chatting and hugs.

It seemed like, other than our little carpool, no one else from the gym made it out. I was expecting at least Mark and Dina to show, but maybe something came up. Jill spotted me from across the room and gave me a lopsided smile and wave. She'd be busy for quite some time it seemed.

Once again, I found myself alone in a crowded room. It hurt, but I wouldn't be a sad sack. This was my vacation after all. There was a jukebox in the corner of the room, one of those old timey machines with lights and flashy brass knobs. I instantly thought of my mother handing me a few dimes every time we stopped at a roadside diner when I was a kid. The towns were always different, but the diners were usually the same with their jukeboxes, cracked plastic booths, and the aroma of coffee and eggs that lingered no matter the hour of the day. My mother would stretch her bright pink lips in a grin and tip her chin in my direction, urging me to go choose a few songs. She knew what I'd pick. It was the same every time. I'd scroll the selections by twisting the handles while listening to the thwap of pages turn until I found what I was looking for—Fleetwood Mac, "Dreams." It was our song. I'd use up all my dimes to play it as many times as I could.

Mom and I would sway in our booth, me with a chocolate milkshake the size of my head and her with a steaming cup of black coffee, and we'd croon the lyrics to each other. It kept us from having to make any real conversation. I would never know where we were headed or how long we'd be there, but I could always depend on Stevie.

Fishing out a shiny quarter from my purse, I slipped it into the machine and watched the jukebox light up, brightening the small corner. There it was, a few pages in, just like I knew it would be. I pressed the corresponding button and waited for the mechanisms to do their duties while tapping my heel in anticipation.

The familiar drumbeat and guitar riffs filled the room as Stevie's haunting voice floated into me. Smiling, I swayed side to side and sipped my thawing drink, letting the music drift through me. My limbs were already feeling lighter and looser. *Thank you, alcohol.*

Halfway through the song, a few people had joined me near the jukebox, dancing and mouthing the lyrics with me. I didn't know these people, not the woman dressed in a leather vest and jeans, not the guy so tall the tip of his head almost skimmed the hanging netting, and not the clearly intoxicated middle-aged woman singing out of tune, but at that moment, they were my kin. I spun slowly, swaying my hips with one arm above my head and my eyes blissfully closed.

When I opened them again, I was facing the bar. That's when I spotted Mia and Shawn peering in my direction, and their faces were oddly giddy considering that we only just started drinking. Someone was next to them, standing straight as a board in front of a barstool. It was the one person I never expected to see here, not in a million years. I felt his gaze searing into me before I met those stone-gray eyes I'd thought about every night for weeks. My breath hitched, and I twisted around so he wouldn't see the shock painted all over my face.

Bastard.

What the hell was Coby doing here?

And why was my best friend talking to him with a huge grin on her face? That traitor. If she knew he would be here and didn't tell me... The car ride. That's why she had been acting so strangely.

It only took me a few seconds to collect myself. It was fine. Everything was A-okay. Coby was here, but that didn't mean I had to acknowledge him. Was it petty? Yeah. Did I care? Nope.

As "Dreams" ended and my fellow dancers dispersed, I stuck my last quarter into the jukebox and chose another Stevie song, "Rhiannon" this time. Turning on my heel, I made my way to the opposite side of the bar to order another drink.

"Another margarita, please. And make it a double." I morphed my face into a forced grin and fished out a few dollars from my purse to leave as a tip.

The barstool next to me squealed as Mia pulled it out, sliding into the seat quietly. It was a few breaths before she spoke.

"Ken, please don't be mad." She leaned closer. "I know you're not exactly thrilled to see him, but he promised me he wouldn't mess with you."

In an extra show of drama, I whipped my head around. "What do you mean, 'he promised you'?"

That sneaky, sneak. She knew about him coming and kept it from me. I didn't know whether to feel hurt, pissed, or slightly happy. I couldn't deny that a minuscule sliver inside me was feeling *something* at seeing him again. What that something was, I did not know.

Mia twirled a curl around her finger and looked at me with those obnoxiously cute puppy dog eyes. "He called Shawn a few days ago…"

Thoughts swirled in my head. Thoughts like, *Wow, I guess his phone did work, after all.* Followed by, *and he chose not to call or text me*. But I wasn't going to act like a wounded animal and mope around. No, my resolve stood. This was my vacation, and Coby or not, I'd have a good time, which meant forgiving my best friend and not being a total brat. I knew she meant well in her own way.

"It's fine, Mi. I don't blame you." I took a blessed sip of lime-flavored goodness before I went on. "Do I wish you would have mentioned him coming? Yes. But if you did, I know I would have stayed home. So don't worry about it."

Mia leaned her head on me, shooting out more apologies and niceties in between sips of her fruity beverage. I only half acknowledged her. The other half of me was keenly focused on Coby who was openly staring from across the bar.

Questions about Mia's conversation with Coby fluttered through my mind. I wanted to pry and find out what she knew about his absence and figure out what the hell she meant by him "not messing with me?" But before I could formulate my questions, the music stopped and Mike's voice boomed across the busy bar.

"Marin wedding guests! Time to get our grub on. Head on over to the dining area."

His loudspeaker voice and the resulting stampede of guests into the adjoining room reminded me of the last bell of the day ringing in a high school hallway with the resounding mass exodus that followed. I pulled Mia's hand down and urged her to wait until the crowd dispersed.

"I guess these guests go apeshit for a seafood dinner, huh?" I laughed, shaking my head at the bustling crowd.

"For real. You'd think it was Walmart on Black Friday or something."

Once the area cleared, we both finished our drinks and got up to join them. In the chaos, I hadn't noticed that Shawn had sidled up next to Mia's other side. Leaving the heartbreaker lingering at my left side, leaning far too casually on the bar with a smirk that told me he was oh so confident.

Good luck with that, buddy.

That smile may have gotten him to second base with me before, but now, he could consider my nether region Fort Knox. My panties, the world's strongest chastity belt. My lips, for all intents and purposes, were sewn shut like a creepy version of Sally the ragdoll.

Coby Barnes could kiss my ass—metaphorically, of course.

Chapter 7

Coby

I HAD A FEELING Kendahl would be pissed at me, and I deserved it, but damn. I wasn't expecting the death glares she was shooting my way. Before this night went completely in the shitter, I had to figure out my game plan. I told Shawn and Mia that I'd leave her alone, but I knew they didn't want an entire weekend of icy-cold tension either.

"Kendahl, hold up a second."

Mia patted her shoulder and continued to the restaurant with Shawn, leaving Kendahl lingering behind. She hadn't so much as turned her head in my direction, but she was waiting for me. That was something, right?

"How have you been?" I asked.

Seeing that I caught up beside her, she scoffed and continued walking. The silence between us only punctuated the jukebox tunes. Hints of her perfume floated my way, and I had to stop myself from leaning into her to get a closer whiff. If she wasn't talking to me, she sure as shit wouldn't want me sniffing her like a creep. Slipping my hands into my pockets, I followed close and tried again.

"I've missed you."

She stopped abruptly and whipped her head in my direction. I almost knocked into her.

"Just stop." Her hands reached out to put a physical barrier between our bodies. "Whatever it is you're doing. I don't want it or need it." Her eyes blazed, icy blue and narrowed.

I took the opportunity of our closeness to take in her features, ivory skin with a few well-placed freckles, her dark lashes, and her kissable lips. After looking at her face every night in a photo, finally seeing her in person felt surreal.

"Why are you staring at me like that? Is there something in my hair?" She fingered her long locks and brushed off invisible dust from her shoulders. My gaze followed her hands, taking in the slope of delicate neck, her black-lace cropped top was fitted against her chest leaving little to the imagination. That slice of skin at her middle made me want to splay my hands around her waist and hide those exposed bits from other eyes.

I cleared my throat, focusing on her face again. "What were you saying?"

"Oh my God. You were checking me out! Subtle much?" She quickened her pace, and her heels clicked against the distressed wooden floors.

She wasn't wrong. I slipped my calm and cool mask back on and strode next to her into the noisy dining area.

"When you look like that, can you blame me?"

"Like what, exactly? This is how I always look." Her tone was razor sharp, which caused me to stop in my tracks before we reached the mass of people.

I wrapped my hand around her arm, pulling her in close, so close I could smell the tequila on her breath. One inch closer and our lips would meet. It took all my restraint not to do just that. Instead, I whispered, "I want to sling you over my shoulder and take you upstairs so no one else gets to see you in that outfit."

She yanked herself out of my grip and stalked toward the tables with her chest heaving and muttered under her breath, "You're unbelievable. Hell would freeze over before I went upstairs with you."

Mia stood from her seat as we reached the empty chairs she held for us. "Everything alright?" she asked tentatively, looking from Kendahl to me.

I pulled out Kendahl's chair and waited for her to plop down, but she looked at me and rolled her eyes before shuffling a few seats to an empty chair near Avery and a woman I didn't know.

"I take that as a no." Mia sat back down and sipped her drink as she made eyes across the table at her best friend.

"I'm fine," Kendahl said through gritted teeth. "I'm just going to sit over here next to my good buddy, Avery, and my new friend, Bethany." Slinging her arm around a bewildered Avery, she flashed the rest of us a forced grin, and purposely shifted her gaze elsewhere.

I motioned to the server for another beer. While the rest of our table was busy placing their orders, Shawn leaned in, speaking low to suppress a chuckle. "Damn, you're in the doghouse, huh?"

"I'd have to have been allowed inside the house first to get banished to the doghouse."

He shook his head. "Well, you are Coby, notorious ladies' man and breaker of hearts. I'm okay with whatever this is as long as they are," he motioned to Kendahl and Mia. "But man, the second they tell me otherwise, you know I have to protect them, right?"

Oh Shawn, always the knight in shining armor. I understood, But I wished he would mind his own business and let me deal with my own women troubles.

Nodding and folding my hands in front of me, I closed the subject. "You do what you gotta do, and I'll do what I came here to do."

He looked at Mia, checking that she was still deep in conversation with the fourth couple at the table. "Remember what Mia said. I'm rooting for you two but, bro, I've never seen Kendahl look this pissed. Tread lightly."

Treading lightly was never my style, but I tilted my chin up at him in the universal guy response for, "I got you, man."

"So," Shawn asked me loud enough for the whole table to hear. "Where in Wyoming were you?"

"West." I cleared my throat and looked down, they didn't need more details than that.

"Oh yeah?" Avery asked. "I've done some camping up there, a long time ago though. Beautiful scenery."

"Uh-huh," I said under my breath. I glanced back up at Kendahl just in time to see her taking me in before darting her eyes away. I remember that wide-eyed look from our first date, she was full of questions.

"Please tell me you didn't drive," Mia said.

"Nah, I flew back home long enough to sleep and then drove here."

"Well I guess not all the rumors are true then," Avery said. "Although..." she hesitated. "I'm sure you must have had fun in Wyoming all the same."

What the hell did that mean? Kendahl scoffed loud enough for everyone to hear. I shook my head, wanting to be done with the questioning about where I was and what I was doing.

Our meal was like a game of ping pong. I'd sling a comment across the table and she'd hit it back at me with vehement angst. I'd comment on the beauty of the island, and she'd meet me with a "looks like your vision works after all." If I was keeping score, Kendahl would've been winning. When the server asked how our meals were, Kendahl replied that her meal was delicious but there seemed to be a rotten smell coming from the opposite end of the table, then pointed nonchalantly toward me. When

I stood up to use the restroom, I heard her attempt to whisper in Avery's ear that she wished I'd get lost on the way back.

I stood in the men's room propped against the sink, trying to hold my breath from the noxious odor and failing. Splashing some water on my face, I stared at the deep blue circles under my eyes. I really fucked things up. I was exhausted. I'd driven straight here the morning after flying to Palm Cove and still had to finish selling the house in Verdant Valley without any help from my asshole brother. I don't know what I expected from this trip, but it certainly wasn't this frigid welcome.

Maybe I was going about this the wrong way. I was Coby Barnes, notorious ladies' man, as Shawn said earlier. I'd never had to stoop, grovel, or beg. Kendahl fell for my charms before, so maybe she'd fall for them again.

"You got this," I mumbled to myself as I smoothed my wet hands through my hair. I wanted to apologize and get her back, but if she wasn't talking to me, then it was time to pivot.

Back at the tables, Jill and Mike were standing in front of the room holding hands. I'd almost forgotten the reason we were here. All eyes were turned their way as I reached my chair, but my eyes slid toward Kendahl who was leaning back in her chair with a slight slump to her shoulders. She met my gaze but quickly shifted her face toward Jill again. I couldn't hold back my grin.

"Thank you all for coming to our wedding weekend. We are so excited to share our love with our closest friends and family." Jill beamed. She looked gorgeous in a long black sundress.

Mike spoke up from beside her. "I'm so grateful to my aunt and uncle for their hospitality. The inn and this restaurant have been in our family for generations. To get married here to the love of my life is nothing short of a dream come true."

A chorus of oohs and ahhs started around the room and a few people dabbed at their eyes. Love was a powerful thing. I remember feeling that way with Amy during our honeymoon period. Too bad those feelings didn't last.

My thoughts were interrupted by Jill. "As you know, Kayla helped me put together a fun itinerary for our weekend. You should have gotten a printout at check-in." She squeezed Mike's hand and continued. "First up is our favorite pastime, well, besides Krav of course." She gestured across the way toward the bar to where a young gangly employee was setting up a speaker and a microphone on a small, raised platform and another slightly less gangly twenty-something was getting situated in an emcee's corner. I inhaled, waiting for Jill to say the word. My palms already felt clammy. "It's karaoke time, all!"

Talk about an icebreaker. There was no better one than getting sloshed and watching people you know belt out the wrong lyrics to Journey. I'd never been a karaoke guy. Hell, I barely even sang in the shower. I didn't have a fear per se of singing in front of people more like a strong aversion. Piano. That I could do. Maybe. It'd been a long time, but singing? No way. There was an incident in middle school involving me and the musical *Annie*. Let's leave it at me hoping and wishing the sun would not come up tomorrow by the end of the night.

Mia squealed and pulled Shawn up from the table. A whole meal worth of crumbs fell from his lap. Others in the group seemed excited too. There would have to be many more beers to get through this night.

A strong breeze blew through the open bar area, knocking over laminated menus and napkins onto the creaky wooden floor. I rubbed my bare arms, which had prickled with goosebumps, and wished I'd brought a sweatshirt. At least my thick layer of Wyoming facial hair still insulated my face a good amount.

"Do we have to do this?" I said to Shawn who looked as equally mortified as I did, maybe more so.

Kendahl slugged back the remnants of her drink and stood up straight before reaching her best friend. "What's the matter, Barnes, scared of a little karaoke?"

It was the first time that night that she'd spoken directly to me, making our verbal ping pong reach a new level.

"Do I look scared, Edwards?" I raised a brow at her and puffed out my chest for emphasis while hoping my actual fear wasn't showing.

"I don't know. What do you think, Mi? It looks to me like tough guy Coby isn't so tough after all."

We reached the bar and snagged seats right in front of the stage. Jill and Mike were already at the emcee booth chatting with the hipster guy.

Shawn looked from me to Kendahl, surely wondering what my next play would be while Kendahl watched me intently. Her face lit up with a sly smirk. In that moment, my stage fright took a backseat to my enormous competitive streak. This girl drove me crazy. I wanted nothing more than to take her back to my room and fuck that smug grin right off her face.

Without another word, I stalked over to the emcee booth and gave my idea to Jill and the DJ. Jill's face lit up, and she laughed her ass off, glancing back toward a confused Kendahl. The DJ, who I learned was named Quake. Yes, that's right, only Quake, no first name or title. Anyway, Quake gave a nonchalant shrug of approval. He must have been the least enthusiastic emcee I'd ever seen. I made a mental note to ask Jill if she was using this guy for her wedding reception. I hoped not for the sake of the life of her party.

A giddy Jill joined Mike in front of the small stage set up, and I turned myself around to face Kendahl. I wanted to watch her expression change, hoping she'd be as nervous as I was. Our eyes connected like magnets to steel as Quake spoke into the mic with the same cadence of Ben Stein repeating "Bueller," he said, "This guy just asked for a battle and, uh, that sounds dope, so yeah."

That's right. Because there's no better way to win a girl's heart than crushing her in a karaoke battle. But instead of Kendahl looking mortified she looked ready to draw blood.

Chapter 8

Kendahl

I STARED DAGGERS AT Coby, and the scene from my favorite childhood movie, *Little Giants,* popped into my head. I used to watch it again and again mainly daydreaming about my future wedding with Devon Sawa. But I'd memorized every scene. The scene where the underdogs pull a stunt involving Alka Seltzer and grunting like wild boars stood out, in particular, because just like football was eighty percent mental and forty percent physical...so was karaoke battling. And I was ready to give 120 percent.

Coby wanted to play dirty? Well, he didn't know who he was playing with.

"Uh, you good, girl?" Mia said beside me. She flashed me a wide-eyed look that brought me back to earth.

"Never better." I downed the tequila shot I'd ordered when we first came into the bar area and wiped my mouth with a crinkled paper napkin.

Quake's voice boomed over his mic. "The bride has given me names for the battle so, uh, come up and see who you're with like, if you want to, or something. Oh, and write down the song you're vibing with."

Without another word, I went to talk to Quake. I had the perfect song in mind. Coby's arm brushed against mine as I went to whisper in Quake's ear. He shifted closer and tensed next to me. Maybe it was the copious amount of tequila in my system, or maybe, it was the fact that I was finally feeling a spark of life running through my veins again at seeing Coby squirm, but I leaned closer to Quake and planted a quick kiss on his cheek, then winked as I backed away.

A muscle in Coby's chiseled jaw ticked, but he ground his heels in and glared at no one in particular. I loved seeing those stormy eyes fill with fire. Karma, baby.

Jill hopped onto the platform. The entire room focused on her, which gave me a sneak peek at what it would be like when it was my turn on the stage. A few nervous flutters swirled in my gut, but I forced myself to focus on Jill.

"I didn't know I'd be starting our wedding weekend by battling my fiancé." She shifted her weight from one high-heeled foot to the other, then focused her attention toward Mike who clapped his meaty hands as he laughed. "But, Mike, I'm here to win, baby."

She nodded at Quake and the opening riffs of Sonny & Cher's "I Got You Babe" crackled through the dusty speakers. Jill's voice matched Cher's deep, husky tones perfectly, and before I realized it, I was sucked in. She swayed her hips side to side and pointed to Mike adorably. I almost forgot about my annoyance at Coby until he inched closer and murmured to me, "If you think that's good, just wait, baby. I'm going to have you crooning for me by the end of the night."

Was it considered uncouth to knee someone in the balls in public? Honestly, I was two seconds away from not caring and doing it anyway. But I scoffed, trying to ignore the treacherous parts of my anatomy that twinged the slightest amount at the way Coby called me baby.

By the third chorus, Mike had climbed the stage to sing. That was when their battle ended and became a duet, which they followed up with a cheesy rendition of "Islands in the Stream."

Guests whistled, clapped, and catcalled. There was no doubt in my mind that Mike and Jill were in love as well as loved by all their guests. They ended their performance with a loud smacking kiss right in front of the mic.

I needed another shot, stat.

Coby clapped beside me and cheered with gusto. For a guy with commitment issues and no game, he really seemed into all this romance.

The sound of Quake clearing his throat shot through the speakers. "Uh, I guess that wasn't really a battle so, next pair?"

Coby turned at the same time I did, wanting to go first. Was he sweating?

Fine, I'd let him go first. I needed another drink anyway. While I ordered another double tequila, I pressed back against the bar, waiting to laugh at how horrible he'd sound. Every eye in the room fixed on him, and I noticed the young bartender watching him with wide eyes.

She handed me my shot and nodded at Coby. "He's cute, huh? I wonder if he's single."

I tipped my head back and let the burn of the tequila slide down my throat. She handed me a chunk of lime. I smiled, then sucked before answering.

"Trust me, you don't want to go there. He gave my friend an STI. And his dick... a baby carrot is bigger."

She cleared my now empty shot glass away, her mouth agape. "Wow, looking at him, I'd never think that."

"I know, right? I was shocked too. I guess there's a reason guys like him look so confident, they need to play a good game to reel a lady in."

She placed her elbows against the sticky bar and leaned in, giving me a view of her cleavage that was entirely wasted on me. "True. Well, thanks girl." She handed me a beer from the cooler under her. "Here, it's on the house."

Flashing a grin and dropping a twenty on the bar, I made my way back to Quake's booth in time for a nervous-looking Coby to begin. A drumbeat pulsed in the speakers, followed by a familiar guitar riff. Coby gripped the mic stand and his tanned hands flexed so hard that the corded muscles of his forearm bulged. His chest rose and fell under his T-shirt.

He pointed his index finger at me when he sang "I want you to want me."

My face flushed and I tried to look away but I couldn't. I was fixated on his damn face, his gyrating hips, and those stupid sexy forearm muscles. What universal being decided it was okay to let this man's hair skim his face in the perfect hot guy way?

He belted out the chorus, gaze fixed on me. Why couldn't he have sang like shit? That same universal being who gave him perfect hair also blessed him with a gorgeous voice. He sounded melodic and angsty. The whole room was captivated by him.

Game on, asshole.

I barely let him climb off the stage after he bowed with a huge shit-eating grin. He grazed my low back as he passed me but I refused to let his touch affect me. A sound somewhere between a growl and a hiss came from somewhere inside me, creepy enough to make me dead stop. I ignored it and precariously scaled the platform, wobblier than I'd been all night and took the mic. Quake was saying something, but his voice was drowned out by the beat of my heart hammering in my chest.

Deep breath, Queen, you got this.

I saw Mia clapping and bouncing in her seat. She gave me a new sense of resolve. I blew a kiss to Quake, then nodded that I was ready before taking notice of where Coby went. The music rolled through my loose limbs as I shimmied and shook. My eyes found Coby's hungry gaze, and I opened my mouth to croon the intro to "You're So Vain" by Carly Simon.

He laughed, but shook his head and clapped. That wasn't the response I wanted, but I went on singing in my best voice. Or at least the best voice I could muster that many drinks in.

I was finding my stride. I'd closed my eyes as I got to the good part where Carly would have been repeating "don't you," when the mic was taken from my hands.

What the hell?

I opened my eyes to see Coby's huge frame next to me. He gestured to Quake and "You're so Vain" was cut off as quickly as it started. I didn't have time to leave the stage before Coby started his next song.

That smug bastard.

This freaking man worked the stage like he was damn Mick Jagger singing "One Way Or Another" by Blondie. Every ounce of the nervousness I saw earlier evaporated as soon as he opened his mouth.

We had drawn a bigger crowd, and there were phones out now, recording him. When the guitar solo came, he shook his ass, and I swear every woman in the crowd, even Jill and Mia, howled and whistled.

No, no, no. I needed this win.

Two could play this game.

Taking a play straight out of Coby's book, I came up in front of him, ground my ass against his front, then dropped it low. He stuttered and was rendered speechless. Just what I wanted. I turned around and yanked the mic away as I pushed him aside with my free hand.

"Damn, that was cold," Quake said over his mic.

Quake was invested. I sauntered to the side of the stage and whispered my next song title into his ear, making sure to linger against his cheek. I wished I hadn't because he smelled like he'd rolled around in a Goodwill donation bin. I tottered back to the center of the platform as he started my next song.

"Hot N Cold" by Katy Perry blasted out, and I didn't bother facing the crowd. I sang the lines right to Coby, not breaking eye contact even when every cell of my body told me to look away. My legs wobbled with every passing line as the mix of emotions, alcohol, and adrenaline bombarded me at once. Strong hands were around my waist before I could falter. Coby held me up, and I took that moment to lean my head on his chest to get my bearings back.

He smelled amazing. How did he smell this good after sweating on stage?

His hands cradled my back and rubbed circles against my lace shirt.

Wait, no. I wasn't doing this.

I shot up, still wobbly, but feeling better. "I can finish. I'm fine."

In that instant his usual mask of smugness lifted and concern shone through. "You should sit and have some water."

"I don't take orders from you." I pushed away and climbed down from the stage. He was right. I needed water, but I wasn't getting some because he told me to. I could think for myself.

Mia caught up with me to lead me into a chair and force an icy glass into my hands. "Oh my God, Ken, you were amazing! Are you okay? You look pale."

I gulped like I had just ran a marathon. "M' fine."

Coby was still on stage, shifting from one foot to the other. It was like the spell we were under had broken, and as he dragged his hand through his hair, I could read the anxiousness on his features.

Everyone chanted his name. "Coby! Coby! Coby..."

What the hell?

I wanted to get up there and steal the limelight back, but I knew when to admit defeat. The tequila had betrayed me, and the thought of walking back on stage again brought bile to the back of my throat. Had I eaten much of my dinner? I couldn't remember anymore. A basket of pretzels sat behind me on the table, and I reached for it, not caring how many germy hands had plundered it all evening.

Shawn caught me reaching and grabbed a handful, placing them on a plate in front in front of me. I was so lucky to have these two to take care of me even if I was still pissed at them for keeping the big, hunky elephant in the room from me.

Coby walked off to the side to say something to Quake, and as he took his place back at the center of the stage, the room fell silent. That muscle in his jaw ticked, and his hand went through his hair again and again causing it to stand up in parts, adorably, of course. Those smoky eyes locked onto mine and all the humor had gone from them. I was almost seeing double at that point, but I couldn't look away. A weight settled into my gut, and I knew he was about to sing something that would break me.

Hauntingly, he sang Ed Sheeran's "Perfect", and the entire time, he never looked away from me.

As the last line spilled from his lips, I rubbed at the wetness on my cheeks, knowing I was making myself look like a raccoon as my black mascara smudged. But I couldn't help it. This man had captivated the entire room. Too many conflicting emotions were churning around my head and my gut.

Before I could stop myself, it happened in slow motion. It was more than emotions churning. Vomit, and not a small amount, came spewing out of my mouth, landing across my chest and my plate of pretzels. The foul odor hit me square in the face, and I retched again. How did alcohol still smell that strong on its way back up?

"Oh God—" The contents of my stomach came up again, and I put my hands out as if they could stop it from coming.

From the depths of hell, where I was residing, I heard Mia's voice like a slow-motion sports announcer. "Ohhh shittt!"

A towel appeared out of thin air and covered me as someone led me toward the exit. "M'okay. I think maybe it was something I ate."

The outside world spun as the wind whipped my hair into my vomit covered face. Wet and shivering, it took every ounce of dignity I had not to burst out crying. I looked up to thank whoever was graciously ignoring my smell to see the underside of Coby's bearded jaw.

Well, fuck.

Chapter 9

Coby

WE ALMOST MADE IT back to the inn before Kendahl realized who was escorting her. Damn, how much had she drank? I'd seen her drunk before, but never wasted like she was tonight.

"No, nosurrr," she said, slurring her words. "Don't need help."

God damn, she knew how to push my buttons. She tried to pull away from me, but I adjusted my hold from her shoulders to her waist.

"Don't make me sling you over my shoulder. I said I'd do it earlier, and I meant it."

Kendahl stopped in her tracks, which made me stumble a bit. Her lip wobbled, and she took a deep sigh. Oh no.

"Look at me. Why would ya wanna touch me. M'dis-gush-ting." Her final words ended in a sob. God dammit. I didn't really want to be covered in vomit, but this situation needed remedying immediately.

My phone buzzed in my pocket, but I ignored it. Instead, before she could fight me, I scooped her up in my arms and cradled her against my chest. The stench hit my nostrils, and I tried not to gag.

"What the—" she slurred.

"Shh, I got you. You're not disgusting. You never could be." Hoisting her up further, I registered that my hand cradled her ass cheek perfectly. I bounded down the path toward the inn. We needed to get out of this insane wind and get cleaned up.

I almost brought her to my room but thought better of it. Everything she'd need would be in her room after all. There was one major problem with the situation. Kendahl was nearly passed out against my chest, and I had no idea which room was hers. I couldn't think straight while I had her ass in my hand.

Only one light flickered in the deserted lobby. The space was eerily quiet save for the ancient outdoor shutters clacking against the walls. Visions of *The Shining* ran through my mind. I could imagine creepy twins appearing out of thin air, pointing their menacing fingers at me. Shuddering, I quickened my pace toward the stairs. I only stopped to glance at a sign propped against the desk where they'd scrawled a phone number.

"Hey, I need to put you down for a second, okay?" I rubbed Kendahl's back and gingerly placed her on one of the steps, silently praying she didn't get sick again or leave remnants of her puke on the carpet.

She mumbled a response, words that resembled a mix between okay and good. Shaking my head at her stubbornness, I opened her small purse and felt around for her room key. I found it at the very bottom of her bag and laughed when I saw the hand-painted urchin adorned on it.

"Urchin room, huh? I was lucky then. I got the coral room." I hoisted her back into my arms with her key dangling between my fingers and continued. "They really took the whole theme seriously. I mean I knew coral was a color, I guess, but I never knew how hideous an entire room of coral would be."

I took the stairs, grateful that I trained like an animal to stay fit while I carried her bridal style. Hopefully my random conversation would keep her alert enough for me to get her cleaned up without feeling like a total creep with a lifeless woman. Luckily, she giggled a bit though the sound was muffled by my chest.

The urchin theme overwhelmed the space, and purple. So much purple. "Wow, I thought my room was bad." I hesitated, taking in the space. "Okay, let's get you cleaned up."

There were a few piles of clothes strewn across a lounge chair in the corner, and some clothes hanging up in the small bureau. I picked up the first thing I found and examined it. Was it a shirt or a skirt? Holding it at multiple angles, I still couldn't figure it out, so I tossed it aside to grab the next thing. It was lacy and the size of my palm.

"Do you own any clothing that doesn't take an engineering degree to figure out?" I kept searching by digging my hand to the bottom of her suitcase but instead of finding a T-shirt I felt something much more interesting—something silicone. I yanked it out to take a peek. Yes, it was a violation of her trust, but I wanted to know what my competition looked like.

It was one of those small rose-shaped vibrators, the kind with the little flicking tip. I'd bet anything she only brought this one because it was her smallest and most discreet. My girl probably had a whole drawer of toys at home. I shoved it back to the bottom of the bag and pushed her clothes over it. Anything else I found was either lacy or not drunken sleepwear appropriate. So I gave up and went into her very purple bathroom, coming back out with a damp washcloth. Kendahl was already laying down by that point, but I knew she'd hate waking up still covered in puke.

She opened her eyes as I dabbed her chin with a cool cloth. "Argh, cold." Her hand shot out like bullet, pushing me away. "Tired. Going to sleep."

"Wait." I sighed. "Let's just get you out of your clothes, they're covered."

In a moment of lucidity, she sat up and leaned forward, bringing her face inches from my crotch. I had to hold her by the shoulders to keep her from face planting right into it. She lifted her arms for me to help her out of her shirt.

You got this. Do not look. Do not linger.

I was holding my breath. It was like I'd never seen a topless woman before. Quickly, like my hands would catch fire if they stayed too long, I yanked her top off, most likely getting more sick in her hair, exposing her black lace bra. The pads of my fingers prickled with the need to feel her skin and to trace the round curves of her breasts spilling out of the top of her bra.

Wait, her skin—she was covered in goosebumps.

"Are you cold, baby?"

Like a robot with an off switch she slumped while murmuring more nonsense. A visceral need to get her warm and settled took hold of me. I undressed her the rest of the way, starting at her heels and ending with pulling her unnaturally tight jeans off, which was not easy. Why did women have to wear their damn pants so tight? My mind lingered on her ass in those jeans earlier, and I guess I found my answer.

Grasping the duvet from underneath her limp body, I wrapped her like a cocoon, making sure she was situated on her side because God forbid she got sick again in her sleep. I'd heard about some miner in my hometown dying that way as a kid. He got wasted and choked on his own vomit in his sleep. His poor wife found him like that when she woke up the next morning. It was one of those town news stories that stayed with me all these years.

After fussing over her for a few more minutes, I realized I needed to go. A pit formed in my stomach thinking about that damn miner. I didn't want to leave her like this. Her chest rose and fell while shallow breaths escaped her lips. Was I really this anxious of a person that I was watching this woman sleep? *Get a grip, man.*

My phone buzzed, breaking me out of my spell. I answered, speaking low so Kendahl wouldn't wake. "Shawn, hey. How's it going?"

With the background sounds of music and talking, I knew he was still at the bar.

"Good, still at karaoke. Bro, everyone is still talking about you guys. I swear it's like you're both celebrities or something. Anyway, I'm jealous. I'm ready to go to bed, but Mia's drunk and wants to sing."

In all the chaos of Kendahl getting sick, I had honestly forgotten about the karaoke battle. I guess we left a mark. That stage fright feeling kicked back up in my gut, making me want to toss my damn cookies too. The adrenaline rush of being up there and trying to impress Kendahl drained away the moment I left the bar. I ran a hand through my hair and brought the conversation back to Shawn.

"Lucky you," I laughed. "I'd come back to see that, but I want to keep an eye on Kendahl a little longer."

"Yeah? Mia wanted me to see how she's doing. I didn't realize she had that much to drink, she can knock 'em back."

Chuckling under my breath I added, "Yeah, I didn't realize either, but I guess I pissed her off enough that she wanted to get shitfaced. Anyway, she's good now. I got her cleaned up and she's asleep."

Shawn got quiet for a second. I knew what was coming—one of his lectures. The dude acted like I was a freaking predator sometimes even though he knew me as well as anyone else.

"Just keep your hands to yourself, buddy," he said.

Knew it.

"Bro, you know I'm a decent guy, right? I'd never take advantage." Even if everything in me wanted to cradle Kendahl in my arms and feel her skin against mine, but I only thought that part.

His voice lightened up and he laughed. "I know. I just gotta say my piece. When I tell Mia that you're taking care of her she's going to screech. She is really rooting for you guys."

I could picture her screeching right into Shawn's ear. The image made me chuckle loudly. Kendahl shifted in bed and blinked her eyes.

"Hey, man, I think I woke Kendahl up. Let me see if she needs anything. Have a good night, and I'll see you tomorrow."

I hit end, not waiting for him to reply.

Kendahl sat up a bit and leaned her head against the tufted headboard. Her eyes met mine, her pupils wide in the dim light of the room. The corners of her mouth lifted in a small smile, and my pulse sped up of its own accord.

"Coby?" Her voice rasped with my name rolling off her lips. I kneeled beside the bed so I could be close enough to hear her.

"Baby, I'm here to take care of you. What do you need?"

"Water." She rubbed at her eyes and darted her tongue out to moisten her lips. I hopped up, filled a glass from the bathroom with tap water, and watched her gulp it down. After refilling it and leaving it on the end table, I waited by the door. She was settling back into sleep now considering the rise and fall of her chest beneath the blanket.

"I'm going to head back to my room. Call me if you need me, okay?" I knew she wouldn't. Her phone wasn't in her purse, so I couldn't leave it next to her.

"Wait," she whispered. I held my breath and turned back around to face her again. "Don't go."

Fuck. My first thought was to hop into her bed and pull her against me, but no. That wasn't right. I eyed the purple lounger across the room. My body would hate me in the morning, but what my girl asked for my girl got. Plus I was anxious about leaving her anyway.

"I'll stay with you. Rest, I'll be right over there."

A smile lit up her sleepy face, and she snuggled back into the pillow. Stiff neck be damned, seeing her light up like that would be worth the pain.

Chapter 10

Kendahl

I GROANED AS I rolled over and watched rain pelt at the sliver of uncovered window. Did someone put a brick on my head? Or a lead pipe? What time was it? For all I knew it could have been three a.m. or noon. Images from the previous night played back in my head like a slideshow with blurred edges. Then the smell hit me. I sniffed a hardened strand of my hair.

Holy hell! How was it possible for my vomit to still smell like alcohol?

As I reached around, looking for my phone, a rustle from across the room made me jump back.

A very bare-chested Coby was asleep, scrunched up and looking ridiculous on the small lounge chair. A knit throw blanket covered the space between his navel and thighs. Seeing Coby and his tan chest, abs like a washboard, and pecs that should be illegal on any human, sleeping like Michael Scott on his tiny end-of-bed bench did absolutely nothing for me. Nope.

My heart squeezed and my treacherous gut fluttered, but I chalked that up to my enormous hangover. Tequila was known to do that to me.

Coby shifted, knocking the throw blanket to the floor and exposing a pair of black boxer briefs. I sat up straight, trying not to ogle him like a creep, but hot damn, that man had thighs like tree trunks. Speaking of tree trunks, I was not seeing what I thought I was seeing. I sat forward and confirmed that yup, Coby's very prominent morning wood was attempting to break free of his shorts.

I cleared my throat louder than I meant to and woke him up.

"Sorry," I muttered, my tongue somehow weighing ten pounds. "Didn't mean to wake you."

Why was I being nice to this jerk? His freaking hot body and morning wood were distracting me from the fact that he had dumped me via text, then bailed out of town for weeks. God only knew what he did during that time or *who* he did for that matter.

A sound rumbled from his lips, making my skin heat involuntarily. I had to get him out of here. Standing up to use the bathroom, I noticed I was only in my bra and panties. I yanked the covers around myself.

"Uh, sorry. I didn't realize I wasn't dressed. I'm just going to go get cleaned up. You can see yourself out," I said.

A husky laugh came from his corner of the room, and I put my hand on my hip.

"What? Ugh, you know what? I don't even care. I'm going to shower." I reached down to grab his shirt and tossed it at him. "Here you go. You can laugh all you want...back in your own room."

While I rummaged around the room mummy wrapped in a purple duvet that dummy just sat there with both his arms casually on the armrests like I was some kind of entertainment and he was the audience. I huffed out another annoyed groan, finding his pants and tossing them over, before heading into the bathroom to pee and run my hair under the sink. When I opened the door he was still in the same spot.

"You don't remember much from last night, do you?" he said it on a yawn while rubbing sleep out of his eyes and cocking his head.

"I remember owning you in karaoke." I straightened my posture, trying to look as smug as I could while being a hungover woman wrapped in nothing but a blanket.

He rubbed at his beard and his eyes lit up in amusement. "Owning me, huh? I don't know. If memory serves, I think I had more applause. I guess we'll have to ask around."

"I guess so." I cast my eyes downward since he chose that moment to stand up, giving me an eyeful of more than I needed to see.

As he stretched and made that suggestive groan again, he added, "So remember anything else from last night? Anything from after your pop star debut?"

He wanted me to talk about getting sick, but I was already embarrassed enough. Did he really have to rub it in?

"No, nothing comes to mind," I said in a sickly-sweet voice.

He walked toward me. His frame was so much larger than mine that I had to lean back against the bureau as I yanked the duvet up to my neck. The room suddenly became ten degrees warmer.

"You don't remember asking me to stay, do you?" He bent inches from my face, rendering me speechless for a moment.

"No, I wouldn't do that." I shrugged away from him and side stepped toward the door.

He chuckled, then reached down to grab his pants and put them on. I eyed him with a raised brow.

"What's the laugh for? And your shirt too please. I've seen enough of your nakedness."

"Am I making you blush, Kendahl?"

I scoffed. "You wish."

Being the jerk that he was, he turned around, giving me the perfect view of his tight ass, and bent to pick up his shirt. I choked on a breath. "Unfortunately, I can't wear this because it's covered in someone's puke," he said, raising his brow. "My room's down the hall though, so it's fine."

"Yes, good. Okay then..." I swallowed down the lump in my throat, walked to the door, and wrenched it open. "Bye."

Two complete strangers stood outside my door. I looked down at myself covered by only a hideous duvet, then over at Coby, barefoot, in nothing but his dirty jeans. We looked like we had a wild night. I turned without a word and shut the door in their grinning faces.

"What the fuck? You think they're housekeeping?" I didn't see a cart, and they hadn't knocked. They threw me off guard. Like who the hell ambushes someone in front of their door that way?

Leaning against the wall, Coby let out a hearty chuckle.

"What's so funny? That was mortifying. I'm going to issue a complaint." I paced. "Yeah, let me call the front desk right now. You think they're here this early in the morning?"

"Kendahl, it's eleven. I checked my phone a few minutes ago."

My eyes opened like saucers. "We slept that long?"

He shrugged like it was no big deal. I never slept this late even hungover. We had the itinerary to think about and I was never late. Today was a morning workout on the beach. Although the rain would have nixed that idea.

"Let me throw on actual clothes. Turn around." I dug through my bag looking for a sweats and a T-shirt and finally found them at the bottom of my bag. Coby laughed again as he faced the wall.

"You know I saw you in your bra and panties last night and this morning, right?" he said.

"Yeah, yeah... that doesn't mean you need another free peek. Okay you can turn around."

Now that I was decent, the only thing left to handle was his still half-nude state. I rummaged some more through my bag and found the only thing that would potentially fit him.

"Here." I tossed my Lilo and Stitch nightshirt at him. "This should fit you. At least it'll be something, so you don't have to walk out of here," I gestured with my palm, "like that."

He held it out in front of him, suppressing a laugh. "Stitch? Cute. But you realize, this will look ridiculous on me? It'll be less attention-grabbing for me to walk back shirtless."

I'd never seen him look this amused.

"No. Just put it on, okay? And go find out what those people want."

He squeezed into the nightshirt, and wow, he was right. He looked hilarious. I tried to hold in my laughter, but I couldn't.

"See, I told you. This thing is skintight. I may have to cut it off."

"Ruin Stitch and you're dead meat mister. Stitch is sacred." I covered my mouth to hide my smile. "Now, go."

He opened the door, and I stood to the side, peeking out to see if anyone was there. Much to my annoyance, the same two people were leaning casually against the hallway wall. The guy looked to be in his midtwenties. He was thin and had longish hair that was tied up in a man bun. He wore baggy shorts and a Ramones T-shirt. Something about his face looked familiar but I couldn't place how I knew him. The woman at his side looked to be around the same age. Before I could notice any details about her looks, my eyes stopped on her hand holding up a cell phone directly at us.

"What the—"

"Kendahl and Coby, right?" the guy said. "Hey, I'm Aiden Aarons. You might recognize me from my YouTube channel." That's where I'd seen him. Lee had shown me one of his videos where he interviewed random people on the street.

I found my voice, but as I was about to speak, he cut me off again.

"I recorded your battle last night. You guys went viral. I'm talking a million views since last night and counting."

My jaw hit the floor.

"You're kidding, right?" Coby said as he laughed.

"Not kidding. Someone even made a song parody," Aiden said.

Phone girl pressed her phone into my mortified face and there it was, an Alvin and the Chipmunks sounding Coby singing a familiar song. Ed Sheeran? I couldn't be sure because he was cut short by the camera panning to me vomiting all over myself. Overly exaggerated retching sounds were dubbed over it, and the clip was replayed again and again to over the top music.

My face felt like molten lava as I turned to Coby. I'd be a laughingstock. I'd never get a dream job now. I'd bet if I grabbed my phone, there'd already be a hundred messages from Claudia in my inbox. I wobbled against the doorframe, and Coby reached for me before I could brush him off.

"Bro, I can't believe you posted that shit. Take it down." His voice deepened.

Aiden held his hands up in surrender. "Hey, hey...it's not just that part that everyone's going apeshit over, man. The whole internet fell in love with you two. Honestly, I was surprised by the comments."

"In love? What do you mean?" I couldn't catch a full breath.

He nodded to his friend, and the camera went back up. Coby looked two seconds away from committing murder.

"Off, now," he said.

The friend lowered the phone, but I wasn't sure if she'd actually turned it off or not.

Aiden continued, "The whole world wants to know. Are you two together? Did he win you back with his serenade?"

This was too much. I needed a shower and coffee. Most importantly coffee. And apparently to check my phone. I took a deep breath to answer truthfully, but once again I was cut off.

"Yes. We're back together." Coby slung his arm around me, ripping the armpit of my favorite nightshirt. "Right, baby?"

I scowled as I hyper focused on the tear before snapping my gaze upward. What did he just say?

As I was about to retort with the truthful answer, Coby shut the door in Aiden's face. With his arms crossed, he looked at me as smug as can be.

Chapter 11

Coby

"WHAT THE HELL, COBY?" She was pissed. I could almost see the steam coming off of her. I had to play my cards carefully.

"Listen, we can use this to our advantage," I said.

She crossed her arms and sank onto the bed. "What advantage? You saw that video. My career will be ruined. I need to do damage control. It's my specialty after all."

I sat next to her on the bed, ripping the ridiculous straitjacket of a nightshirt off so I could breathe again.

"You of all people know how good this could look for you. Think about it. You talked about wanting to move up the ladder when we were dating. This could be the kind of thing that could launch you into the career of your dreams."

She brushed me off before she reached over the side of the bed and came back up with her phone in hand. "Great. My battery died."

"Did you hear what I said? What do you think?" I asked.

Without answering, she plugged in her phone. My mind whirled, and I laid back on her bed, letting this whole thing sink in. Going viral meant a lot for me too. I thought about this YouTube guy finding Clyde and interviewing him. That would be my worst nightmare come to life. It meant the past I left behind in Verdant Valley might get drudged up to the people I cared for here in Florida, the life I'd created away from the toxicity of my family and that town brought into my present. Nothing good would come from that.

If we played the nice and boring couple, then everyone would back off. There was no story if there was no drama. I haven't watched much reality TV, but I knew enough to know, nobody thought twice about the happy couples. It was the rocky ones who made ratings.

Her phone chirped to life and kept chirping. It beeped for what felt like a full five minutes. Kendahl stared at the small rectangle, her messy blonde hair flopped forward in the bun atop her head. I waited for her to speak and scooted closer so I could try and peek at the screen.

Come to think of it, I hadn't checked my own device since the previous night when I silenced it, apart from looking at the time. I had been worried about someone from work or even another check in call from Mia and Shawn waking her up early in the morning. Those two meddled more than a pair of new mothers. I hoped my phone wouldn't be blowing up the same way.

"Is everything okay?" I asked.

Her answering voice was shrill as she spoke through closed teeth. "No. Everything is not okay. Every person I've ever known plus God knows how many random strangers are blowing up my socials. My boss texted me multiple times, and..." She scrolled and her eyes widened. "Oh my God."

My heart rate hitched up a notch and I jerked to hover behind her. "What?" I couldn't get a read on the change in her tone. She almost sounded in awe.

She flopped backward and clutched her hands to her chest, then turned her head toward the foggy windows before meeting my gaze. "I got an email from my dream PR firm this morning. They want to schedule a Zoom interview with me."

I wanted to hold her in my arms, praise her, and show her that she's incredible. But I came back to reality and remembered she pretty much hated me.

"That's great news. When do they want to have the interview?"

"Monday morning. I don't know if I could do this. I mean, I sent my resume out on a whim. I was having a crappy day and figured, what the hell, I'll move to LA. I never thought they'd get back to me. What would Mia say? Or my mom?" She groaned, then rolled onto her stomach and pushed her face into the plush pillow. "Plus," she continued speaking but I couldn't make out what she said with her face attached to a pillow.

"What? Kendahl, look at me. I can't help you if you're talking into a pillow." I flipped her around like she weighed next to nothing and waited for her to tell me again, but annoyingly, she tossed her arm over her face and groaned some more.

"Come on, if you don't move your arm and talk to me, you're going to force me into extreme measures," I said.

I knew how to get to her. She slid her arm to the side, and her wide blue eyes peeked out from behind her palm. "Extreme measures?"

I kneeled facing her, thinking wicked thoughts, and took in how perfect she was lying next to me. She had no fucking idea what I wanted to do to her or how much I wanted to taste every inch of her. I'd only ever gotten to taste her lips when we were dating, and she had been exquisite. How I kept it in my pants then, was beyond me. Then again, I never did have the opportunity I had now with us side by side in bed.

"I bet I could make you spill every single thought in your mind to me right now." I trailed my fingers lightly from her hip down the outside of her thigh. Her breath hitched, and she ripped her arm away to look at me with blazing eyes. "Now, what did you say?" I trailed the same hand up and down the midline of her thigh. Her breaths became faster as she clenched her thighs together. "Should I keep going?"

"What if they see the video?" The words escaped her lips in a rush of breath, and I stopped, leaving my palm flat against her thigh.

"Good girl." I gathered my thoughts. "I wouldn't worry about it right now. If you want this job, we'll figure everything out." I let my eyes bore into hers, waiting for her response and watching her react to our closeness.

"They'll ask questions... like everyone else."

Her eyes were icy saucers as she evaded saying what I knew was on her mind. *What if they asked about us?* I had told that jackass YouTube guy we were together, but that was easily remedied if Kendahl didn't agree.

Every one of her thoughts played out on her face as she chewed her lip. Finally, as she was about to open her mouth to speak, someone knocked on the door. She jumped, and I mean literally jumped from the bed like she was an Olympic pole vaulter.

"Do you think it's that Aiden guy again?"

"You want me to get it?" I sat up at the edge of the bed, missing the heat of her body.

She hesitated against the wall but adjusted her hair and stomped forward. "No, I've got it."

They knocked again. "Ken Dolly?" This time there was no guessing who was behind the door because Mia squealed loud enough for her voice to travel through multiple dimensions. "Time to get up, my little diva."

Kendahl yanked the door open before Mia attracted any more attention in the hall. "Come in, come in," she whispered.

Mia stepped into the room, took one look at me and my shirtlessness, snapped her head back to Kendahl who was still disheveled as hell and squealed again. The sound went through my skull, and I wasn't even hungover. I couldn't imagine how Kendahl must have felt.

"I knew it," she singsonged. "Shawn said he couldn't get ahold of you this morning," she said pointing at me, "and I knew this was why."

When I didn't correct her assumption, Kendahl piped in. "It's not what it looks like. It's ju—"

"Everyone is going bananas about you two. Do you guys even know? You freaking killed it last night and, apparently, some famous YouTube guy got it all on video and well..." She stared at our faces and noticed our lack of shock. "I guess you know. Olivia sent me some TikToks this morning of you both. I'd bet the whole country has seen your karaoke show." She winced while she took in Kendahl's appearance. "And your unfortunate accident afterward. Luckily, it doesn't seem like that's the focus, at least this morning."

Mia flopped on the bed next to me and shook her head while smiling.

"We know. That guy bombarded us this morning, and my phone is blowing up." Kendahl groaned.

"Yeah, and Kendahl got a—" She put a hand over my mouth and stood in front of me. I didn't mind the view, but what the hell? Mia looked over at us with her brows raised.

"What he meant to say was I got new followers on my Insta-gram. Right, Coby?"

Her eyes pleaded into mine, so I bobbed my head up and down in agreement. She released her hand and wrenched her palms together.

"Okay..." Mia drawled. "Anyway, everyone's at brunch. Obviously, the morning workout on the beach got canceled. You guys should get ready and meet us next door. And spa day is later. I cannot wait."

"Sounds good. Coby was just leaving, weren't you, Coby?" Kendahl walked over and started to open the door.

As I got up, Mia asked the question that was apparently on everyone's mind. "So, before I go, inquiring minds want to know, are you guys back together?"

I kept my mouth shut, waiting literally on the edge of my seat for her to answer. She pursed her lips and pressed herself against the door. This had to be the worst hangover of her life.

"Yes, we're back together. Right, Coby?"

Both women peered at me. Mia had a wide grin and bounced on the heels of her feet, and Kendahl forced a smile through gritted teeth.

"Right, babe. We worked everything out last night and this morning," I answered.

Shit, that sounded sexual.

Kendahl cleared her throat and guided Mia out the door. "And now my *boyfriend* needs to go get cleaned up. Come on, Coby."

I wanted to talk more, but she was right. We both desperately needed to shower.

"Okay, okay." Mia held her hands up in mock surrender. "I'll see you two lovebirds in a little while."

After squeezing Kendahl, Mia stepped out and waited for me to join her. I didn't know how to play this. Should I give Kendahl a goodbye kiss? A hug?

I kissed her on the cheek, but she spun at the last second, making me kiss the side of her scalp. Not that I don't love her hair, I do, but getting a mouthful of it, still smelling like vomit wasn't fun.

She was frazzled. I wanted to stay and calm her nerves. I'd never seen cool, calm, and collected Kendahl this spun out. Then again, we didn't date for long.

"Okay, bye," she said in a clipped tone.

Bam.

She pushed the door closed, very close to my face, not exactly the picture of a happy relationship, but I couldn't blame her.

Mia turned to me and gave me a knowing look. "Looks like you have your work cut out for you. May I suggest a healthy dose of groveling?"

Chuckling and running a hand through my hair, I turned toward my room. "You know, you're probably right. I fucked up badly. I know I need to make it up to her."

"I hope you can. I want to see my best friend happy and herself again. See you in a bit," Mia said before heading back downstairs.

As I reached my room, I thought about the insane situation we were in. Did Kendahl actually agree to date me, or was she blowing smoke up my ass? Only one way to find out. I'd have to have a conversation with her if, and when, we could get a moment to ourselves.

Chapter 12

Kendahl

As the steaming water pulsed over me, I let my mind whirl. How were the last twenty-four hours real life? Could I be living in some kind of twilight zone or was I actually still asleep? Coby's hands on me had been very real, too real. I didn't want to be thinking of the way he eye fucked me with his smoky eyes or the way my thighs clenched to feel some sort of relief.

Thank God Mia interrupted us when she did. It was already a complicated mess, and we didn't need to add sex to the plate. I don't know what he was thinking, but there was no way I was dating him. No freaking way. I had more self-respect than that even if my body thrummed every time he was near.

This would have to stay pretend. Maybe, and I mean *maybe*, if he helped me tamp down this whole viral video thing long enough for me to get this job offer, then I'd consider forgiving him. But if we were going to do this charade, I had to set some ground rules and a time frame.

As soon as he had left my room and I could think straight, I reread the email from Victor Moss's personal assistant spending way too much time formulating a response that didn't sound too eager but also conveyed how interested I was in meeting with them. Victor's assistant would interview me on Zoom in a few days, and if that went well, they'd fly me out to LA for an in-person interview with Victor Moss himself, and lastly, a trial period. I had to keep my embarrassing video out of the picture.

I transformed into a prune in the shower while letting myself mull over all the details. All I had to do was tell a little fib for a few days and then pretend Coby and I broke things off amicably. No harm no foul. My potential new boss would never find out about my embarrassing fifteen minutes of fame, and I'd get to figure out if a move to LA was what I needed.

I tried not to think of how hurt my mother and Mia would be when I told them I'd be leaving Florida. Thinking of Mia's puppy dog eyes and how long we'd been only a few minutes away from each other on top of my mother's train wreck of a life without me physically in it was not a fun feeling. I'd have to wait to tell them, but there was no point in upsetting either of them until it was necessary.

The familiar weight of guilt sat heavy in the pit of my stomach at all the lies I'd be telling the two most important people in my life over the next few days. Ultimately, I had to do what would be best for me in the long run. I couldn't mope around Palm

Cove for the rest of my life when golden opportunities like these were ripe for the picking. I knew as difficult as it would be, they'd both understand.

Finally, all clean, and dressed in a loose tan romper with a cable knit cardigan to cover my exposed shoulders, I made my way down to the lobby. I was starved and in need of coffee. I should have coordinated with Coby so we could have walked next door together, but I shrugged the thought away figuring he was a big boy and knew where to find me.

A woman was sat at the large wooden front desk as I made my way through the lobby toward the restaurant next door. With just a glance at her, I could tell she had a big personality and was most definitely Bethany's mom. Her dyed red hair was styled in an almost conical-looking beehive do, and she wore a nautical patterned sweater with layers of silver necklaces. She called out to me as I tried to sneak by. If I had to have another conversation before coffee, I'd die.

"Yoo-hoo!" She waved me over and put her book on the counter in front of her. I sighed and plastered on my best PR smile while waving back and walking to the desk. "You must be Kendahl. A nice-looking man was waiting for you, but he got hungry. He asked me to give you this."

She handed me a black umbrella from behind her desk. "Isn't he a sweetheart? I'm Ginger by the way, Ginger Marin." I took the umbrella she offered, and she grasped my hand in hers, shaking it so vigorously that I was afraid the umbrella might launch out of my grip and become a deadly projectile.

Smiling politely, I retrieved my hand and thanked her. I was being kind of rude by not striking up a conversation, but as I said before, coffee and food were at the top of my to-do list and anything keeping me from them would have to wait.

"I say rain is just confetti from the sky." She looked out the window with a frown. "But I do wish Mother Nature would finish up her business. I'd hate for my poor Mikey's wedding to be rained out. I know how much they're looking forward to a beach wedding."

I nodded along offering a chorus of "uh-huhs" and "you're rights." When she started asking me if I was married to that "big hunk of a man," I snapped back into the present.

"No, we're uh...," I hesitated knowing I should have this answer at the ready if we were going to do this thing before nodding again and adding, "just dating. It's all very new."

Releasing a breath, I let the thought of me and Coby having a beach wedding pop into my mind before the bubble popped with Ginger replying, "Well, you better get on that. Boy oh boy, if only I were ten years younger." Shaking her head and laughing, she looked off wistfully. "And single, of course. I have my husband, Tim, bless his soul. But between us girls, what I wouldn't do for a little peek of the goods if you know what I mean."

I suppressed my laughter as I said my goodbyes. I knew all too well what she meant.

As soon as I stepped outside, I was instantly grateful for the umbrella. Rain pelted the top of the umbrella's canopy, and I had to grip it with two hands to keep it from blowing away. Gray skies thick with clouds went on as far as the eye could see. I only hoped this storm would pass quickly.

The windows that were wide open letting in a salty breeze the night before were shut tight, and I felt like I was walking into a completely different place without the boisterous noises and music drifting through the windows.

My eyes zeroed in on Coby the moment I walked into the dining area. I hadn't even mouthed a hello to a single person before I noticed he was sitting next to Shawn soaking wet. His hair reminded me of a spilled bottle of ink, drenched and pushed to the side of his forehead. I couldn't tell if he was wearing a black shirt or if it was a lighter-colored shirt that was darkened from being soaked through.

Looking side to side, I saw that no one else was wet, at least not more than I was from the breeze misting drips toward my face.

If it bothered him, he didn't show it. As soon as he spotted me checking him out, his face broke into a bright smile.

"What happened to you?" I asked.

"What? You mean I'm the only one who thought this was a wet T-shirt contest? Damn, I was hoping you were signed up too."

Coming across the table to sit at his side, I elbow bumped him but couldn't suppress my grin. "Seriously. Aren't you freezing? It's not exactly beach weather out there."

"Nah, I'm good, nothing a strong cup of coffee won't fix. I'm glad Ginger caught you on your way out. I didn't want you getting soaked." He pulled his chair closer to me, then leaned in to whisper into my ear, "At least not soaked in the way I want you to be."

He smelled so good, like mint and shaving cream, and his voice melted over me like warm chocolate. It took me remembering that we were at a table with an audience for me not to nuzzle into him like a cat.

"Wait." I cleared my throat. "Did you give me your umbrella?" That had to be it. Ginger's words replayed through my head about Coby asking her to make sure I had it.

Head tilted to the side, he scratched his beard. "It was the last one. They only had a handful to give out."

Okay, that was sweet of him—really sweet. "Thank you. I'm sorry you got wet. You could have waited for me."

He shrugged, looking back toward his menu. "I didn't know how long you'd be." His eyes lit up and his voice boomed, "Plus, I'd do anything for my new *girlfriend*."

Reality snapped back into place. Shit, it was real. Coby and I were going to fake this thing. Only, with the way he was looking at me, I didn't know if he realized it wasn't real for me.

As the servers came around to take orders and drop off drinks, the comments began. "It was meant to be." A random relative of Mike's remarked from across the long table. "After last night, everyone has been placing bets. I better go find Don; he owes me a twenty."

I exchanged looks with Mia and Shawn who nodded and laughed. "I told you everyone's invested." Mia reached across the table and squeezed my hand. "I'm happy for you. Both of you." Her eyes connected with Coby's, and she gave him a look that said, you better behave or else.

"Yeah, man," Shawn added while gulping down a sip of coffee. "I'm honestly surprised she took your sorry ass back. You must have done a lot of groveling."

Coby draped an arm around me, making my insides clench from the close contact. "I'm surprised too. And I'm nowhere near done with my groveling."

"Yeah, if I know my bestie as well as I think I do, you're going to need to up your game to get back into her good graces," Mia said.

Mike's gruff voice had me glancing away from Mia. He reached the table with Jill by his side, both looking somber.

"Hey guys." He pulled up a couple chairs to join us. "This damn weather messed up our plans." Jill put a reassuring hand on his shoulder, giving him a gentle squeeze through his plaid flannel shirt.

Despite her bummed-out appearance she pushed a smile through. "It'll be okay, love. There's nothing we can do about the weather. No reason not to improvise and make the best of it."

My big cheesy omelet arrived, fluffy and warm, with a side of diced potatoes and toast. An otherworldly sound came from my stomach, and while listening as closely as I could to Jill, I scarfed down the food in front of me only pausing to take generous sips of my creamy coffee from the oversized mug in front of me.

"As long as the forecast I've been hearing is wrong, everything should be fine." Dejected, he slugged back his own coffee like it was a shot. It might have been more than coffee, but it looked like he needed a little added spirit. "I'll find a way to make it up to you, Jilly."

Shawn cut in. "What have you heard about the forecast?"

Everyone at our table leaned in, although between my food and Coby's closeness I was having a hard time concentrating.

"I don't want to cause a panic, but Uncle Tim told me this morning that there's a chance of a tropical storm rolling though Serenity. As of now, they think it'll pass by us and head straight out to sea. He doesn't think there's any cause for concern, but I can't help but worry about it."

Voices dropped to a low hush as everyone processed Mike's news. I'd hate for their guests to up and leave them in the lurch when their wedding plans were already getting messed up by Mother Nature. It seemed the rest of the table agreed.

"We're here for you guys. Krav family forever, remember?" Mia said, sweetly. "Plus, Kendahl hasn't melted from the rain yet, so I guess we're all good."

"Haha, very funny." I showed her my choice finger from across the table.

"Speaking of melting," Jill said, "How are you feeling after your performance last night?" She waggled her brows at me, too cute for me to be sassy with her.

Aiden Aarons stood up from the next table and leaned behind Jill's chair like she had summoned the devil himself. He was like a damn ninja. I hadn't even noticed him in here, but there he was, bobbing man bun and all.

Jill turned around, giving him a cheerful grin. "Oh everyone, I don't think I introduced you to my nephew, Aiden. He traveled here for the wedding with his girlfriend all the way from New York."

Her nephew? Well wasn't that just great.

"Of course, anything for my favorite aunt." He hugged Jill and grinned. Nephew or not, I still didn't trust him. I knew he was only creeping around us to get more content for his channel.

Aiden grabbed a piece of toast from my plate, took a large bite, and added, "Aunt Jill, you'll have to read some of the comments on my video from last night. These two might help me hit a million subscribers."

That little shit. How dare he steal my extremely valuable carbs. I narrowed my eyes at him.

"Listen, while Kendahl and I are glad that your channel is gaining views, this weekend is about your aunt, not some drunken karaoke battle." Coby cut in while handing me his piece of toast. He really was trying to get on my good side.

Nods started around the table along with a few yeahs murmured. Aiden took his time responding, thoroughly chewing my stolen toast, then tilting his head to the side.

"I see what you're saying, bro. How about this? You two give me an interview for my channel before any other content creators get to you, and I'll leave you be for the rest of the weekend." He snagged someone else's orange juice, gulped it down, and leaned closer. "What do you say?"

What I wanted to do had nothing to do with words and everything to do with a few moves I had learned in Krav. But thankfully, Coby answered for us with his voice deep and gravelly.

"I won't speak for my girl, but if it'll get all of this nonsense to stop so we can focus back on the wedding, then I'm in." Turning to me, he asked, "What do you think, babe?"

My face flushed, and I tried not to show him the reaction that his *babe* caused.

"Okay, I'll do it."

Chapter 13

Coby

I WRAPPED MY ARM possessively around Kendahl's shoulders almost as if she'd disappear if didn't keep that physical anchor.

"Right on, right on. Let's get this party started." Aiden began to type on his phone lightning fast before Kendahl cleared her throat, interrupting him.

"Actually, Aiden, let's schedule the interview for later today. I want to get myself camera ready first."

She glanced up at me, eyes wide.

"Right. How about before dinner later? Meet in the lobby around five?"

That would give us plenty of time to get on the same page.

Aiden's shoulders slumped as if he wasn't used to having to wait for what he wanted. Jill noticed right away.

"Aiden, let my guests be. You'll get your interview, but for now, go find your cousin. I haven't seen her since last night."

The change in Aiden's expression after the scolding from his aunt was night and day. It reminded me just how young he really was.

"Alright, Aunt Jill." He reached out to grip my palm and give me a handshake. "I'll see you two later."

Once he was out of hearing vicinity, Jill released a breath through her teeth. "Sorry about him, guys. I love my nephew dearly, but he wasn't raised the way I've raised Kayla. My lovely sister hasn't taught him the word no, and I have to say he's a bit on the selfish side." She sipped water from the glass in front of her. "I learned that after my fire. He didn't care enough to use his platform to help out his own blood."

Her face flushed and chest slumped in. I couldn't let Jill be upset on her wedding weekend. Reaching past Kendahl, I gave her upper arm a light squeeze.

"Hey, that's why your Krav family has your back, always. Let's finish eating. If I remember correctly, we have some spa appointments to get to."

It hadn't escaped me that Kendahl relaxed into my side or that the corners of her lips turned up. I'd cheer up the whole island if it meant seeing her mood boost even a fractional amount.

"Thanks, Coby," Jill said.

Mike gave his bride-to-be a side hug and a quick kiss on her cheek, then said, "Krav family forever."

A warmth spread to my chest. Being here, with Kendahl by my side and my chosen family surrounding us, cemented my plan to get myself out of this limelight and keep Wyoming far away from my life.

As we dispersed clutching our umbrellas, I took Kendahl's hand and pulled her away from the others.

"I think we should find somewhere quiet to talk," I said.

She looked down at our connected palms, then back up to my eyes, her expression unreadable. We watched each other for a moment, hand in hand, before she gulped a breath. "Yeah, sorry. It's just I'm not used to your touch anymore. I'd be lying if I said it wasn't...I don't know, kind of weird."

I circled my thumb against the outside of her palm. "Just *kind of* weird? I can work with that." I glanced out the foggy window at the sideways rain battering the outside of the bar. "Let's go over here."

I found us a little table in the back of the bar. It was still early enough that the place was empty anyway, but back here, tucked away, we were sure to be left alone. Kendahl situated herself in her chair and sat up straight as she pulled her hands away from mine and placed them on the table. This was her business persona, and the switch up was jarring.

She pushed a lock of hair behind her ears and finally met my gaze. I feigned a relaxed, couldn't-care-less look even though my stomach was in knots, and I was waiting for her to speak first.

"I thought about our situation while I was in the shower."

My ears perked up. "Oh yeah? How did our *situation* look in the shower?" I scooted closer and lowered my voice. "Better yet, how did it feel?"

"Oh my God, Coby. Keep it in your pants." Her cheeks turned an adorable rosy pink.

I chuckled and gestured for her to go on.

"As I was saying, our situation...you know, the one *you* got us into when you told Aarons, and his one million viewers, that we were back together."

She crossed her legs, shaking them violently enough to vibrate the table. Her brows knitted together, and she chewed at her full bottom lip.

"Okay," I put my hands up in mock surrender. "So I had some wishful thinking. But it wasn't me who started this whole going viral thing. That karaoke battle was all you. I merely showed off my superb singing ability."

Scoffing, she rested both forearms on the table. "You're kidding, right? I know for a fact that you started it. I may have been a little bit tipsy." A little? I had to put my hand across my mouth to keep from laughing. That only pissed her off more. "But I remcmber that it was you who asked for the battle in the first place."

"Only after you baited me. You know I'm competitive."

That rosy glow migrated up from her cheeks toward her entire gorgeous face. She was pissed, and I didn't know why, but I loved watching her get fired up. Something about pulling the brat out of her made my dick hard.

She huffed. "None of that matters now anyway. The fact of the matter is, not only do our closest friends think we're back together, but a million other freaking people out there do as well. And," she leaned close enough that I could feel the warmth of her breath on my skin, "most importantly, my dream job is on the line now. Freaking Stratestar Agency. Do you even know who they represent?"

"Uh, no idea. Do you want to enlighten me? You seem to be getting yourself a little worked up there," I said.

"Of course I'm worked up," she yelled before looking from side to side, realizing where we were. She took a deep breath, dropped her voice back down a few notches, and added, "This is the job of my dreams, and I'm struggling to believe that my entire future is riding on us convincing the world that we're together so Aiden and everyone else will stop talking about that video."

I guess I got my answer. This wasn't real for her. She was in this for her gains and that was all. For all I knew, she probably still hated my guts. Thinking about that made me clench my jaw almost painfully. Everything in me wanted to use humor to defuse the situation and make her feel not so freaked out by all of this. But that's how I always did things, and clearly, that hadn't gotten me very far. I sucked in a deep breath.

"So just to be sure I have this right, you want us to pretend to date so you can get this dream job that's all the way in LA? What if they've already seen the video, and it bites you in the ass? And what we just lie to Mia and Shawn and everyone else?"

I thought about how, not more than ten minutes ago, I was reassuring Jill of how we were a family and how we took care of each other. A lump formed in my throat at the thought of lying to them, but I guess it was me that technically started this whole mess. Goddamn I was an idiot sometimes.

Kendahl watched my face closely like she could pick through my unspoken thoughts.

"I hate to lie as much as you do. But, yes, this job means that much to me. To at least have the chance to go through with the interview..." Hesitating she added, "It would mean the world to me."

It was like my fucking heart was in a vice grip. I knew then and there that I'd do anything to make her happy. Maybe that's why I hadn't thought twice about it. I wanted to earn her forgiveness even if that meant I knew I couldn't keep her.

"Okay then. Fake boyfriend checking in for duty. I can tell by the look you're giving me you have more to add?"

"I do. We need to lay down some ground rules especially if Aiden Aarons is going to be lurking around all weekend recording and live streaming whenever he can."

"Agreed." I ran my hand through my beard, interested to hear what her rules would be.

Tapping her fingers on the table and chewing that bottom lip again, she finally looked back up at me.

"Rule number one, no PDA. That means no kissing, intentional touching, and one hundred percent, no sex."

Chuckling, I leaned in. "Now wait a second, aren't we supposed to look all lovey-dovey? You said yourself that the little twerp would be live streaming. I think it would look a bit suspicious if we didn't have a little bit of PDA."

She glared at me as I watched her mind work on a rebuttal.

"Fine. Only PDA when we know Aiden is around, but nothing crazy." She narrowed those big blue eyes at me. "I know how your charm works. I'm on to you."

For the second time, I held my hands up in mock surrender. "I have no idea what you mean."

I knew exactly what she meant.

"Rule number two, no fooling around or flirting with anyone else. We need to make this look real," she said.

Well that was easy. She was the only one I wanted anyway even while we were a thousand miles apart.

I nodded. "Gotcha. What else?"

Tap, tap, tap. Her pink painted nails clinked against the table.

"Rule number three, no taking on any interviews or important conversations without consulting with each other. That means no answering DMs, no scheduling interviews, and absolutely no reaching out to any press. I'm in PR, this is what I do. We need to swing the narrative in the direction we want it to go. Better yet, we need to do whatever we can to make the video disappear."

Leaning back in my chair, I nodded. Another easy one. I had no desire to make this into anything more than it already was. If anything, I wanted the opposite. The more attention we received, the greater the chance of people finding out about my past.

"Yes, warden. Anything else?" I purposefully gave her my widest smirk, knowing it irritated her. With a sharp look straight into my eyes, she nodded.

"Yes, one last rule, absolutely no sharing a room. Last night was an anomaly. A mistake. It can't happen again."

"I don't know. Like rule one, I think people will talk if they don't see us together," I answered.

I brushed my leg against hers under the table, and she jumped in response.

"It's a hard no for me. No sleeping together. If people delve into us that closely then they can just fuck off. It's healthy to have some boundaries anyway. Let Aiden's viewers learn a thing or two about that."

"Yes, ma'am, your urchin room will stay yours. I will stick to the solitude of my coral room."

I so badly wanted to remind her of the way she had urged me to stay the night before. And the way her face lit up when I said I would.

"Good. Now that all of that's settled, we should go get ready for spa day."

The downpour was drenching everything in sight, and the wind beat against the walls. I wondered how the hell we'd even get to the main strip of town intact. I held up the umbrella, which was almost pointless to use with how insane the rain was and let my palm rest on the curve of her low back. She twisted her neck to look at where our bodies touched and her eyes widened.

"Rule number one, Coby."

I removed my hand with a huff, but every fiber of my being itched to touch her, to have a possessive hand on any part of her body. Before we reached the exit, Kendahl stopped short, causing the umbrella to knock into the old wooden door.

"I just realized something."

"Yeah?"

"You never told me what's in it for you? Why go through with this whole charade? I know you're not a guy who shies away from the spotlight." I grinned at that. "But to play these games, there must be something in it for you?"

I shrugged, feigning indifference. "Maybe I feel like an ass for walking out on you the way I did. Maybe I want to make it up to you in any way I can."

Her eyes narrowed. "I don't buy that for a second. There must be something in it for you."

I positioned my mouth right over her soft earlobe. "Maybe I'm waiting for the moment that you admit you want me as much as I want you. Maybe I like to watch you squirm so badly that you won't be able to think straight until I've made you scream my name."

I grazed her skin, ever so lightly, with the edge of my teeth and felt a shiver course through her body. She shoved me off and huffed away from me.

"The only screaming I'll be doing is when I'll be telling you to fuck off."

I had my work cut out for me but watching that perfect ass as she strutted through the door and out into the pouring rain without the umbrella made me want to earn every second I could with that woman.

Chapter 14

Kendahl

Ginger corralled our group of six women into her transporter van. We tried to argue that we were fully capable of driving, but she insisted that the girls and guys get split up. Jill whispered to Mia, Avery, and me to go with it.

With the way the rain pelted the van and the wind howled, I was glad to have someone who knew where they were going behind the wheel. It wasn't long before we arrived at the island's only spa located directly across from the beach. Thanks to the foggy van windows, I couldn't make out much of the exterior of the spa, but it was much larger than I would have thought.

"Here we are, Serenity Spa. Out you go." Ginger idled, waiting for us to unload like a group of schoolchildren. "Tim will be back to pick you up in a few hours. Enjoy!"

We ran toward the doors, screeching and avoiding massive puddles in the sandy parking area.

"Oh my God," I huffed as we entered the dimly lit lobby. "I feel like a drowned rat." I breathed in the comforting lavender scented air while I wiped drops of water from my brow line.

Mia chuckled and readjusted her bun. "But a cute, drowned rat though."

I swatted her, but we were interrupted by a pair of spa employees dressed in black polo shirts and loose-fitted pants.

"Welcome. You must be the Marin wedding party?" one of them asked in a serene voice that was a direct contrast to the pelting rain. "I'm Sara, and this is Liam." She gestured to her right at the ridiculously tall and insanely handsome man beside her. He waved and flashed us a friendly grin. "We're going to get you all checked in. It looks like the rest of your party hasn't arrived yet?"

Jill stepped forward. "Not yet, we took separate vehicles. I'm Jill, by the way."

"Our lovely bride," Sara beamed. "We're so happy to have you all today. Thanks for braving the weather. It's pretty wild out there."

I nodded along with everyone else, thinking about how I couldn't wait to get out of my soaking wet clothes and into a cozy robe and slippers. While Sara rambled on with the normal spa niceties, describing the spa offerings, and handing out forms, I couldn't help but notice Liam checking me out. He was all muscular arms, sharp jawline with stubble, and dark hair cut close to his scalp. I met his gaze, but only for a second, before bringing my attention back to Sara.

Kendahl you are not here to flirt with guys. Not anymore. You're technically in a relationship now.

"If you'll follow me, I'll show you to the changing facilities." Sara led the way down a dimly lit hallway lined with treatment rooms.

Mia leaned in to whisper, "You think Liam is one of the therapists?"

My pulse picked up speed. "If he is, I hope one of the guys gets him. I don't think I could focus with that man's hands all over me."

She giggled. "Same. Plus Shawn would lose his mind if another guy laid a finger on me."

"So possessive," I snorted, causing Sara to turn my way. I waved my hand in an apologetic gesture and gave Mia the stink eye. "You're going to get us in trouble. We need to use spa voices."

"Right. Spa voices." Mia bobbed her head, before busting out another giggle. Sometimes we were like two teenagers when we were together.

"This is more like it," I said while tying my plush robe tight against my waist. I lounged back on a chaise in the locker room while the rest of our group peeled off their wet clothes in exchange for spa robes. "It's starting to feel like a vacation now," I said to Mia.

"Totally," Mia said as she flopped next to me. "Although these robes were not really made for ladies like me." She pulled the two sides closer and readjusted the tie. "My goodies are spilling out."

"Here," I tossed a throw pillow her way. "Just keep this in front of your chest all day and you'll be fine."

She huffed. "That's not a bad plan. But I may need a bigger pillow. If I move my legs at all, I'll flash some poor unknowing soul."

A laugh made its way up from my belly, and I spread out laying my legs over Mia's lap. "There, all covered up. I'll walk in front of you whenever we have to go somewhere. Problem solved."

Mia rested against the pillows. and I took a moment to enjoy the warmth of being snuggled up. "I can't remember the last time we've had a spa day," Mia said.

"I think it was that time Spa Perfection gifted me those packages for helping them launch their grand opening." That was a few years ago when I first started working for Claudia.

Mia sat up. "Oh dear Lord, I hope today will be better than that nightmare."

"You're being dramatic. It wasn't that bad." It was, but I was not going down this rabbit hole with Mia again.

"Not bad? I'm not sure if you have a temporary case of amnesia, but my face was bright red for a week. No amount of makeup could cover my reaction to that facial." She narrowed her eyes at me, which only made me want to push her buttons more.

"So their products were a little strong for you. Luckily, all it took was one round of steroids and you were good as new." I flashed my brightest smile at her.

"Thanks for the reminder," she deadpanned. "Now I'm anxious. Do you know what treatments Jill signed us up for? I forgot to ask."

I found Jill dressed in her robe and chatting with one of her relatives, but before I could ask her what the plans were, Sara came back in holding an iPad to usher us out into the relaxation room.

Lounging on one of the couches with one leg crossed over the other and an arm resting casually on the back cushion was Coby. His eyes were laser focused on mine, and I couldn't help but peruse him. The spa robe was comically short on his tall frame. Like, another inch and everyone in the room would know if he preferred boxers or briefs (or nothing). It was unfair that legs like his were wasted on him. Seriously, how were they so long and lean yet strong and muscular at the same time.

Sara stopped short before regaining her composure. "I see the other half of your group has arrived. Perfect." She scurried around adjusting pillows and handing out water glasses while we joined the guys. "Make yourselves comfortable. Your therapists will be out shortly to take you in for your treatments."

Coby raised a brow at me and patted the cushion next to him. I guess we were starting our little performance. I watched Mia join Shawn and give him a kiss and Jill flop across Mike's lap, giggling at him in his tiny robe and I internally groaned. Who would have thought a spa day would turn into such a PDA fest.

I plopped next to Coby, inching as far away from his body as I could and double checked that my robe stayed firmly closed. The sooner I could get into my appointment, the better. Hell, I'd rather get a chemical peel and a full body wax than have to sit this close to Coby while all my friends smooched with their boyfriends.

I breathed deeply, willing the lavender to seep into my every pore, but all I could smell was Coby. He smelled like warmth. Like the very first time my skin soaked up the Florida sunshine. I had basked in the bright light, lifting my arms to the sky and immediately knew I was where I needed to be. I wanted to hate my sense of smell and its ability to transport me in time and space. It almost always brought me to moments I didn't want to think about. But Coby's smell had brought me to a happy place and dammit if I didn't want to bottle that shit.

"This is the relaxation room you know." Coby's husky voice broke me out of my thoughts. He inched closer so that our thighs touched and then slung his arm over my shoulder. I jerked at the contact before self-correcting when I noticed Jill looking at us with a cheesy grin.

"I know it is," I gritted out.

"You look anything but relaxed," he whispered. He played with a strand of my hair, inching his fingers closer to the curve of my neck. It felt way better than I wanted to admit. "Why is that?"

When I didn't reply, he moved his large palm to the outside of my thigh right where my robe ended. My breath caught in my throat. Chuckling, he came even closer and drew slow teasing circles with the rough edge of his fingertip.

"Coby," I said through tight lips. "What are you doing?"

"Helping you relax. Like I said, this *is* the relaxation room." He scraped his fingertip up and down the slope of my neck. I shivered beneath his touch. Warmth spread up my chest and neck. "You look beautiful all flushed like that."

I squeezed the edge of my robe to keep my hands from doing something that my head didn't want them to do. Not wanting to meet his heated expression. I aimed my gaze down, but I had to admit, his fingers set my skin on fire.

He slid his index finger underneath the hem of my robe, just an inch, continuing the slow circles. My pulse thumped as he inched higher, and I shivered, releasing a shaky breath. "That's it, baby, let go for me."

His warm breath whispering against my ear brought me back to the present, reminding me that we weren't alone. I jumped and pulled my robe tighter. "I'm going to get some water." Icy cold water to be exact. Coby chuckled under his breath. That bastard knew I was turned on.

There had to be a way to turn the tide in my favor because letting Coby know he was affecting me would surely get to his head. I looked at my cup of ice water, grabbed an ice cube, and grinned.

I made my way back to the couch and sat close to Coby, intentionally leaning into him. He flashed me a smug grin that made his dimples show. "Feeling better?" he asked.

I turned to face him and slid my hand across his shoulder and around his neck until I reached the front of his robe, then I dropped the ice cube right down his front. "Much better," I crooned.

His eyes dropped to his lap, and he hissed before jumping up. "What the he—"

Before he could get the words out a slew of therapists entered the relaxation room calling on their clients one by one. I heard a deep voice say my name and looked up to see none other than Liam, waiting against the wall for me.

I looked back to Coby, smiling smugly. "I thought you might have needed to cool off before your appointment." Coby looked between Liam and me and his lips pursed tightly. "I guess I was right. Have a good treatment, boyfriend." Giving him a little wave, I sauntered over to Liam, shaking his hand and smiling brightly.

On our way out into the hallway, I chanced one more backward look at Coby who was standing stick straight with his fists clenched at his sides and a look that could kill on his face.

Liam led me through a maze of corridors lined with dimly lit glass sconces and framed beach-themed artwork. Jill and Mike were a few paces behind us holding hands and speaking in low voices to their therapists.

"So, you're a massage therapist?" I asked, mostly to make conversation.

"No, I'm actually a dentist. Didn't you know you're here for a root canal?" He chuckled, his voice was low and husky.

"Good one. I'll have you know that I don't mind dental work. I get drugged up every time and take a nice little vacation into dreamland," I quipped.

"Hmm, well I guess I picked the wrong profession for messing with you then," Liam said while he turned down yet another hallway. How big was this place? "I take it the bride didn't share what services you signed up for then?"

"Nope." My voice popped the P sound dramatically. "I'm just along for the ride."

We finally reached door number fourteen and Liam opened it wide, letting me inside. "Well, don't worry. I'll make sure your ride is nice and smooth." My normal cool and calm demeanor crumbled a bit, and I felt my face heat. A sly grin tugged at the corner of his lips. "Your first treatment is with me, a sixty-minute essential oil massage. Then you'll have a break for lunch and a facial with London, one of our estheticians. She's—"

He was cut off mid-sentence by Coby stalking into the room followed by a young female spa attendant who looked nervous as hell.

Chapter 15

Coby

"Coby?" Kendahl gritted my name through her teeth. "What are you doing in here?" She bounced her gaze between me, my confused massage therapist, and the other guy in the room. The guy who looked at Kendahl with a heated expression I knew all too well. That look alone told me, he wasn't as professional as he should be in his line of work.

I forced a breath into my chest, letting it out slowly so I could regain my composure. Kendahl had a hand on her hip and a scowl lining her face. "My therapist," I gestured to the confused woman behind me, "recommended the couples suite for us." The lie slid off my lips as I continued to spin my story. "It has two massage tables and comes with champagne. Isn't that right," I scanned her nametag before continuing, "Katie?"

"Uh, sir…" the douchey guy started as I cracked my knuckles and glared right at him. He zipped his lips. *That's right kid.* I had never been like this before. But when I pictured the douche's hands rubbing Kendahl with hot oil, a burning sensation rose from my belly into my chest.

Katie looked to the douche, then back at me and nodded. "Okay, we can make this work. Couple's suite number three is open. If you're both ready, you can follow me." The burning made its way back down into the deep pits of my gut where it belonged.

"Are you serious, Coby?" Kendahl rolled her eyes.

"Of course I am." I stepped to her side and pulled her against my chest. "I didn't want to be separated from my beautiful girlfriend for a whole hour. Don't you feel the same way?"

"Oh I feel some kind of way." She shrugged me off and stalked ahead of me.

Now I just needed to swap therapists, which meant I'd have another dude rubbing me. I shuddered. I was secure enough in my sexuality to let a guy massage me. Better him working on me than on Kendahl. As I followed a peppy-looking Katie, a baffled douche, and a pissed off Kendahl through the corridors I tried to formulate another plan to turn this spa day around.

They weren't kidding when they called the couple's massage room a suite. It was nothing like the cramped room Amy and I had once gotten massages in at a chain right after we were married. Two massage tables with soft looking blankets were placed in the center of the spacious room. A river-rock-lined shower large enough for five people was to my side and more framed beach artwork lined the cream-colored walls. Dimly lit sconces set the room in a soft glow, and the sounds of rain pelting from outside mixed with meditation music set the perfect ambiance for relaxation. Yet I was anything but relaxed. My jaw clenched as the douche, or Liam as Kendahl corrected on our way down the hall, led Kendahl toward one of the tables.

Katie started to do the same by turning down the corner of the sheet. "I was thinking we could swap therapists," I blurted out.

Kendahl swung her head in my direction, her brows raised. "No, I think I'd like to keep things as they are." She flashed a sweet smile that was in direct contrast to the tone of her voice.

I huffed. Should I push the issue? Make a scene? Glancing at my therapist who had that same perplexed look on her face as earlier, had me resigning. "Fine."

Liam's brow gleamed with sweat as he stepped toward the door and gave us both their spiel. He avoided making eye contact with me all together instead focusing only on Kendahl. We were to get undressed to our comfort level and lie face down underneath the sheets. They'd be back shortly to begin. I heard the two of them whispering to each other as they closed the door behind them.

"What's your issue? You're acting like an animal during mating season. All that's missing is you marking me with your scent." She scoffed and turned her back to me, untied her robe, and hung it on the hook against the wall. She kept her thong on, and I narrowed my eyes trying to make out the small pattern on it.

Her silhouette in the dim light had me stumbling over my response. The slope of her neck as she pulled her hair up in a ponytail, the soft curve of her hips, the tiny bit of exposed side breast as she shimmied beneath the sheets still facing away from me. I bit back a moan, cursing the fact that I couldn't go to her and trace every inch of her body.

"No issue. Everything is fine," I said through clenched teeth as I disrobed and slid myself onto the heated table. "But if you really want me to mark you as mine, I have far better ways."

Lying on her stomach, she lifted her head out of the face cradle. "Right... you're fine," she said sarcastically. "Have I hit my head and been transported into one of those shifter romance novels? You know what? I don't want to know. Stop this pissing match and relax. I'm going to save the discussion of your temper tantrum room switcheroo for later."

She breathed deeply and settled her head back down into the cradle but not before I replied, "Don't worry, pussycat, I'll show you my bite later."

With her head buried in the face cradle all I could make out was a muffled, "for the love of—" before one of the therapists knocked on the door.

"All set?" It was Katie's tentative voice sounding like she had no idea what she would find when she opened the door.

Kendahl let out a muffled "yeah" as I attempted to make myself comfortable in the face cradle. Being a physical therapist, I knew a thing or two about massage and used these tables daily on my patients, so I took it upon myself to reach around and twist knobs, moving things exactly the way I wanted them to go. Katie came to my side to help, but I had already pretty much gotten myself comfortable at least physically, mentally I was still on edge.

I tried to tune out Katie's questions to better focus on what Liam was asking Kendahl a few feet away. His voice sounded too smooth, and I didn't like the giggle that came out of her. What the hell was he saying to make her laugh?

"Mr. Barnes?" Katie placed her warm palm on my upper back. "I was asking if there are any areas you'd like me to focus on?"

"No."

"Okay. Well if anything changes, feel free to let me know."

"Uh-huh," I grunted out, straining my ears to hear Kendahl's low voice. All at once the room quieted, and I believe the lights dimmed even more from what I could tell face down. Squelching noises sounded awfully close to my ears as Katie rubbed oil into her palm.

Just relax, Coby. I needed this. It had been a hellish few weeks, and my body hurt from sleeping on that shitty couch and missing my Krav classes and regular training routine. Katie pulled back the sheet and exposed my back to the cool air.

"Take a deep breathe in," she instructed me.

Ah, lavender. I filled my lungs with the calming aroma.

"And breathe out," Katie whispered.

I released my breath slowly in a hiss...but what the hell was that sound?

"Mmm...that feels perfect."

What the hell? I jerked, lifting my head out of the cradle so fast that Katie jumped. Liam was hovering over Kendahl's exposed back, spreading oil in long fluid motions.

"Mr. Barnes? Everything okay?" Katie added more oil to her palm, squelching her hands together again, and I stuffed my face back into the padded cradle.

Freaking Kendahl. She had definitely moaned like that to fuck with me.

Katie made contact with my skin and massaged in flowing strokes down the sides of my spine and back up, hooking at the notch where my head connects with my neck. She had strong hands for such a small person, but I learned in my physical therapy classes that you could never judge a book by its cover.

By her third pass, my breathing calmed, and I almost forgot that my girl was getting felt up by another dude right next to me. *Almost.* Until I heard Kendahl moan again. Every muscle in my body tensed as I lifted my head. He was still massaging her back, paying extra attention to the curve of her low back this time.

"Mmm..." she moaned low.

It was a sound I may not have heard had my head been in the cradle. Nothing looked unprofessional, but that didn't stop red from flaring across my field of vision. Katie stepped back up to the head of the table after also working my low back. I wish I could have actually enjoyed her craft, but there would be no melting of muscle for me. Not in here.

"If you're more comfortable, you can keep your head to the side like that Mr. Barnes," Katie said sweetly. "You may get a crick in your neck though."

Fuck it. My neck was already tense, and there was no way that would change, so I nodded and let her go about her business.

Midway through a super eerie track of wolves howling set against somber piano music, I felt Katie re-drape my back and move on to my legs with a gentle palm against the sheets. That was when I lost my shit.

Chapter 16

Kendahl

LIAM UNDRAPED MY LEG all the way up to my inner thigh. My exposed skin pebbled from the cool air. I peeked my head up an inch to spy on Coby inconspicuously. His therapist was still working his back, and he actually looked peaceful. Maybe I should stop messing with him. He already went all alpha male before. I didn't need to goad him more even if it was fun.

Liam cupped my feet with his warm hands and slid them upward in one long stroke that ended at my bikini line. Trailing his hands down, he repeated the move but with deeper pressure. Everything felt great, amazing even. I certainly didn't want to disrupt Coby again; I was done messing around with him. I don't know exactly what happened when he started on a third pass, but a sob slipped out of my lips from some unknown depths in my chest. Liam stopped moving. He didn't say a word just waited.

I was fine.

He started again, kneading into my foot with his thumb. It felt so... freaking... good. Before I knew what was happening, the most harrowing banshee moan cut through the quiet room. I tried to control it and stuff it back down, but it was no use. Liam's freaking angelic hands had massaged something loose and whatever it was needed to be released.

Being facedown I couldn't see Liam's reaction but felt his hands still as soon as the wailing began.

"Kendahl? Did he hurt you?" Coby's voice was laced with venom.

I ignored Coby and attempted to control my breathing. Liam moved to the head of the table and placed a reassuring palm on my back. "Are you okay? Did I use too much pressure?" He sounded panicked.

"No." Sob. "You're fine." I sniffled. "I just need a minute."

"May we have the room?" Coby's commanding voice sounded closer, maybe he had sat up. I was too embarrassed to look. Embarrassed and *very* snotty.

"But Mr. Barnes...your treatments aren't over and..." Coby's therapist hesitated. "Sure. No problem, take your time."

I breathed in through my stuffy nose. It felt like I was trying to fill up a balloon through nothing more than a pinhole. The door closed with a click, and I still didn't want to get up. My head was too heavy anyway. There was no explanation as to why I was in hysterics.

Coby kept seeing me at my absolute worst. Then the thought crept in. *No wonder he left just like Ben and everyone else.*

I choked on another sob.

"Baby, did he hurt you? I'll rip him apart limb from limb." He spoke slowly, his voice thick with barely-contained anger.

The air stirred around my still undraped leg. Coby pulled the covers over me and gave my foot a comforting press. I still wasn't ready to look at him, so I shook my head. "He didn't hurt me."

He released a breath. "Do you want to talk about it? What's upsetting you?"

Yes. I want you to hold me. Bring me in to your comforting chest and let me spill my soul out. My insecurities, my fears, my failures.

"No," I squeaked out, shaking my head.

The room was quiet for a beat, the only sound being a rather unfortunate playlist of wolves howling that reminded me of a haunted house soundtrack.

He placed a hand on the table beside my shoulder, reassuring me that he was there and that I wasn't alone. "Can I touch you?" he asked in a low voice.

He was already so close to me. Without seeing anything at all, I knew. Warmth radiated from his fingers like an aura. But he waited, even as his index finger moved the slightest bit toward me. My body wanted...needed to feel his touch. My head said otherwise. His finger danced along the curve of my shoulder gliding over nothing but air. I stayed quiet wanting to see how long he'd wait for me.

One breath, then two, until my sobs were replaced by needy pants. Dammit.

"Coby?" I hardly recognized my muffled voice.

"Kendahl."

My name from his lips sounded so incredibly sexy.

"Was there something you wanted?" He spoke against my ear just close enough that I could imagine the stubble of his beard nuzzling the side of my face.

What was I doing? I wasn't some meek woman who let a man lead the way. That's never been me. Taking a deep breath in, I found my voice.

"Touch me."

He let loose a long breath next to my ear that sent a flush of warmth between my thighs. Without teasing me and without another thought, his hands were on me. His warm palms splayed across the tops of my shoulders gliding ever so gently at first across the small, uncovered area.

"How's that, baby?"

I hummed in response, unable to form words. He continued to glide and knead the oil-slicked skin of my shoulders and neck with an expert's touch. My hum of pleasure must have sent him into more of a trance. It seemed as though hours went by. He massaged my scalp, working his fingertips in slow circles. His thumbs pressed a path down the slope of my neck and stopped above the tucked in sheet.

"Feeling better now?" he asked, stopping his movements. Was I? I had stopped crying so that was a plus. The tightness in my chest seemed to have loosened, and my attention was squarely focused on the aching between my thighs.

"Yes."

He slid one finger under the sheet. Just one finger. He kept it still at first, before tracing a pattern slowly from one side of my back to the other. My stomach fluttered and that ache grew heavy.

He grazed the bottoms of my shoulder blade and the ridges of my spine, he slowed as he reached the side of my breast and let his finger linger along my ribcage. Every part of me was waiting, longing to see how far he would go.

He skimmed the swell of my breast and trailed his finger back up along the edge of my tight shoulder blade. The anticipation was going to kill me. I had never been this needy in my life. He made another pass down my back this time lower and lower until he was hovering above me at the head of the table so closely that I could feel the heat of his body and hear his ragged breaths escaping his lips.

The need for his hands to be all over me and for there to be no fabric between us overwhelmed me. "Mmm, Coby."

"God, Kendahl those sounds you're making. You're killing me." He splayed his palms out again and let his fingers hover just above my panty line. My pulse pounded, filling me with liquid heat. His fingers smoothed along the lace band, tracing the outline lightly. He played with the material before dipping one finger beneath it, drawing across the ridges of my hip slowly and deliberately.

"I love to toy with you and watch you writhe and squirm," he growled into my ear before palming my ass with both hands. "I know you're wet for me. Tell me, did you soak the sheets?"

Fuck yes, I did. "You're an asshole," I told him between a breathy moan. I was so close to grinding my hips into the table to get some relief. He chuckled low and deep.

"Looks like you want to break rule number one." He kneaded my cheeks, gently pushing my center into the warmth of the sheets. It felt too damn good. "Rules are meant to be broken, baby."

He glided his fingers closer to my slit, trailing them along the crease of my ass. Another inch and he'd be exactly where I needed him. I squirmed against the delicious weight of his body hovering over me. The pressure only added to my need. He hooked his finger under the seam of my thong. If I lifted my ass, he'd be right there, but he stopped and nuzzled into my neck causing another shiver to course through me.

"Tell me, Kendahl. Do you want me to fuck your wet pussy with my fingers?" His dirty mouth was something I wasn't used to. Yes. God yes, I wanted him inside me. I kept my mouth shut though, letting the anticipation of his next move stoke the flames within me, wanting him to feel all the need that I did.

I was about to sit up and take what I wanted when we were interrupted by a knock at the door.

"Mr. Barnes? Ms. Edwards? You're treatment time is over. May we come in?"

"Oh my God. Coby get off." I pushed myself up, knocking Coby forward so that he almost landed on top of me. He grumbled, and righted himself, taking a step back toward his table. As I fixed my ponytail and tried to calm my heart rate, I glanced down and my eyes went directly to Coby's dick which was...erect.

I cleared my throat, "Jesus, Coby, get your robe on." He pulled a hand through his hair and followed my gaze down to his boxer briefs.

"Fuck." He turned toward the hook on the wall, grabbed his robe, and tossed me mine as I stood up.

They knocked again. Damn, Katie, take a hint.

"We'll be right out," I yelled. "Coby, fix your boner," I said in a whisper. "This is a nice establishment."

He chuckled, that smug, infuriating laugh. "What do you want me to do with it?"

"I don't know. Think of something unsexy...lizards, owls, snakes. No not snakes, don't think of anything long and tubular." I frantically threw back the sheets, noticing a wet patch. Christ.

"What's with all the animals?" He laughed again.

"I don't know," I said exasperated. "That's where my brain went."

He shook his head. "It's fine. Calm down. It's not like they haven't seen someone all riled up after a rub down before."

I grabbed a towel from the counter and tried to blot the wetness away to no avail. "Ugh, you're gross."

"Not gross." He crossed the room toward me still very much at attention. "What would have happened if they hadn't knocked?" He watched me intently as I bunched up the towel and hid it under the sheets.

"Nothing. We have rules remember." I lied through gritted teeth.

"Rules...right," he said sarcastically.

Katie knocked again. "Is there anything you need in there?"

"Come on." I gave him a gentle shove toward the door and adjusted my robe. "And tie that robe tighter. This poor therapist has dealt with enough trouble from you today. She doesn't need a heart attack."

"I don't think this robe can hide what's going on under here," Coby joked.

Feeling hot, bothered, and past my limit of witty comebacks, I closed my eyes and shook my head following Coby out into the hallway of the spa.

Chapter 17

Coby

Once Kendahl was led into another room for her facial, I was shown the Jacuzzi, steam room, and sauna where Shawn and a few of the other guys were hanging out. We spent the next hour or so lying back in the hot water goofing around and telling stories about our early days at Krav. Shawn admitted he wasn't my biggest fan when we first met. Like I hadn't known that. But even he hasn't been immune to my charms. The usually quiet and gruff Mike was full of laughs and stories about how him and Jill hit it off after she stepped on his toe in a group activity a few months ago.

Who would have thought that a gym where people quite literally choke and kick each other would be such a matchmaking haven. Thoughts of Kendahl swam in the back of my mind the entire time I marinated in the water. We had been so close to taking things to the next level in that couple's suite. The noises that came out of her had been small and needy. Fuck. I didn't need to be thinking about those while sitting in a hot tub with a bunch of dudes. I hoped she was okay. I'd dealt with clients having emotional releases on my table before. We store all kinds of shit in our muscles and have no control when or where they come out.

Back in the locker rooms, I toweled dry and pulled my clothes out from the crumpled pile they were in. Shawn did the same beside me. He rubbed some deodorant on before slinging on a black T-shirt. "How are things going with Kendahl?"

I sat on the wooden bench that separated the rows of lockers, thinking of a response. "It's going as well as can be expected."

"That good, huh?" He smirked as he sat down to put his socks on. "I have to admit, I was shocked when Mia told me you guys got back together. That was fast considering how she reacted last night."

If only he knew. "No one was more shocked than me. Believe me, I still have a lot of groveling to do."

He chuckled. "Knowing Kendahl, I believe you." He quieted for a moment before continuing, "And you may want to drop the whole Casanova act. Tell her why you left if you haven't already."

My mind spiraled. Had I told Shawn about my father in a moment of weakness? No, I'd remember that.

"Helping a friend isn't a bad thing, man. Plus, it's better to set the record straight than have her stewing on all the rumors that have been going around." Shawn finished tying his sneakers and stood up to close his locker door.

"My friend...yeah, you're right, man. Honestly, I was waiting for her to bring it up. But maybe I should do it first and clear the air."

I stood and rubbed my towel through my still damp hair. Not that it would help, I could still hear the rain pelting the roof. Shawn waited for me against the row of lockers.

"Oh, and take it from me, you can never go wrong with wine and chocolate." We chuckled. When had he become so soft?

We arrived back at the inn before the women and all went our separate ways. As much as I liked these guys, I was thrilled to get a minute to myself. In the solace of my room, I watched the wind spray rain sideways out my rattling window.

Staring at the faded geometric patterns on the throw rug in front of me, I decided to give mama a call and check in. I reached her room after dialing the main number and hitting her extension.

"Caroline Barnes speaking," she answered in her unsteady voice. Sounds from her television were playing in the background.

I stood up to pace the length of the small room. "Hey, Mama, it's me, Coby." I could picture her sitting on that little loveseat in her studio, flipping through the early evening news channels.

"Hello, dear. Thanks for calling."

"How are you settling in?" I asked, forcing myself to speak louder so she'd hear me over the noise.

"Very well. I've been playing every day, and the food here is much better than I'd ever imagined. We're having chicken pot pie tonight."

She sounded relaxed and happy. My heart swelled.

"I'm so glad to hear that." Searching for something else to say, I asked, "Has Clyde called to check in?"

I made sure to text my brother her new number, and he told me he'd call. Not that I counted on him to keep his word for a second, but maybe his wife called.

"Not yet, but I'm sure he's busy. You know how busy your father used to get at the mines this time of year."

So busy at the bar more like it. "Yeah, I remember. Hopefully he'll call soon. Is there anything you need, Mama? I want you to be comfortable."

She tutted. "No, no...I'm great here. What I need is for you to take care of yourself. Are you eating enough? What about that lovely girl? Did you talk to her yet?"

She was really hung up on Kendahl. I couldn't blame her, considering I hadn't talked about a woman with her since Amy.

"Not yet, but don't worry. I will when the time is right." I let a breath loose. There was no need to get her excited for something that may end up going nowhere.

"Good. Once you tell her about your father passing and all the work you've had to do, she'll forgive you. I know it. Remember what I said. Honesty, trust, and love."

I ran a hand across my beard as I stared at the storm through the window again. Hesitating, I said, "Maybe. I don't know."

I heard shuffling noises from the other side of the phone and then the background noise went silent. "Son," she said softly. "You're nothing like him, you know?"

"Yeah," I gulped. "I know."

"You deserve love. Your father never taught you how to love a woman but somehow here you are. My beautiful kind-hearted boy. I wish Amy saw what I see."

I dropped my phone onto the window ledge, pressed the speaker button, and sank onto the floor. With my head in my hands, I let my mother's words sink in.

"Son?" her quiet voice cut through the speaker. "Did you hang up?"

I reached for the phone, "No."

"I love you. Thanks for calling. I'm fine. You go get your girl." She laughed, a sound no louder than a tinkle, but hearing it had me grinning like a fool. Knowing she was happy was the most important thing in the world to me—well one of them anyway.

I took an hour after hanging up with my mama to think over her words. Was I afraid that I'd turn out like him? No, that wasn't it. Relationships got too complicated. Too real. Honesty and trust didn't exist for me. Not after I'd given both freely, only to have my past thrown in my face and used as a reason for her infidelity. And love...I wasn't capable of it. Not anymore.

Someone like Kendahl, who dreamed of moving to LA and working with the stars, would never want to settle down with me, a divorced loser from Nowhere, Wyoming with baggage from a drunk abusive prick of a father and a brother who took after his dad in every way.

Maybe if I got her out of my system that would be enough and I could stop replaying her laugh or picturing the swell of her lips as she parted them for me every time I closed my eyes. Once we worked out our frustrations, my skin could stop itching to be near her every second.

I raked a hand through my hair and put the conversation with my mother out of my mind to focus on the task at hand—the interview. I checked my phone for the time—4:32. The interview was at five in the lobby.

I pulled myself together and checked my appearance in the mirror before making my way down the hall to Kendahl's room.

Chapter 18

Coby

"KENDAHL?" I KNOCKED AT her door, right in the center of the urchin placard. The room sounded quiet, no blow dryer or TV on. Was she asleep?

Knocking again, three times firmly, I leaned my arm against the door frame. I was about to pull my phone out to call her when she opened the door a sliver showing nothing but her big blue eyes out of the crack. When recognition sparked, she opened the door a few inches wider, so I could slip inside.

I took her in. She was dressed in distressed gray jeans and a thin cream sweater. While her outfit and hair looked put together, she had a slump to her shoulders and a dejected sort of frown lining her face. "Are you ready for the interview?" I asked as she turned back toward the bathroom.

"I need to finish up my makeup." No emotion, no teasing remark.

I sat on the edge of the bed watching her apply a layer of mascara to her already thick lashes. "How are you feeling?"

She scoffed. "You mean after my outburst?" Sticking the wand back in the tube, she tossed it onto the counter and grabbed a makeup brush. "I'm fine. I just want to get this interview over with."

I needed to tread lightly but also get her to talk through her feelings. That release happened for a reason, and it wouldn't help to stuff it back in. "I wonder what kind of questions he'll ask."

She swirled the makeup brush all over her face. Watching her was kind of mesmerizing if I was honest. She was like an artist but with an already perfect canvas.

"Are you covering up your beauty mark?" I asked.

Dropping her hand down toward her waist, she turned. "What?"

Damn my lack of filter. "Don't cover up your beauty mark. The one right above your lip." I got up to lean against the bathroom's doorframe and watched her posture straighten. "I think about it all the time, that little bullseye." I wanted to take her upper lip between my teeth and nibble and graze that tiny dot with my tongue.

"Bullseye?" she laughed. "Are you hiding a bow and arrow somewhere I don't know about?"

"Something like that," I murmured. She shook her head and continued applying her makeup. "I saw you crack a smile. Come on, tell me what's wrong. Besides the interview, you know we're both going to nail that."

I watched her apply a layer of fire engine red lipstick and smack her lips together with a pop. What I wouldn't give to have those lips wrapped around my— "Wait, what did you say?" With my mind in other places, I missed her words completely.

Narrowing her eyes and slinging a hand on her hip, she repeated, "I don't know. I guess I'm drained. I have no idea where those emotions came from. God, I haven't cried like that since..." she wavered.

"Since?" I encouraged keeping my gaze firmly on her.

Sighing, she came and perched on the bed next to me close enough that I could smell her perfume. Honey with a hint of spice. "Since Ben."

Ah, Ben, the first asshole that broke her heart. She'd told me bits and pieces about him when we first started dating, but not much. "Do you want me to beat him up? Because I'm more than willing." I cracked a smirk.

She didn't laugh at my joke, only silently toyed with a loose thread on her sweater. "Joking. You know that right?" I nudged her with my shoulder, wanting to feel some kind of connection between us. "You can talk to me. Maybe I can shed some light on the subject, seeing as I'm also a major dick who hurt you."

A small smile lit up her face. "I can agree with that." She sighed again. "We were together for two years. The longest relationship I'd had before him was a month if that. Everything seemed perfect. We were going to move in together. We talked about the future..."

Here was the part where the other shoe dropped. I knew all about that, not that I'd ever tell her or anyone else details about Amy. I set my palm on her thigh like a reassuring anchor.

"Things changed. He grew more distant, ignoring my calls and texts. He would always meet me at the office after work, and we'd go to dinner. He meant to surprise me every time, but he did it so often that I came to expect it, to expect him leaning against my car in the parking lot with a cheese grin on his face, opening his arms wide the second I got close enough to reach him." She laughed, a sad sardonic sound. "Up until the last time he did it, I faked being surprised. I knew how much he loved to see my face light up."

Fuck, my heart was cracking in two. Maybe I wasn't joking. This prick needed an ass kicking. "What happened, baby?"

She sniffed and sat up, continuing with a clear voice, "He was away for a work conference with some coworkers. His responses were short and unlike him the entire trip, but I figured he was busy. I knew he was coming back on a Friday, and he hadn't told me otherwise. By Sunday, all my messages from the weekend had gone unread, so I went to his place. I was getting worried that something might have happened to him. Well, I wasn't wrong. Something was happening to him." I squeezed her thigh gently, knowing what was coming. "I slipped into his house with the key he'd given me and found him lying flat on his back with some woman riding his face."

My chest tightened, and I forced myself to focus on her instead of reacting like I wanted to. "I'm so sorry." I wanted to make a joke to defuse the situation, but for the first time in a long time, nothing came to me.

She stood and paced the space in front of me. "Yeah, me too. The kicker of it was, that for two years he told me he didn't like giving oral. He said it made him gag." A cynical laugh slipped through her lips.

"What? You're kidding, right?" I yanked at the scruff of my beard, not sure what to do with my hands.

Shrugging she said, "Nope. Two years and he didn't go," she pointed down with her index finger, "more than a few times."

"That piece of shit wasn't a real man then," I nearly growled. What kind of idiot wouldn't devour every inch of this woman if they had the chance?

"Apparently, it was only me that made him gag, since Melody, that's her name by the way, was like an all you can eat buffet." She cast her eyes toward the rug and leaned against the wall.

Rules be damned. I stood up and walked toward her slowly to give her enough time to tell me to fuck off. I boxed her in with my body, placing my hands against the wall beside her head and leaned in. Her kissable red lips were so close, her rapid breath warm against my face. I had time to savor her lips later, at that moment, I needed her to hear my words.

"Baby, he's a fucking idiot. If you were mine, I'd lick and suck every inch of your body. You'd be my every meal, the only sustenance I needed. I wouldn't let a drop go to waste."

Her eyes glazed over and warm puffs of air escaped her lips. Even her breath smelled sweet. It took every ounce of strength in me to back away from her.

I walked closer to the door, letting her regain her composure.

She cleared her throat, then grabbed her purse from the side table, tossed a few things inside the small bag, and yanked the zipper closed before stomping behind me. "I bet you said that to all the women you fooled around with in Wyoming."

We were back to this then. "You know that's not true." I reached for the door and let her out in front of me. Lowering my voice, I stepped closer so she could hear me. "I thought about you the entire time I was gone. I had to help a friend. That's all."

"Right," she emphasized the T, but stopped to look directly at me. "You're telling me that the whole time you were gone, three whole weeks, you didn't hook up with a single person?"

Fuck. She had me there. Thoughts of that redhead in the bar bathroom popped into my head. Scoffing, she added, "That's what I thought."

My poker face sucked. "Baby, I didn't sleep with anyone. I only wanted you. Only *want* you. I was an idiot. I should have called you...explained everything."

"Keep your voice down," she said through gritted teeth. "Come here." She grabbed onto my arm, led me around a corner, and pushed me against the wall. Damn my cock was hard. She could push me around anytime. "New rule. No bringing up the past." Rising on her tiptoes to get as close to my face as she could she added, "This thing between us, this game, it'll be over soon. So why bother rehashing things. The past is the past and the damage is done. Whatever you did," I threw up my hands to break in, but she cut me off, "Or didn't do, is frankly none of my business. I still don't know what's in this for you, nor do I care. After this weekend, we are done, Coby."

I watched her back away, one step, then another, before she stormed down the hallway leaving me standing there feeling like the biggest piece of shit that ever walked the earth.

Chapter 19

Kendahl

How fitting that the weather mirrored my mood. I watched the rain pound against the lobby window. Maybe I had been too harsh with Coby. No. He hesitated when I asked him if he hooked up with anyone while he was away allegedly "helping" a friend. I did not need another cheater in my life. Technically we had been on a break, but if he'd missed me that much, he could have kept it in his pants.

He showed up after a few minutes and joined me on the couch. I was expecting a remark or joke to break the icy tension between us, but he was uncharacteristically silent. The only sound came from Coby scraping his hands against his beard.

The chilly room had me scootching closer to feel the heat of his body. This vacation was going to hell. It had been one disaster after another with shitty weather as the cherry on top. He must have taken me moving closer as his queue to chat.

"If this kid doesn't get here soon, I say we bail." He sounded as tired as I felt.

I checked my phone. Aiden was five minutes late. "Let's give him five more minutes. Only because he's Jill's nephew," I said.

Coby chuckled but didn't respond.

I turned to him. "What are you laughing at?"

He stared into my eyes, a look that felt too intimate to be given in a lobby with random senior citizens walking around searching for the coffee maker. "You. The way you use your business voice sometimes."

"Can you be more condescending?" I scoffed.

He put his hands up in surrender. "Sorry, okay. It's cute." He leaned in so only I could hear what he said next. "It makes my dick hard."

My face heated from a mix of anger and other emotions that I would be ignoring. Stupid hormones. "I hope you like having blue balls because that thing isn't coming near me."

He chuckled again, an infuriating husky sound that sent heat straight to my belly. Jill's nephew better be on his way. I needed to get some space from this man.

As if summoned directly by my thoughts, Aiden Aarons and his partner came traipsing into the lobby carrying to-go coffee cups looking completely unbothered. I forced a breath into my chest so I wouldn't lose it on them. *Remember Kendahl, it's Coby you're pissed at. Keep it together.*

"Hey, my bros." He raised his hand in a gesture that wasn't quite a wave, but I guess could be considered one. "Sorry we're late." *Yeah, you look so sorry,* I stewed.

"It's all good, man. Let's get started," Coby cut in sounding stern and boss like. Interesting, he had a business voice too. I'd have to tease him about it later.

No. That was flirty behavior.

"Okay, no worries. Zara and I need a minute to set up and then we're good to go." They pulled some items out of a suitcase. The equipment looked professional for a pair of young kids, a mic, camera, and lighting set up. My stomach churned. I had never been the subject of an interview. It was always me setting things like this up for my clients. Who would have thought I'd be feeling this nervous. Coby glanced at me, scrunching his brows, and before I could protest, he slung his arm around my shoulders. The warmth and weight of him had me sighing in relief.

"Okay, lovebirds, act natural and say whatever comes to mind." He gestured to his partner to start recording.

"Helloooo, everyone, and welcome back to my channel. I'm Aiden Aarons, as you already know." He smirked at the camera while his voice boomed loud enough to shatter glass. "I have a special treat for you all. The internet exploded last night when their onstage singing battle ended with a vomit-induced grand finale." I cringed internally but tried not to show it. "It's the Karaoke Couple here for an exclusive interview. Kendahl, Coby, welcome to my show."

Zara turned the small camera in our direction. My tongue suddenly felt like it weighed ten pounds. "Thanks for having us," Coby said as he gave my shoulders a reassuring squeeze.

"Let's get right into it. The burning question on everyone's mind is are you two dating?"

Coby looked at me, urging me to answer with his eyes. I cleared my throat. "Uh, yes. We are together." I sounded robotic.

Unfazed, Aiden continued, "Wonderful. I think we were hoping for that answer. Can you tell us a little bit about how you ended up battling it out karaoke style."

As I reached for the cup of water in front of me, Coby answered the question. He spoke about our recent breakup, saying he had to leave town unexpectantly to help a friend and thought it would be better to end things.

"I never would have thought that she would occupy every corner of my mind. When I woke up, it was her smile that would push me out of bed. I'd daydream about her laugh and the way she'd bite her lip when she was concentrating. I'd think about this tiny beauty mark she has above her lip." He shook his head almost as if he was waking himself up from a trance. "Needless to say, I realized I'd made a mistake."

My heart was beating like crazy. I had no idea how I was supposed to respond to that. He sounded so sincere, nothing like the Coby I'd known for the past few months. "So, Kendahl," Aiden asked me directly, "was it you who decided to start the battle?"

I sipped my water again to clear my throat. "No, that was Coby."

Aiden gestured his hand in a way that said, "go on," but I had nothing else to add. After a moment he redirected.

"Okay, well, I think we're all glad the battle ended up the way it did. It was epic. Coby, has anyone ever told you that you're a natural on stage?"

Just what he needed, an even bigger ego.

He played with a strand of my hair, which caused me to shiver as he answered. "No, I'll admit I have a healthy dose of stage fright. I was nervous as hell last night."

I shot my gaze in his direction. "Seriously? You were like Mick Jagger up there. I highly doubt you were nervous."

"So you liked my moves?" He said in that annoying smooth voice.

I huffed and turned back toward Aiden. "Next question, please."

Aiden put on a mask of seriousness like a child playing pretend news reporter. "What does the future look like for the two of you?"

Damn, we hadn't prepped for this question. Coby opened his mouth, closed it, then opened it again before he answered in an uneven voice. "I don't want to speak for Kendahl, but I know that I'm all in. This is it for me. She is it." With his strong arm possessively around my shoulders and the closeness of his touch, I was feeling all sorts of confused. He was saying all the right things. I had to respond.

"I'd say we're taking things day by day. This weekend is all about our friends Mike and Jill. They're getting married in a few days, and I'd love to give them back the spotlight they so truly deserve."

"Well said," Aiden added. "Love is in the air this weekend. That and rain, lots of rain." Laughing at his own joke, he redirected, looking over a list on the laptop in front of him. "We have a few fan questions, if you're up for that?"

"Bring it on," Coby answered for us both. I would have said no. I'm done and ready to take my leave.

"From @spicysmutlover," Aiden laughed. "What a name. Okay, Coby, this one's for you. She'd like to know if you're available for hire? It's her bachelorette party next week and she'd love to—actually never mind. I try to keep my show PG-13."

Coby shook his head and laughed as he gently squeezed my shoulder again. "Uh, sorry ladies. I'm taken."

I wanted to facepalm. Thankfully this interview from hell was almost over.

"Kendahl, a question from @SwiftyTara in Arizona, 'How are you feeling? I felt so bad seeing you get sick like that. Also, if you need someone to nurse you back to health DM me.'" I couldn't help but smile at that one. I can respect someone for shooting their shot.

"Wow! The thirsty people are out in full force for you two." Aiden chuckled. "Let me scan down my list to an actual question. Here we go. Aiden read the question before lifting his eyes to Coby. "This one is from a follower in Wyoming."

Coby's entire body tensed beside me.

"@YellowstoneCowgirl asked—"

"Can we take a break?" Coby cut in as he reached his arm out to block the camera. Aiden looked up from his screen, head tilted.

"This is live. We don't take breaks." Coby rubbed his palms against his pant legs and nodded. What was that about? "Back to the question. Let's see. Whoops, I was mistaken. @YellowstoneCowgirl from Texas, not Wyoming. My bad. Geography was never my thing. Don't unfollow!" If I could rub my temples I would. His voice grated on my nerves. Coby sagged back against the cushion but he didn't return his arm over my shoulders. "She'd like to know about your ideal date night. Kendahl, you want to answer this one?"

"Okay. That's a tough question. It would depend on what type of mood I was in." I thought for a moment, staring across the lobby at a framed art print.

Coby's palm settled on my thigh as he spoke. "Either a night of dancing with loud music, interesting conversation, and fun atmosphere." I found myself waiting for him to continue, in awe that he'd remembered that much. "Or staying home in comfortable pajamas, eating too much cheese, and watching movies. Disney or horror, depending on your mood."

My mouth hung open.

"By the look on Kendahl's face, you hit the nail on the head," Aiden said. Coby pinned me with his gaze.

"I pay attention when it comes to her."

I needed to remember all of this was pretend. A show put on by a man who probably wrote the book on saying all the right things at the right times. Coby talked smooth, and I couldn't fall for his words.

"Clearly," Aiden laughed. He took a minute scrolling through his list while I composed myself. It would have been nice if he was more prepared, but I guess he didn't have much time. "Here's a good one. Not so much a question though, from @RitaK in Florida—wait, aren't you two from Florida?"

We both nodded, and I waited on the edge of my seat, eager for a shift from the previous question.

"Kendahl and Coby, I'm Rita and I'm eighty-five years old. My granddaughter showed me your video. I wanted to say what a beautiful couple the two of you make. I know life is tough and relationships take work. As someone who was lucky enough to spend over fifty years with my true love, Paul, I know a thing or two about challenges of the heart. Watching the way you sang to each other on that stage I knew deep in my soul that you've got what it takes. You're meant to be. Keep at it, kiddos. We're all rooting for you. Love, Rita.'" Aiden quieted, for once not booming over everyone else. I felt warm tears beginning to leak out of the corner of my eye and quickly blotted them away with my index fingers.

I couldn't look at Coby. Not after hearing that beautiful story. Finally, Aiden spoke, more gently than before. "That was lovely. Thank you, Rita, for your kind words. Kendahl or Coby, do you have anything to add?"

I shook my head and forced a smile that didn't reach my eyes. Coby gave a wave and a low thank you while Aiden chattered at the camera, wrapping up. I had not expected to be left absolutely wrecked by one comment, but it was as if all the air drained out of my lungs and I was left flat and lifeless. I stood to walk my paper cup to the nearest garbage can.

We were supposed to go to dinner next door with the whole crew. It would be another long night of conversation with all the happy couples. After I tossed the cup away, I hung out near the garbage can to peek at Coby without him noticing. He looked as affected by the interview as I was. His head hung low and his shoulders drooped in a way that made him look like a different person. After a moment he looked up and our eyes met. Slate gray orbs that seemed to reach deep inside me. I watched him slowly stand and run a hand through his dark hair before joining me.

"You don't want to go to dinner, do you?" he asked.

I shifted from one foot to the other as I pretended to mull over my response. "No." I hesitated. "I think I need to be alone for a little while."

He stepped closer until he was right up against me. I hadn't realized how much taller than me he was until that moment. My breathing picked up, and I angled my gaze directly at his shirt. I couldn't look into those eyes again, not feeling as confused as I felt.

He placed one hand against the wall above my head to brace himself while his other cupped my chin. His grip was soft yet strong, and the feel of his skin against mine had me wishing we were not in the middle of a busy lobby. He angled my face so I had no choice but to look into his eyes.

Seconds passed, or maybe minutes, I didn't know. Our breathing synced and heat passed between us until finally Coby said, "Whatever you need. But know this, Kendahl, with me you're never truly alone. I'm here to stay."

He stepped away and walked toward the exit. I finally released a breath I hadn't even realized I'd been holding.

Chapter 20

Coby

THE RAIN COULD SOAK through my clothes and I wouldn't give a shit. We'd all need kayaks to get from the inn to the restaurant soon enough. I pushed through the door and was greeted by the sounds of laughter and the scents of fresh bread and garlic. My mouth watered.

But I didn't have it in me. My pulse was still racing like crazy. The second that kid said 'Wyoming' I figured it was over. Someone was about to ask if I was *the Coby Barnes*, from Verdant Valley. The same Coby Barnes who'd dumpster dive to feed his family. Who'd get bullied at school for wearing too-small shoes and holey shirts. The same Coby who'd drag his drunk, belligerent father out of the Cowboy Club night after night and got his ass beat for doing so. The Coby who left Wyoming as soon as he could.

Then when I realized Aiden's mistake and could breathe again, the air got knocked out of me once more hearing that elderly woman's story. Over fifty years happily married to the same person? I couldn't even fathom that. Hell, it had been years since I could stand to be with a woman for more than a few hours up until I met Kendahl. I needed to get inside her head and find out what she was thinking. She was obviously affected by the interview too. I knew that bullshit pissy attitude was an act. She was angry, yes. And with reason. I behaved like a scared little boy when what she needed was a real man.

I clenched my fists together as a gust of wind rattled the door behind me. Taking another quick glance across the restaurant at my group of friends smiling and laughing, I made a snap decision. I'd order Kendahl and I some food to go, and drop it off at her room.

Twenty minutes later, after making a vague excuse to Mike and Jill, I headed back to the inn with soaked plastic bags containing about half their menu. Hopefully Kendahl would like at least one of these choices. I shifted the bags to one hand and knocked on her door. My heart pounded like I was a teenager going on my first date. Get it together man, she said she needed space.

"Who is it?" she called tentatively from behind the door.

"Room service," I answered in a goofy high-pitched voice. She opened the door with her hand on her hip. "Don't worry, it's just me. You're free to cuss me out."

She shook her head and sighed. "You're soaked." An internal battle played out in her eyes as she took in my state, then the bags of food until she opened the door wider to gesture me inside.

I grabbed a towel from the bathroom, plopped the bags on top of the dresser, and made myself busy unpacking the containers. "Did you order the whole menu?" she asked.

"Everything but the special, some kind of fish I'd never heard of. Didn't want to risk making your room smell like an actual urchin."

That got a small laugh out of her. "Appreciate that."

As I busied myself emptying the third bag, my stomach rumbling took precedent over my overactive pulse. I almost jumped as she slung a dry towel around my shoulders. "I'm running out of nightshirts."

"There's always sleeping naked." I took the towel and rubbed my hair to a somewhat dry state.

"I already do." She winked and settled down on the bed. Only then did I take in the fact that she had changed into tiny cotton shorts and a loose fitted long sleeve tee. The makeup I watched her meticulously apply had been washed off, and her long hair was pulled back. She was so beautiful it hurt to look at her.

"In that case, I think it's bedtime." I put down the container filled with a pasta and chicken dish and pretended to go turn off the lamp.

She laughed. "Don't be a tease, bring over the goods." She had spread out a quilt over the queen bed mock picnic blanket style and patted the side across from her.

I hesitated, "Shit, I think I forgot to order something for you. All of this is mine." I flashed a grin. She scrunched her nose and narrowed her eyes. It was too fun to tease her, and I needed that to pull myself out of my post-interview funk. "Kidding, no need to laser blast me."

I put that container and a few others in front of her along with plastic cutlery. "Laser blast?" she asked as she opened the lids.

"Yeah. That thing you do with your eyes. It reminds me of Cyclops from X-Men when he shoots his deadly laser things and destroys enemies." I stuffed a piece of garlic bread into my face.

"X-Men? Who would have known Coby Barnes was a comic nerd," she said as she swallowed a bite of pasta.

"Did I reveal too much?" Her face lit up whether it was from the food or my revelation, I didn't know. "Yes, I'm a nerd. But come on, what little boy didn't want to be a superhero with cool powers? Laser eyes, ice powers, sharp claw hands. Plus Jean Gray—hot as hell. I think she was my first crush."

She was laughing, like a real true laugh. "Oh my God. This is the best thing I've heard all day, all year even. Have you read all the comics?"

"Um." I grinned. "I don't know if I want to answer that." I cut into my steak with a plastic knife, which was working out about as good as expected.

"I'm kidding. I love that you have a nerdy side. It's refreshing." She got up and walked over to the corner of the room, grabbed a bottle of wine from who knows where, and uncorked it. "I'm about to give away all my secrets but...I'm a nerd too. I saw those movies. Wolverine is hot. I always wondered if that metal stuff was in *every* part of his body?" She took a swig out of the bottle, wiping a drop off her lips before offering it to me. "Sorry, no glasses."

I took a sip of the full-bodied red. I wasn't a wine snob, but I knew it was a decent bottle. "You dirty girl. Are you asking if he has an Adamantium dick?" Thank God I had swallowed because I might have choked and spit wine all over the place.

"Inquiring minds want to know," she quipped, taking the bottle back from me.

"Since I already revealed the true depths of my nerdiness...no, his dick is a normal dick. The metal is only in his bones." I raised a brow at the face she was giving me. "Not that bone." I chuckled.

"That's a missed opportunity. I bet there's a porno out there with a metal-dicked Wolverine. Should we Google?" She grabbed her phone and tapped it on before busting out laughing. "Okay, even I can't go there. Who knows what my search history will look like after that rabbit hole. Dicks...too many dicks."

"You have to stop saying dicks." I shook my head and attempted to swallow a bite of meat.

She lowered her voice to a husky whisper. "What's wrong? Having trouble with your meat?"

"I never have trouble with my meat. My meat is perfect."

"Prove it." She got on all fours and crawled closer to me. I zeroed in on the outline of her bare tits through her loose shirt, and my cock stiffened. The plastic fork speared with a hunk of steak dropped from my shaky fingers as she inched closer. I stared at the outline of her full bottom lip, wanting to feel it between my teeth.

She parted her lips, letting a small sigh escape them, and I leaned in ready to feel her, taste her. Then she sat up and grabbed my fork. She brought the bite of steak to her lips and slowly, too slowly, bit down, sliding the piece into her mouth. As she chewed, she moaned again. "Ooh yeah, your meat is pretty perfect. Might need a bit more salt though."

With a grin, she scrambled back to her side of the bed and took another swig out of the bottle. I cleared my throat. "You're evil."

"What?" she asked innocently. "You don't like to share?"

She passed the bottle my way. We had already finished half of it. I slid the rest of my container of steak in her direction. "My meat is all yours."

With a full wattage grin she pulled it closer and said, "Good boy."

Two bottles of wine and many empty containers later, we sprawled out on Kendahl's bed keeping a good foot of space between us. I listened to the sounds of her breathing mixed with the constant beat of rain and wind against the windows. A warm bubble of contentedness enveloped me at being near her. "So today was..." I stopped, searching for the right words.

"A hot mess express," she added.

Sighing, I stretched my arms above my head before turning on my side to face her. "Pretty much." Her blue eyes bore into me. I closed my eyes to get out the words that were swirling around in my head. "But it was one of the best days I've had in a long time. I..." Shit, why was this so hard? Everything in me wanted to make more jokes, laugh up the chaos that this trip has been so far. Maybe it was the wine, or the nearness of her skin inches away from mine, but I wanted to tell her the truth. I needed to. "I haven't been one hundred percent honest with you. The real reason I left was—"

A massive gust of wind rattled the windows, and the room went pitch black. Kendahl jumped. "Shit, we lost power."

Chapter 21

Kendahl

"Where's my phone?" I grumbled. I've tried not to look at it since the going viral thing started, but it was the only source of light I had. I planted my foot directly onto a takeout container. "Oh God, I think I spaghettied my foot."

Of course this would happen when the floor was a mine-field of half-empty food containers, and I was happily wine buzzed. Another gust rattled the window. Hopefully our friends were back in their rooms safely, especially Mia. My chest tightened at the thought of her stuck outside in the dark storm. We'd always taken care of each other. Although she laid it on thick in that department, I worried about her equally. We had different ways of showing it.

"I hope Mia made it back okay," I rambled. "But then again, she has Shawn. I mean she's a strong independent woman. It's like I know this but can't help but worry. Do you think they're back? Want to call Shawn?"

I made my way to the dresser across the room, only stubbing my toe once miraculously. My eyes were getting adjusted to the darkness, but I still felt around for my phone like a blind baby animal. "Ah-ha, I found it." I tapped the screen to life and immediately saw white spots in my field of vision. My battery was low, and there were no missed messages from Mia. Fingers crossed she was already in bed.

"No messages and my battery's low. How's your phone?" I asked as I tapped on Mia's text thread shooting off a quick "Are you ok?" message. "Coby? Did you fall asleep?" Phone in hand, I had a much easier time navigating back to the bed by the glow of the screen. The walls shuddered as another gust lashed at the building. I hoped this place was stronger than it felt. "Coby?" I asked again. How was it that guys could sleep through anything? Ben used to sleep like the dead too. His alarm would wake me up, and he'd stay asleep, unbothered until I shook him for ten minutes straight. And now I was comparing Coby to Ben. Ick.

The first thing I noticed, besides him not answering me back in his joking Coby way, was his breathing. Rapid and shallow. I turned on my phone flashlight and put it down on the side table so I wouldn't blind him. That's when I saw that his eyes were open so wide I could see the entire white area surrounding his irises.

I recognized it immediately. Mia had her first panic attack during freshman year. It was my first time being there for someone in the thick of it. Instinct took over as I ran my hands though his hair and spoke gently. "It's okay. We're safe. I know it feels like we're not. Every feeling you're having is real, but I promise you, this will pass." I massaged his scalp, using the tips of my nails for extra sensory stimulation. After Mia's first attack, I'd looked up some ways to help in the moment. Most sources said to use as many senses as you could to keep yourself grounded and out of your head.

Coby closed his eyes and brought a shaky fist to rest under his nose. "Sorry." He mumbled through his fist.

"There's nothing to be sorry for." His breathing seemed to be slowing. "Can I help you?" He took a ragged breath in through his mouth and nodded. I could see that the air barely reached his chest. Chest breathing was a big no-no. "Let's breathe together." I ran my hand down the side of his neck and over the slope of his corded shoulders, giving them a gentle knead before reaching right below his collarbones. I massaged small circles around the tight muscles there as best I could with him lying on his side.

"Deep breath in through your nose," I followed suit, filling my chest with as much air as I could and holding it for three counts. "Now release it slowly." I watched him do as I said, but I could still tell he wasn't quite there yet. "Here, let's sit up." I pulled at his fist, tugging it away from his face and adjusted my position, so I'd be sitting directly in front of him. He'd have an easier time with his breathwork sitting instead of lying down, another fact I could thank Google for.

I dropped his fist, and his eyes widened. "Don't go. Please," he begged, his voice so much smaller than I'd ever heard it.

"I'm not going anywhere." I took his hand in mine and brought it to rest over my sternum. "Feel the way I'm breathing." I took another deep inhale, pushing the air all the way down into my belly before releasing it in a slow stream. His eyes burned into mine. "We're going to do that again. This time you follow me. Feel my breath expanding my chest." I reached out and settled my palms one on top of the other in the same spot between his pecs and used my fingertips to massage small circles into the tight muscles.

He nodded and let out a strangled moan as I paid extra attention to a knot there. "That's good, babe. Let your chest open up." I scooted closer, feeling the body heat between us. Sweat formed on my brow, and I wanted to wipe it away, but at the same time, I didn't want to move my hands from Coby's body. His eyes were closed, and the tightness in his face seemed to be softening. "Let's take another breath. Follow the movement of my chest." I laid one of my palms over his, keeping the other centered at his heart. His hand was so large it rested on the edges of my breasts. I tried not to think about the feelings his touch stirred within me. It wasn't the time.

Another gust shook the walls, and his face tensed again. "Focus on my chest, the rise and fall." My heart was breaking seeing him like this, but he seemed to be responding to me. I continued to rub small circles throughout the tight muscles surrounding his sternum. "That's it. I can feel the air reaching lower now. Let's do it again. This time hold for three counts. In...and one...two...three. Now let it out slowly."

He opened his eyes as he released a steady stream of air, and I felt a zap of electricity between us. With nothing more than my phone light illuminating the small space, his eyes looked like pools of dark water. I couldn't look away. Now I was the one who was breathing rapidly. I parted my lips, darting my tongue out to moisten them and saw his gaze focus on the movement. I went to pull my hand away from his chest. It felt different with him looking at me that way, but he caught it and placed it back into the same spot.

Another rattle shook the walls and then I was the one trembling. Our eyes stayed locked on each other, and we breathed in sync. One breath, then two. With the third release, I felt his hand flex, bunching up my loose shirt. "I'm going to kiss you now." He pulled me closer until I was almost straddling his lap. So close that I could taste the next words leave his mouth. "Tell me you're okay with that, baby, because if I have to wait one more second to feel your lips again, I might die right here." I nodded, unable to get words out, and he closed the space between us, crashing his lips against mine.

I let go as soon as I felt our skin meet and opened to him. He explored me with his tongue, devouring me like a starved man. Every inch of my skin was burning for him—his taste, his smell, his warmth.

"Coby." His name slipped out of my lips in a small needy moan. I scrambled onto his lap and wrapped my arms around his neck needing to get closer. He pulled me flat against him, tangling one hand in my ponytail while he gripped my hip with the other.

"God, Kendahl." He kissed me deeply before nuzzling the side of my face and peppering kisses onto the space below my ear. "You taste like I remember. So fucking sweet." I ground into him as he took my earlobe into his mouth with a hot suck. I needed to feel the delicious friction against my aching core. "So perfect," he rasped into my ear. I moaned again, soft but needy. My body was on fire. How had I gone so long without this?

He tugged my ponytail loose and fisted my hair using the strands to pull my face back down to his. Our tongues tangled and lips explored with such urgency that I thought I might explode from the heat that was building inside me.

His hand moved from my hair to my breast, teasing my nipples through the thin fabric of my shirt. "Mmm," I hummed, which made him circle the peaks faster as he sucked my lower lip. I was grinding shamelessly against his length, chasing the growing need within me.

"These tits are mine," he growled before pulling my shirt up and over my head. He pulled back but only for a moment to take me in. Without my shirt or the heat of his body the cool air was almost too much for me to handle. My nipples hardened into tight peaks. He took one into his mouth and sucked hard before pulling off with a pop.

"So fucking perfect." I arched and pulled his face back by his hair wanting him to take more, to take all of me. With another growl, he explored my tits, cupping them, then bringing each one to his mouth nipping, licking, and sucking until I was a puddle on top of him.

I pulled his hair again, wanting to see his face. I knew what I needed. I needed to come more than I think I'd ever needed to before. But taking that next step with Coby would break all of our rules. I wanted love more than anything. I was tired of casual sex. The way his eyes burned into me didn't feel casual. Not at all. My decision was made. I wanted him. We'd figure out the rest later.

I moved my mouth over his, slow and soft at first taking control of the situation. If I was a puddle, I needed him to be too. I gave his hair another tug, and he grunted as he nipped at my bottom lip. I drew my hands down his chest and felt the carved planes of his abdomen over his still damp shirt. I was dying to feel his skin against mine with nothing between us.

When I reached the bottom edge, I slipped my hands underneath his shirt and played with the light dusting of hair slowly and teasingly. I let my fingertips graze the band of his boxers that peaked above his jeans. He shuddered and met my lips again. I bunched the bottom of his shirt in my hands about to bring it up his body and over his head, but I stopped short. My phone was vibrating on the end table with a buzzing that made me jump.

"Shit," Coby grumbled. "You should probably get that."

"You're right. It could be important." My phone was on low battery. If it was important, it may be the only chance for me to find out. I pushed myself off Coby's lap and grabbed the phone. It was Mia. Thanks for the cockblock, bestie. But I was happy to see her name on the screen.

I grabbed my shirt because it felt weird to talk to her topless and turned on. "Hey, Mi. Are you guys okay?"

The room was dark again since my flashlight had turned off, but I could still feel Coby's eyes burning into mine.

"We're okay," she said. "Just got back to the inn. I can't believe we lost power. Mike told us a few minutes ago that the storm got upgraded from a hurricane watch to a warning. They're thinking category one, and it'll make landfall tomorrow."

"Oh shit," I said biting my lower lip. "So what does that mean for us? What about the wedding?" Coby reached for my hand giving it a squeeze.

She took a deep breath in and released it slowly. "I don't know. I guess we'll have to figure stuff out in the morning. But for now stay in your room and stay safe. I'm sure the owners will fill us in more tomorrow. Before I forget, Ginger said to look in the top drawer. You'll find some candles and matches."

"They must have had a feeling. Thanks, I'll see you tomorrow. Love you, Mi."

"Love you too. Oh, and Ken? Tell Coby goodnight from us too," she said in a teasing tone before hanging up.

Well shit. This trip got a whole lot more screwed.

Chapter 22

Coby

Kendahl's face fell as she finished her call with Mia.

"What's going on?" I was sure they were safe otherwise Kendahl would have gone to her friend.

"We're officially in a hurricane. Mike just spread the word." She hopped off the bed and went to the dresser to dig through the drawer. Her phone stopped emanating its glow and my pulse picked up. Thank God I was a healthy guy with a strong heart because going from panic attack to being more turned on than I had ever been in my entire life, I was pretty sure anyone else would have needed an EMT.

I heard a scrape and smelled sulfur. Suddenly Kendahl's beautiful body was illuminated by the glow of a candle.

"A hurricane? Damn." My first thought was how dumb we all had been for not digging into the weather forecast before we left for this island. But then I thought about Mike and Jill and how much this sucked for them. "I feel so bad for them. Their wedding is all kinds of screwed."

"I'm sure we'll figure something out. What's important is that we all stay safe." Safe was a word that got thrown around a lot especially in my friend circle. What was safe, really? Yes, I could protect myself or Kendahl from "bad guys" or do my best to watch out for danger, but what happened when my body was the culprit. When the chemicals that flooded my bloodstream sent danger alarms. Darkness meant trouble. It meant that someone was going to be on the receiving end of a fist, and that I wanted it to be me and not her, not Mama.

The flickering of the single candle stole my focus, and I tried to push those thoughts away. "We'll be okay. At least we have each other." I searched my brain for something lighthearted to brighten the situation. "And we're only steps away from a fully stocked bar, so that's something."

She laughed. "When life gives you lemons, grab tequila." We both leaned back against the pillows, and I watched her lips turn down. She pulled on the comforter, bunching it in her hands. I could almost see the unspoken thoughts swirling around her mind.

I reached out to stroke the side of her face. She nuzzled into my hand. "Let me see those beautiful eyes." I held her chin and turned her head so we were facing each other. The singular flame dancing behind her blue eyes reminded me of sapphires. "What's on your mind?"

"Too many things." She sighed and chewed her lip for a few seconds. "This crazy storm, your panic attack," another beat passed and she added, "what happened after."

What happened after will live in all my wet dreams for eternity. I stroked her chin. "I'm sorry for freaking out the way I did."

"It's okay. I've helped Mia get through them before. It's not something you can control."

"Thank you. The way you brought me back by guiding my breathing. Incredible." She was more than incredible. She was perfection. I watched her lips tip up in a small, satisfied grin, and my heartbeat picked up. My girl had a thing for praise. Not that she shouldn't get praised every second of every day. But it was something to remember when my idiot senses took over.

"Was it the storm? The wind has been scary as hell." I rolled over onto my back and scratched my chin.

"No, not really." I squeezed my eyes shut and forced the air down deep. "I'm afraid of the dark. Well not afraid, but it sets me off sometimes. I think the storm added another layer and my body gave me a big fuck you."

I held my breath waiting for it. The laughter, the teasing, the pull away. What kind of grown man was afraid of the dark? In my time with Amy, I never let her in this deep. She'd question why I always kept the hall light on or owned an obscene number of flashlights. But I'd just turn it into a joke. Anything to hide my insecurities. When Kendahl didn't respond right away, I forced my lids open to peer over at her. She wasn't smiling or laughing. She looked calm and contemplative.

"Do you want to talk about it?" Did I want to talk about it? No one had ever asked me that. Talking about it would open up a floodgate of crazy that anyone would run from. That's what Amy did, but Kendahl wasn't Amy. She was so much more.

"My father was a real prick. He..." I hesitated. It felt like I was pushing each oversized word through a tiny pinhole. "He was a drunk. A mean drunk. He'd work all day at the mine, then drink all night. Wasted about every dollar that my mother couldn't hide away on booze and gambling." I rubbed at my beard again, enjoying the scratchy feeling against my skin. "It was never enough money. Not to feed us or pay the bills. The first time our lights got shut off, I was young, maybe five. I thought it was a fun game. My brother and I played Crazy Eights by candlelight, lying on our bellies on the living room rug.

"But then he stumbled through the door late, yelling for one of us to come help him out of his boots. He didn't notice the candles burning or the lack of lamps switched on. There was too much darkness in him I think. When he sat down on the couch to try to turn the TV on and it didn't work, he lost it." I'd told her enough that she could fill in the blanks. There was no need to tell her that he smashed the TV that night or that he yanked my mother by her hair and screamed at her for wasting his hard-earned paycheck on those spoiled fucking brats instead of paying the bills. She didn't need to know how Clyde and I hid behind our bedroom door and prayed to anyone or anything that he'd stop. That he wouldn't come to us next. And that was only the first time our power got turned off. There were countless other times after. Times in the dead of winter when the three of us would huddle around the wood-burning stove and plan who would go through his wallet when he passed out that night.

Her face fell. "I'm so sorry. He sounds like a terrible man." I could see her fighting with herself, wanting to say more or ask more.

"Terrible is an understatement. I don't know when the panic attacks became a thing. It was almost like I'd always equated darkness with fear. Mark's helped me through a lot though with some of the drills in class. When I first started level one, I thought I was such tough shit until he turned those overhead lights off for our first dark drill. I almost pissed myself, but I got through it and each one got a little easier."

I let loose a breath and turned to face her again. I wanted to pull her to me, run my hands along the curve of her waist, and finish what we started earlier. But that moment had passed.

"Thank you for telling me all of that," she said gently.

It took most of the energy I had left to smile in response. Quiet blanketed the room. Even without checking a clock, I knew it had gotten late. "So…" I cleared my throat. "You think you'll be okay for the night?" It sounded like I was fishing for an invitation to stay. "I was going to head back to my room and let you get some rest."

That lip bite, fuck, it was hot. I forced my eyes away from her face and held my breath waiting for a response.

"Yeah, I'll be fine. I'm so full. I'll probably knock right out."

I picked up some of the containers and stuck them back into the plastic bags before making my way to the door. "Coby?" she asked as I was about to leave.

I leaned against the doorframe and turned to face her sure she was about to ask me to stay. "Get some rest."

"Will do." The tiny amount of hope I had sank to the bottom of my gut like a weight.

Out in the hallway, I could hear Mike's aunt and uncle scurrying around the lobby over the rattling of the walls. They must have come through with a few camping-style lanterns right after we lost power since the way to my room was lit by flickering light. I still clenched my jaw the whole few feet back to my room.

After finding the candles in my own room and getting cleaned up, I stayed in bed for what felt like hours replaying every small detail of the day from waking up in Kendahl's room to the conversation with Aiden to the massage. Shit, I shouldn't think of the sounds she made on that table, not with her being rooms away.

With the way she comforted me tonight followed by the fucking passion afterward and the way she wasn't afraid to grind into me and take what she wanted, I'd have to jack off or there was no way I'd get any sleep.

I slid my hand into my boxer briefs, trying to imagine the way Kendahl would do it and how her hand would feel as it wrapped around my cock. Would she be firm and give me a squeeze? I gripped myself at the base and pulled my tight grip all the way up my shaft picturing her soft hand instead of my own. Would she slide her fingertips over my head first and feel how I dripped for her.

Fuck yeah.

She'd glide over my tip, spreading my pre-cum with her perfect fingers. "Shit," I hissed a breath. "Yes, baby you feel so so..." I pulled my hand away. "You'd feel a hell of a lot better if you weren't my own damn hand."

I rolled to my side. I was sick of jacking off. It didn't even take the edge off anymore. There was too much shit swirling its way around in my messed-up head that it would take more than images in my mind to get me to where I needed to be. The conversation about my dad, along with every other twist and turn the day brought kept replaying on a loop. I was shocked I'd told her as much as I did.

I rolled out of bed and paced the threadbare rug, letting my eyes focus on the candles dancing flame. I'd text her, but she'd said her phone was dying.

Fuck it.

I didn't want the night to end the way it did, awkward and quiet. That wasn't us. We teased and joked. She sassed me like a brat, and I gave it back like a dickhead. We didn't do polite. If I really wanted her, I couldn't lie back and do nothing.

Chapter 23

Coby

I STARED AT THE urchin placard, overthinking the situation and the fact that I was associating freaking urchins with feeling turned on. There wasn't enough therapy in the world to address that issue.

I figured I'd try her door. If it was locked, I'd turn back. The last thing I wanted to do was wake her after our exhausting day. I turned the handle, expecting the door to be locked, but it wasn't. As much as that made me want to scold her, another part of me breathed a sigh of relief. I pushed it open an inch. Going in guns blazing wasn't a great idea. We were all already on edge. I held my breath, listening.

Those sounds. I knew those sounds. I inched the door open a bit more and stuck my head inside, feeling like a Peeping Tom, but I needed to know.

I was right. Buzzing and small whimpers...my girl was making herself come. Fuck. I was so turned on that I wasn't sure I could trust myself not to pounce on her like a man on death row. But I was glued to the spot, unable to turn around and leave.

Unmistakable bed squeaking noises broke me out of my thoughts, and I acted on instinct. I pushed the door open and walked inside, confident that she'd either scream at me or be happy to see me. There was no middle ground in this situation. I caught her mid moan and took her in before she realized I was there. She was lying on top of the covers still wearing that loose shirt, but it was hiked up revealing the taut skin of her stomach. Her legs were bent at the knee and spread wide, giving me a perfect view of her glistening pussy. I watched her rub that little rose toy in rhythmic circles, bucking her hips with each pass.

I wet my lips, wanting to devour her whole. I must've let a noise slip out because she stopped abruptly and snapped her legs shut.

"Don't stop on my account."

"Why'd you come back?" she asked, breathless.

"You know why." She looked up at me, and her blue eyes filled with heat. Since she wasn't telling me to get the fuck out, I assumed the opposite was true. Time to do what I did best. "Spread those legs and finish what you started. Let me see that pretty pussy of yours." I walked over to the lounge chair and pulled it so it faced the bed. She looked like a goddess by the flickering candlelight, and I wanted to take in every detail. Her breathing picked up as she slowly let her thighs drop apart.

"Good girl. Now take off your shirt. I want to see those tight little nipples."

She yanked it off like it was burning her skin. With her bared to me I could see the rapid rise and fall of her chest and the way she squirmed against the bed needing release. She slid her palm over her abdomen to cup her breast. "Look at those hard nipples. Do you want to pinch and flick them until you're soaking that blanket?"

She closed her eyes and said, "Yes. I want to."

"Show me." My hungry gaze watched her writhe against the bed with each pass over her hard peaks. My cock was straining against my sweats so hard I thought I might explode. But I wasn't a fucking punk ass kid. I could keep my dick in my pants. "You're perfect. How bad do you want to come, beautiful?"

She answered with a low moan.

I studied her rhythm, her noises, hell even the way she screwed up her eyes as she pushed herself closer and closer to the edge. When I finally got to touch her, I'd practically have a master's degree in how she liked to come. "You're close, aren't you? Let me see you slip a finger into your tight pussy."

"God, Coby," was her answering moan as she obeyed like a good girl. It was almost too much. I palmed my cock through my sweats reveling in the small amount of friction as she fucked herself. This was my wildest wet dream come to life. Every second of fantasizing about this woman for the past few months couldn't hold a candle to the real thing.

"Keep going, Kendahl. Just like that."

Her beautiful thighs parted wider and trembled as she rode the waves of her release. "Oh. My. God." She moaned, bucking her hips and grinding herself against her vibrator, "Mmm." I gripped the edge of the chair to keep from reaching out for her. The need was visceral like she was the sun and I was nothing but a lump of rock being pulled into her orbit. The rapid rise and fall of her chest matched my own as she tossed her toy to the side and pulled the covers over herself.

She didn't invite me into her bed, and I wouldn't overstep. I'd take the victory, small but fucking incredible, and be happy she gave me a sliver of herself. I stood to head back to my room and jerk off more times than should be humanly possible but stopped at the foot of the bed. "Sweet dreams, beautiful."

The only sound apart from the shuddering walls and pounding rain was our breaths, but as I reached the doorway a quiet, "You too," floated across the room. My dreams would be sweet all right, but a little spicy too.

The next morning, I found the rest of our group huddled around a few couches in the lobby sipping coffee from paper cups. Kendahl chatted with Mia, using her hands to accentuate whatever point she was making. It seemed as though the wind had died down to a whipping breeze, but rain still pelted the windows in sheets.

As I reached them Kendahl stopped mid-sentence and looked up at me with a gleam in her eye. She didn't show an ounce of embarrassment or shame for what happened the previous night. If anything, she looked rejuvenated and confident, more like the Kendahl I first met.

"Looks like the generator is running for necessities." I pointed to her coffee cup.

"Look who finally decided to join us. Morning, sunshine." Shawn said as he stretched his arm around Mia's shoulder. "Go fuel up, and we'll fill you in."

I nodded and let the scent of coffee lead the way. Compared to yesterday, the lobby was practically empty. Besides our Krav group, a couple who looked to be in their sixties chatted near the counter, and another dude around my age was hanging by the coffee maker. I had no sense of time with the sun being hidden behind walls of clouds and my phone dead. It could have been five a.m. or ten a.m.

I filled a paper cup and grabbed a muffin from a nearby tray making it halfway back to the couches before I thought about it and grabbed a second muffin for Kendahl. I squeezed in next to her on the small couch and handed her the muffin. "It's chocolate chip," I whispered into her ear.

"Thanks." She spoke softly, so only I could hear. "I could use something sweet."

"You're sweet enough to eat already." I nuzzled into her neck and breathed in her perfume.

"Coby," she scolded low enough that only I could hear. "The rules. Remember?"

"Aww, you two are so cute." Mia broke me out of my Kendahl-induced haze. "Shawn, you never cuddle me like that in public." She wore the cutest scowl.

Shawn put his coffee cup down and with determined hands grabbed her face and kissed her hard. I'm talking open mouth to the point where I could see tongue action. He pulled back with a satisfied grin. "Better?"

She sat back against the cushion before grabbing her coffee again. "Be right back. I need a cold shower."

"You need to get a room... oh wait, you already have one of those." Kendahl joked and then bit into her muffin. A tiny chocolate chip fell to her lap, and I reached over to brush it away. Feeling bold, I decided to leave my hand on her thigh and test the rules a bit. She looked at me over her cup but didn't tell me to move.

I cleared my throat. "So what's going on? You guys talk to Mike and Jill yet?"

Mia answered, "Yeah, and Ginger. In a nutshell, most of the guests left this morning, The county didn't issue an evacuation of the whole island, but they are urging everyone ocean side to take shelter elsewhere, if possible."

"Damn, I hope everyone got home safely. I'd be worried about downed power lines and flooding and shit," I said between sips.

"That's why we opted to hang tight. Mike said they have a generator for necessities, and the restaurant next door does too," Shawn said.

"I feel so bad for Jill. She's gone through so much this year. I want to figure out how to make her wedding happen," Mia added. "Kendahl and I were brainstorming a bit already, and I think we have some good ideas."

I faced my girl. "I bet you do. With the two of you here putting your heads together, you'll make her wedding even better than it was going to be." I rubbed circles against the smooth fabric of Kendahl's leggings with my thumb.

"I say we hunker down and plan a good old-fashioned hurricane party tonight. Coby, you want to help me buy some bottles from next door, and I'm sure we can find a deck of cards at least to get ourselves all set for a night of fun in this chaos." Shawn looked genuinely excited. He never showed more emotion than a well-timed head nod here or there unless it came to Mia, of course.

I looked at Kendahl to try and gauge her thoughts. "As long as the ladies are good with it, I'm down to help." I gulped down the last dregs of coffee and swallowed the last bite of my half-stale muffin. When they didn't object, I added. "Let's go find Mike and see if he needs some help getting windows boarded and sandbags set up. I don't know about you, buddy, but I could use some kind of workout. You want to spar?" I had way too much pent-up frustrated energy coiled around my tight muscles. I'd gone for a few runs and done some pushups in Verdant Valley, but my body missed the fluid movements of grappling with a partner. I craved that moment where I'd barely miss getting punched in the face and bounce back full of adrenaline, ready to strike.

"Hell yes, I do. I miss punching that pretty boy face of yours." Shawn taunted, which made the women laugh.

"You mean you miss me knocking you on your ass." I gave Kendahl's thigh a light squeeze and pushed up from the couch.

"We'll see about that," Shawn replied.

Kendahl added, "No need to get into a pissing contest. You're both big and strong." She imitated a cartoonish caveman grunt making Mia crack up.

Before I could respond with a wise crack of my own, Jill made her way over to us with Aiden at her side. Great, everyone left except the only guy I'd love to never see again.

Chapter 24

Kendahl

"Hey guys," Jill said as she reached us. Poor thing looked worn out. Her shoulder drooped, and the worry line in her brow stood out more than normal. "Is everyone doing okay?"

"Don't worry about us, Jill. We're fine. How are you holding up?" I asked as I reached out to squeeze her hand.

"Terrible," Aiden cut in. "I have absolutely no service. The Wi-Fi went out at some point last night and none of my content has been uploaded." He stared at his phone screen, which somehow still glowed brightly. Jill looked up at the ceiling as if to say, why me?

"We were asking your aunt how she was doing. But wow, this must be so hard for you... being without the internet for a whole day." I let the sarcasm drip from my lips.

"Funny, karaoke queen. The two of you will get buried with the rest of the internet's failures if I don't upload your interview. Do you know how fast people move on? Well, I'll tell you. Faster than you can say loser, which is what we'll all be if I miss a day of posting content." Jill placed a hand on his shoulder.

"Aiden, why don't you go get some coffee. I'll talk to Mike in a bit about the internet situation, okay?"

He inhaled and blew a breath out slowly. "Fine. But please hurry."

After he scurried away to the coffee bar, Jill let out a hollow laugh and rubbed her brow. "If I don't laugh, I'll cry."

Mia gave her a hug. "It'll be okay. Hey, Shawn, why don't you guys take Aiden with you. I'm sure Mike and Tim could use another pair of hands to help out." Shawn narrowed his eyes toward Aiden's retreated figure before giving a resigned sigh.

"Wait, before you guys head out, I heard from Tim that we're going to be taking in some families who had to evacuate from their beachfront homes. I'm not sure how many, but he asked me to see if any of you minded doubling up in rooms." Jill looked between Coby and me, knowing full well that we were the only ones in the group, other than Avery, who had our own rooms. Speaking of Avery, she hadn't shown up all morning. I made a mental note to go check on her. "I didn't think it would be a big deal seeing as you two are back together." She gave us a sweet, maternal grin.

"No problem at all. Coby and I are practically sharing a room already. Right, babe?" I widened my eyes at him so he'd go along with it.

"Yup. I can grab my things and move them into Ken's room right now." A gleam danced in his gray eyes. I knew what he was thinking. "Can I have your key?"

I cleared my throat and stood up to dig it out of my purse. "Here you go. Don't go moving all my stuff around." I hated when my organized makeup system was disrupted.

He raised a brow and said in a deep teasing voice, "Not even your flower?"

Heat rose to my cheeks. That bastard. "Especially not my flower. It has delicate petals."

Mia watched our conversation with a hand on her hip and a raised brow. "What flower? Did you bring a new accessory you haven't shown me?"

Coby didn't miss a beat. "She did. It's probably the best accessory I've ever seen. I'd love for you to show it to me again later."

"I want to see it too," Mia added excitedly. "Ooh we can get dressed cute for the party, and you can wear it."

Coby barely contained his laughter. "I'd love to see that. Maybe you can go show it to Mia right now," he said, holding his hand in front of his mouth.

Ugh, he was such a man child. "Great idea, Mi, but," I took Jill's hand, "let's go chat wedding stuff with Jill." As Coby followed us with his gaze, I flipped my hair out and called over my shoulder, "Alone, please. You two or three I mean," remembering Aiden, "have fun."

We took some much-needed girl time in Jill's room, painting our nails by the light of the window and solidifying plans, so Jill wouldn't have to cancel her wedding. She was upset that most of their guests left, but she admitted that a part of her was relieved it would be a small gathering.

"Mike's family is amazing, but since it's his first wedding, they really went overboard with the guest list. He wants to give me the best, and I love him for that, but this is my second marriage, and I didn't want a big to do. The perfect wedding for me would be a beautiful space where Mike and I can recite our vows to each other, seal our lives together from there on out, and enjoy a nice dinner and some dancing with our guests. Nothing crazy."

I thought about what my perfect wedding would be, and it sounded exactly like what Jill had described. A beach ceremony with a handful of close family and friends, me in a simple dress with my hair blowing in the ocean breeze. I let my mind drift, imagining the waves crashing and the heat of the sun warming my exposed shoulders. I looked over at my soon to be husband and gasped. Why was I seeing Coby in a thin white button down and sleeves rolled up? A few buttons were undone to expose his tanned chest.

No, nope, no way. I shook my head willing my brain cells to erase that little presentation.

"What do you think, Ken?" Mia asked. I turned my head in her direction, staring blankly. I completely missed what she asked me.

Clearing my throat I responded, "Yeah, sounds great." She beamed.

"That's what I was thinking too. The lobby will be perfect for the ceremony. We'll go talk to Ginger about moving some stuff around and maybe you and Kayla can show me what you brought in terms of décor?" The wheels in her head were turning and it showed. I loved when Mia got a fire under her booty about something.

By the time we left Jill's room, each of us had a to-do list, and Jill was all smiles again. I wish I could say I helped out, but it was all Mia. As much as I tried, I couldn't help replaying that image of Coby standing at a beachfront alter staring at me like I was the most precious thing he'd ever seen. The image should have revolted me. He was still an asshole who had ghosted me and broke my heart. So why did my daydream seem so right?

An hour later, Mia and I were sifting through Ginger's stash of décor in an unused room on the top floor. Families were arriving carrying suitcases and baby gear. They brought cases of water and bags of groceries. Someone even brought a scruffy poodle mix. In the crowded mess, we decided we'd be of better use to make ourselves busy elsewhere.

The wind was picking back up again causing the unboarded shuttered windows of the top floor to make ominous banging sounds. I shivered, hating the chill in the air. My blood had thinned since becoming a Floridian, and anytime the sun wasn't shining, I froze.

"I don't know what we can use in this mess," Mia said pulling out a huge floral bow. "Ginger is a sweet lady, but her taste is somewhat questionable."

I kneeled to look through a large plastic bin that mostly held Christmas decorations. I fished out a red tablecloth that smelled like damp and mothballs. "This is probably a lost cause." Plopping on my butt and crossing my legs, I yawned. "What were they originally going to use as décor?"

Mia pushed her pile aside and sat next to me. "It was mostly going to be outside. A beachfront ceremony and the reception next door at the restaurant's patio. Maybe they have a different idea of what constitutes wedding décor than we do?" She added lifting up a semi-usable lace doily.

"That may be salvageable." I said and put it in the small keep pile.

"The theme could be grandma-core meets nautical holiday." Mia laughed as she found a Christmas-colored wooden anchor knickknack. We laughed until tears sprang at the corners of my eyes.

"This is a mess," I said. "And honestly, I feel like the storm isn't the worst of it."

She clutched her ribs and wiped at her eyes too. "For real." She fell back, and her curly hair spread out atop her head like a halo. "Let's catch up. What else is bothering you? Beside this trip gone wrong, I mean."

I flopped next to her on the dusty rug and stretched out my legs. "I haven't been able to reach my mom today. I have no idea if she made it to her meeting yesterday. My freaking phone died, and even if I charge it, there's no service anyway. It makes me uneasy when I can't check in."

Mia was the only one who knew about my mother's addiction. I'd shared that part of me with Ben like a fool. He'd brushed my worry off, of course, even after the accident.

She turned on her side and propped her head up in her palm. "I'm sure she's okay. But I understand. It's a scary thing to let go of the people you love even for a day."

I let a breath loose. "She's such a hot mess. I'm twenty-six years old for the love of God. I should be moving on with my life and not worrying about my disaster of a mother."

Mia reached out to play with a lock of my hair. "You're right. She's never going to change, Ken. I understand you wanting to check in, but she's a big girl and can take care of herself. If she messes up, she'll have to face the consequences."

Since when did my best friend become so mature and strong? The last time we had a serious conversation about my mother, she urged me to stay on her like a barnacle and run her daily life. To be fair, it was right after the accident, and we were all afraid that she would hurt someone again or hurt herself.

"You've changed, you know," I said. I put my arm under my head for support. "Months ago, didn't you suggest that I move back in with her?"

"Oh God, I did, didn't I?" She laughed, sounding horrified. "I'm so glad you ignored that advice."

"Me too. I think I'd have a thousand dollar a week therapy bill if I went through with that plan." A bitter laugh escaped my lips, and I looked at my friend, really looked at her. She was literally glowing even in this dusty shitty old room. Is this what real happiness looked like? "I have something to tell you."

It was like I saw happiness and had to squash it away like I was throwing dirt on a flame. But it was killing me to keep these lies from my best friend. Looking at her now, hearing how much she'd changed in these last few months. I knew she could handle it. I'd keep the secret about Coby and me to myself, at least for a bit longer, but I couldn't hide the interview from her, not anymore.

She gave my shoulder a light squeeze and concern knit her brows. "What is it?"

I started by taking a breath in and opening my mouth, but the words wouldn't come. Her big brown eyes beckoned me to say it.

"I think I'm going to move out of Palm Cove to maybe LA or New York. Hopefully LA. I have an interview on Monday. My dream job, Mi. It's still surreal that they want to meet with me." I wrapped my arms around my chest feeling an odd mix of pride and dread. I realized in that moment how badly I wanted that job. So badly that I was willing to leave my best friend, the town I called home for almost five years, and maybe even leave Coby and whatever the hell we were doing.

Mia was quiet as she took it in. Months ago, I would have expected her to low-key freak out. Maybe not full-blown anxiety attack, but she would've wanted to make a pros and cons list focused heavily on the cons. But instead she sat up and carefully pulled her hair into a messy bun.

"Whoever they are, they'd be lucky to have you." I sat up and dabbed at the stupid tears forming in the corners of my eyes.

"Yeah?" I said on an exhale.

"Of course. Palm Cove is too small for you. You were meant to shine so much brighter. I want the world for you, Ken. No matter where you are, we'll always have each other."

I released a breath, letting the tears slide down my cheeks. I think I was waiting for this conversation before I let the idea fully take shape in my mind. "Thank you. You don't know how much I needed to hear that."

She embraced me in a warm hug, and I breathed in the comforting scent of my best friend as rain pelted the outside walls in sheets. "Don't worry about your mom either. She'll be fine. I'll keep an eye on her."

I found an old ratty rag and wiped my running nose on it. It made me sneeze, which blew more dust into the air. "You're the best."

She batted her lashes dramatically and tilted her head to the side. "I know, what would you do without me?" She added,

"What about Coby? You guys just got back together. Did you tell him about the interview?"

I looked down, playing with a frayed edge of the makeshift handkerchief I'd used. There was no way I could look into her eyes and lie. "Uh, yeah. He knows. I'm not sure what's going to happen with us. It's still so new. But I have to think about what's best for me."

"You're right. I've always said, if it's meant to be, it'll be." Shrugging, she pushed aside the bin behind her and squealed so loud I jolted.

"Oh my God, is there a spider? Or a snake? What is it?"

In her hands was an ancient-looking tape deck, circa 1985. "Music will make this so much better."

"You scared the crap out of me!" My heart was about to burst out of my chest.

"Sorry! I couldn't contain my excitement. Let's see what we're working with." She hit eject with a click and pulled out a gray cassette. "Hell yes! Footloose soundtrack."

"Good find!" I joined her, scattering more bins to make space in the room. "Hit play on that baby and find out if the batteries are still kicking."

Kenny Loggins's angelic voice belted out through the speakers and we danced and sang our way through the rest of the bins. I was having so much fun I *almost* forgot about my Coby daydream and the stress of the interview.

Chapter 25

Coby

SHAWN, AIDEN, AND I found Mike at the back exit of the inn. Him and his uncle were taking trips back and forth from a shed on the side of the property, carrying sandbags and wooden boards. We jumped in to help out carrying as much as we could, except for Aiden, who found out where the router was and insisted that he'd be more help seeing to the WiFi situation. I was happy to have him out of my hair. Seeing Shawn's unmistakable smirk as Aiden shuffled away, I knew he felt the same.

The four of us worked for the entire morning, pairing up and securing every window with plywood, locking the ones with shutters, removing the last of the outdoor furniture, and placing a few sandbags around the entrances that were vulnerable to flood water. Tim assured us that in all the years of the Marin's owning the inn and restaurant they'd never had any flooding or major damage, but he liked to err on the side of caution. The hum of the fridge and our labored breaths filled the space.

"Beers on me," Tim said. He pulled out four cans and slid them to each of us and then grabbed a container of meats and a loaf of bread from another shelf in the fridge. "I've got the generator running this fridge and a couple lights and outlets over here, then another one for the walk-in next door." He took off his ball cap and ran a hand over his peach fuzz hair with a groan. "I don't know how we're gonna feed all these people though."

Mike piped up, "It'll be okay. Most of the guests left and the locals will have to pitch in. Don't worry about it. Let's make the best out of the situation."

"Here, here," I added and clinked cans with Mike. "I know the girls are planning something nice for you and Jill tomorrow. As for feeding us, we'll figure it out." I held up my turkey sandwich, "This kinda thing is perfect."

Tim sighed. "Well don't think we'll be taking a dime from you for the room charge. This is not the guest experience we promise."

I laughed. "Try and stop us from paying."

Shawn added, "Not like you can control the weather. Plus if you're Mike's family, then you're our family."

Mike's round face lit up as he thanked us. Tim continued to apologize a few more times in between swigs of beer, but by the time we finished eating, Ginger had found us and beckoned him and Mike away to help fill more jugs of water.

"Ready for me to kick your ass?" Shawn grinned and took his last swig of beer before swiping his hand over his mouth.

I stood, pushed my chair in, and cracked my knuckles. "You mean, ready for me to hand your ass to you, right?"

"Eh, I don't know about that. You've been away for a couple weeks. I'd be willing to bet you've barely gone for a jog all month."

"Willing to bet, huh?" I scratched at the rough stubble of my chin. "Let's say I have a lot of pent-up frustration to get out and leave it at that."

We headed next door to the empty restaurant, re-soaking our shirts. The wind was picking up and Shawn had to holler for me to hear him.

"Listen, I don't need to know about your pent-up sexual frustration. Save that for your girlfriend," Shawn chuckled.

"Look who's being a creepy pervert now." I laughed as we went inside and moved tables and chairs to give ourselves an area to spar. I almost had the knee-jerk reaction to correct him when he called her my girlfriend. That label was still so new but I liked how it sounded.

"Takes one to know one," he said.

"Touché. Enough flirting, square up." My limbs itched to move and to get into that flow where I could shut off my mind and let my focus be the opponent in front of me.

We didn't need pads or gear. The trust was there that we'd keep it clean and not get carried away. I pulled my shirt up and over my head, tossing it aside like a wet rag. Shawn followed my lead and did the same. We faced each other, hands in defensive positions in front of our faces and sidestepped. Each of us waited for the other to make the first move. It was a dance, a violent one.

Shawn came at me first by throwing a low punch to my abdomen, which I blocked at the last second. While he was open, I took my chance and went in for a kick. He saw me coming from a mile away and blocked me with a knee.

We circled while throwing punches and blocking most of them. Shawn tried to get me in a headlock but didn't succeed.

Breathing heavily, I threw another low punch. "Still want to wager that bet?" I was talking shit since neither of us had landed much of anything, but I was holding my own.

He crouched before countering with a knee to my chest. Air whooshed out of me in a grunt. Shawn laughed. "Yeah I think I do."

"Asshole," I groaned.

Still chuckling, he circled me again. My plan was to knock him to the ground. I always beat him when we grappled. For Shawn being such a big guy, once I got him down, I could pin him fast. I glanced at the floor realizing the worn wood wouldn't be the softest place to land, and the last thing we needed during a damn hurricane was a trip to the emergency room. As I was letting a new plan of action form in my mind, a gust of wind shook the walls, and in that moment of being unfocused, Shawn found his in and pinned me under his armpit in a headlock.

"Dude," I wheezed, "I do not need to be this close to your nipple." He let go, laughing, and we fist bumped.

"Want to go again?" he asked as he wiped his hands against his damp gym shorts.

"And get my ass handed to me? Nah, I'm good. I'll walk away with my dignity intact." He walked around the bar, grabbed two glasses, and filled them with water from the soda machine.

"You'll get me back soon enough," he said. "Remember how long I was out of shape after I missed a bunch of classes over the summer? You caught me off guard and got me in a chokehold from behind."

"I do." I took a long sip and sat in a nearby chair. "It's one of my fondest memories."

We were quiet as we finished our waters and caught our breaths. It would have been nice to have this kind of brotherly relationship with Clyde. My brother and I had a decent relationship until he hit his teenage years and started working at the mine.

Yeah, Shawn and I piss each other off here and there, but I knew he had my back and I had his. Maybe it was sentimentality or some shit, but when I opened up my mouth to speak, the thing I never expected to say slipped out.

"I didn't leave to help a friend. My father died." I examined my empty glass, knowing that if I looked up, I'd regret opening my damn mouth. "That's why I had to up and leave so quickly."

Shawn stayed quiet, listening and waiting. There was nothing more for me to say. I didn't even know why I gave up the information to begin with. After a few breaths where I watched the last drips of water slide down the side of my glass, he spoke. "I'm sorry, man."

"I'm not. Son of a bitch can rot for all I care. It was complicated. I had to sell their house and get rid of so much shit. Still have to finish up actually. I don't know why I'm telling you all this. Sorry."

The scratch of chair legs across the hard floor had me looking up. Shawn took a seat across from me, his face unreadable.

"Just cause someone had it coming and deserved their end doesn't mean it makes it any easier to process that shit." He sighed as he opened and closed his fists. "It's not my business why you didn't want anyone to know what happened. Hell, I get it. I'm a private guy. You don't have to justify shit to me or anyone."

"Thanks, man. I guess I needed to get it off my chest." I leaned back and stretched my legs out in front of me, feeling the painful pull of my hamstrings.

"One word of advice though, I made the mistake of keeping things from Mia, and it fucked me over in the end…" he said.

He screwed himself over by thinking he was never going to be good enough for her, or anyone. Was I trying to sabotage any chance of a real relationship with Kendahl because I was scared I'd turn into my piece of shit father? I knew deep down that would never happen. But that involuntary impulse was testing my limit.

"I hear you loud and clear." If I wanted everything with her, the real deal, then I'd have to come clean even if that shit scared the hell out of me.

"Good." He stood up, stretching his arms up. "Plus, I'm sure whatever family issues you have aren't half as bad as the rumors that made their way around the gym while you were gone."

"For real? Ken hasn't said much just kind of implied that stuff was said." I scratched my jaw wondering what kind of nonsense was spread around.

"Yup. You got someone in Palm Cove pregnant and were running out on her.... you have a wife and kid somewhere in the Midwest..." I chuckled. "Or my personal favorite, you're a, how should I say it nicely... an adult film actor and had to go off to shoot a movie."

I couldn't hold my laughter in at that one. "Wow, I could get behind that rumor."

"Your man-whoring all of Palm Cove really got into the rumor mill, so I wasn't too surprised to hear that one. Between us, Kendahl's jaw dropped to the floor when she heard them though."

I shook my head, not believing what I was hearing. "I have a lot of work ahead of me to fix my reputation."

"Too bad. I was enjoying the entertainment." We laughed our way back out into the rain, shirtless because what was the point.

I moved a sandbag aside and held the door open for Shawn, but before he made it inside, I was sure to call him an asshole one more time for good measure.

Chapter 26

Kendahl

MIA AND I SPENT a few more hours finding anything and everything that we could salvage for the wedding. All in all, I was pleasantly surprised with what we came up with. After seeing Ginger's decorating sense, my bar was set pretty low.

I fished the spare key I got from Bethany out of my bag and made a ridiculous amount of noise unlocking the door. Part of me expected Coby to be there doing who knew what, and I didn't need to catch him off guard. *Like he caught me last night.*

My cheeks heated at the thought of his eyes on me. I hadn't come that hard in years. The euphoria was short lived though as panic ran through my body when I came back to earth. I didn't know how to react or what to do about what transpired between us. A line had been crossed, and I was still unpacking how I felt about that. Still, I wished I'd done more than pull the covers over myself. The way I let his praise penetrate my skin and sink into the deepest recesses of my soul.

Good girl. His husky voice was so commanding like every word he said was thought out with care. He sounded nothing like the man who never took anything seriously. Even when we were dating, he never let that part of him out. I wanted more.

I used a washcloth to wipe some of the grime and dust from my body. I wished I could take a long, hot shower instead. But I had no idea what the hot water situation would be without power and didn't want to use it up. Dirty hippie mode would have to do. Wrapped in a towel, I brushed out my tangled hair, tied it away from my face, and swiped on some fresh eyeliner and mascara. I dug through the remainder of my packed clothing and opted to wear a cute off-the-shoulder black top with some distressed jean shorts. Even if I felt grimy, there was no reason I couldn't dress cute. Rose from Titanic knew that even with the ship going down and people dying, she still rocked her dress and curls. *Damnit, Rose.* There was room for Jack on the door. I will die on that hill.

The lobby was chaos by the time evening rolled around. Subconsciously, I scouted the room for Coby and found him near the desk. He had two children literally running circles around him. He looked disheveled in a wrinkled T-shirt and gym shorts with his dark hair sticking up on end like he'd gone through a wind tunnel. I held back a giggle at seeing him in such a state.

About fifteen people including children, mingled around the comfortable lobby space. These must be some of the local families who had to take shelter here. Every couch was taken and board games and coloring books were scattered across coffee tables. One solitary lamp cast a glow in the darkening space while a few small battery-powered lanterns sat waiting to be used. Someone had set up trays and bowls of food along the coffee bar table. It looked like a crudité platter, a few cheese trays, and some bowls of chips. A niggle of guilt tugged at me that while I was relaxing in my room, the others were busy working down here.

I felt a familiar tingle and looked up. Coby's wide eyes were cast in my direction. The children had decided to climb his legs like tree trunks and were hanging onto them giggling like small maniacs. He mouthed, help me. With a barely suppressed giggle, I went to rescue him.

"How did you end up on babysitting duty?" I asked, bending down to say hello to the little guy attached to Coby's leg.

"No idea." He laughed. "One look at me and these little ones decided I was the perfect jungle gym."

They weren't wrong. I let my gaze rest on his tall, lean frame. He did have an extremely climbable body. *Kendahl, focus.* There were children present. "Let's see if I can distract them," I said to Coby before focusing my attention on the little boy. "Hi there, little guy. What's your name?"

Big brown eyes met mine. "Henry," he said, the 'ry' in his name sounding like 'we'. He had to be no more than three years old.

"And you?" I gestured to the little girl on Coby's other leg. She looked a bit older, maybe five or six, and she had the same brown eyes and squishy face as Henry.

"Isabella. I'm six, and that's my little brother. He forgot his favorite dinosaur toy at home. Mom said we can't get it." Isabella spoke with the eloquence of a grown adult. What a precocious little thing. I wondered where their parents were.

"I'm so sorry, sweetie. Mom's right. It's safer here for the night." I looked around to see if I spotted anyone looking even mildly concerned to be missing a couple of kids, but everyone around seemed preoccupied.

"What should we do with them?" Coby asked, running a hand through his crazy hair.

I had no idea. I wasn't really one of those naturally maternal women. As an only child who raised her adult mother, taking care of kids was never something I wanted to do. The closest I got was Alex, Mia's ten-year-old nephew, and that's only been recently since Olivia moved them to Florida.

"Let's try and get them preoccupied. They must be nervous. I mean think about how you'd feel in a dark scary storm away from home." His face fell, and I realized what I'd said. Insert foot into mouth. I didn't want him to think I was mocking his fears. "Sorry, that's not what I meant."

"No, it's fine. You're right. They're probably nervous." He reached down and pried Isabella off his leg and lifted her into his arms. She instantly rubbed his beard and giggled. I took his cue and picked Henry up. His adorable little face peered into mine, and I felt him relax into my arms. He yawned and put his head on my shoulder.

I inhaled his sweet scent, cookies and apple juice. "Come on, little guy, let's go find your parents." Rubbing his back, I turned to Coby. Isabella was also resting her head on his shoulder. My heart flipped, and I nearly let an explicit word slip out of my lips. Him holding a child made me suddenly one hundred times more attracted to him. That image of Coby and I standing under an archway on the beach crawled its way back to the forefront of my mind especially the way he smiled at me and his dimples were on full display as the waves rolled behind me.

I stopped short and Coby almost crashed into me. "Sorry." I cleared my throat. "I don't know where I'm going. Want to lead the way?"

He hoisted Isabella up an inch and nodded. "Yeah, let's go check the kitchen."

"Good plan." I stepped aside to let him walk in front of me, trying to shake away the image I'd conjured out of thin air.

I knew the inn must have been built as a large vacation home ages ago, but I hadn't thought about the fact that there was a kitchen down here. We'd had all our meals next door, so the thought never crossed my mind. We passed a family of three who were gathered around a small table playing Uno and an elderly couple munching on some cheese and crackers chatting quietly. Rain and wind battered the boarded-up windows, which made overhearing their conversations difficult.

Down a long hallway lined with a few closed doors, we finally made it to the kitchen. Just in time too because my arm was going numb. The dead weight of a toddler was no joke. As we pushed through the door, I heard Mia's unmistakable laugh and Shawn's gruff voice muttering something. The kitchen had been turned into a sandwich-making factory. Ginger and Tim stood around the stove fussing with a package while Mia, Shawn, and another young couple slapped fillings between slices of bread in an assembly line.

Isabella lifted her head from Coby's shoulder. "Mommy! Daddy!" The couple lifted their heads in unison to take in the scene before them. Mia and Shawn also looked at us with confused grins.

"Bella, oh my goodness. You were supposed to be playing with Mrs. Lancaster." The woman said as she dropped the sandwich she had been making. Both parents shuffled over to us, apologizing profusely. The children were supposed to have been looked after by their neighbor, so that the parents could help with dinner, but apparently, the children were a handful for the elderly Mrs. Lancaster.

"It's no problem," I assured them. "They're sweet kids."

"I think they tired themselves out running circles around me," Coby added, laughing.

"Well, in that case, you deserve the first sandwiches." Their mother said lifting Henry's sleepy form from my arms. I tried to ignore how I immediately missed the warm weight of him against my chest. Their father scooped Isabella from Coby and thanked him again, making a joke about how they should have gotten another dog. I laughed absently at his joke, but my mind hung on the fact that holding little Henry and seeing Coby being sweet woke some dormant instinct deep inside of me. I needed a drink.

"Why don't you guys go have something to eat. Coby and I can take over in here." She nodded, and I watched them juggle two sleepy kids and four sandwiches as they made their way out the door.

"We should play truth or dare," Mia announced, a few drinks in. A group of us were getting the party started in the lobby. Stacks of red Solo cups and bottles of liquor replaced the mugs and K-cups at the coffee station. Someone had brought over an open ice bucket from next door and filled it with cans of beer and soda. Along with the drinks were more snacks like pretzels and chips on tables for people to grab. The whole thing reminded me of the parties Mia and I went to in college only without someone puking in a corner. Mia remembered the tape deck we found earlier and had it blasting the Footloose soundtrack again in the background.

I groaned and took a small sip of my vodka cranberry. "Mi, I love you, but we're not teenagers."

Avery, with her arm slung around Bethany's shoulder on the couch, cut in, "There's not much else to do."

"Yeah, Ken, when did you become such a party pooper?" Mia added. A few drinks in and she was already acting goofy.

I sighed, resigned to go with the flow. I was not choosing dare though. Yet truth wasn't much better. Coby was seated next to me on the worn area rug, close enough that the bare skin of my thigh grazed against his pant leg. He took a sip from his Solo cup, and his gaze locked on mine. The Coby I knew would have been the first one to initiate a wild drinking game. That is unless he was too busy putting the moves on someone.

I thought about the night I met him for the first time. The moment we connected, all of his focus shifted to me. Our conversation flowed so easily that I hadn't realized hours had gone by. Tonight, he had the same air about him but more reserved and intense.

"I'm in. But nothing scandalous. Can't be kissing other guys the night before my wedding." Jill laughed, and Mike squeezed her closer.

"I don't think Coby or I are looking to get our asses kicked by our girls," Shawn said as he leaned in to nuzzle Mia's cheek. "Or Mike. But I'm honestly more afraid of Mia and Kendahl."

Mia beamed. "As you should be." My friends volleyed playful insults back and forth, finishing up drinks and pouring refills. A few other guests were scattered around the lobby in conversations of their own, and I was glad for that. It was hard enough for me to socialize with my friends. I was exhausted.

"Miss Bride, you ask first." Mia said with a wide grin.

Jill leaned forward using her pointer finger to aim at her target. I knew the moment her eyes met Coby's and she gave a mischievous smirk that he was her victim. "Coby, truth or dare?"

Everyone murmured ohs and ahs, and Shawn reached over to smack his knee. "Better choose right, buddy," he teased.

Coby scratched his chin, then swung his arm around my shoulders. Sounding as confident as a politician delivering their victory speech, he said, "Truth."

I let out a shaky laugh. I would have taken him for a dare-guy especially with our dating arrangement hanging over us like a shadow.

"Ooh, I better make it good," Jill laughed. She chewed the side of her lip, deep in thought. "I got one," she said.

I held my breath.

"What were you really doing when you dipped out of Palm Cove? Wyoming, right?"

My breath released in a puff. We were safe, for now. Laughing, Avery added, "Good one, Jill. Tell us all about your family in middle America."

Taking a swig of her drink and nearly choking on a swallow thanks to laughing Jill piped in, "Or was it the porn thing?" Her face turned beet red.

"Come on, buddy, I'm about to be a happily married man tell us the juicy bits." Mike slurred, clearly drunk. "How many women did you have hanging all over you?"

Coby stiffened and pulled his arm away from me to wring his palms together. It was only a moment until he leaned back again and morphed his face into his signature smile. "I plead the fifth."

Shawn's eyes met Coby's in a look of irritation while everyone else groaned. Everyone except me. "Not fair. It's literally truth or dare. You gotta give us something," Mike said. He continued talking, but I couldn't hear him over my pulse. God, I was so stupid. Here I thought he was changing and that he was over that player bullcrap.

I grabbed my cup and pushed myself up to a stand. They quieted and shifted their gazes toward me. Mia started to get up too, but I put my hand out to stop her. "I need some air."

Chapter 27

Kendahl

I DIDN'T LOOK AT him or anyone else as I bolted from the lobby. How could I have let myself get that invested? Yet again, another man was showing me that I was not enough, and like an idiot, I let him crawl his way into my heart.

This is why there were rules, Kendahl. Play by the rules and no one would get hurt. Liars and cheaters are what they all were, and I was done. He didn't have to spill about our dating arrangement, but playing into the rumors was almost worse. I'd told Mia about the move, so all I had left was to break the news to my mother, then I could kiss Palm Cove goodbye and start fresh.

Without thinking, I pushed the front door open and walked out onto the covered wraparound porch. Rain pelted my face and wind whipped at my exposed skin. I dipped my tongue out to taste the cool drops that collected on my upper lip. My shirt quickly soaked through, but I didn't care. If anything, I wanted to step off the porch and feel more, let the rain wash away my every thought until there was nothing but empty space.

I breathed in, expanding my lungs as much as they'd go. The briny smell of the rising tide mixed with something sharp and fresh filled my nostrils. I looked out into the blackness imagining what it would be like to get carried away on the next gust of wind like a broken tree branch and the absolute freedom in having no control over where I'd land or if I'd make it in one piece. I spread my arms out and closed my eyes, letting the next gust wrap itself around my limbs and push me backward a step.

"What the fuck are you doing, Kendahl?"

Coby.

I opened my eyes and dropped my arms to my sides but didn't turn around. While I no longer felt anger coursing through me like lightning, I still didn't want to look at him. Keeping my gaze trained at the darkness, I crossed my now pebbled arms over my chest.

His large hand grasped my shoulder, and he came to stand in front of me, blocking the rain from lashing my body with his frame. "It's not fucking safe out here. Let's go inside and talk."

I cast my eyes down, so I wouldn't crack and look at his face. Those gunmetal eyes always pulled me in. "No. You go inside. There's nothing to talk about."

The sole of his boots splashed against the old wooden planks as he paced in front of me. "Is this about truth or dare? It's a stupid game. It doesn't mean anything," he pleaded.

An involuntary scoff made its way out of my lips. "Nothing you say means anything. I shouldn't have forgotten that this is all pretend."

The tips of his worn boots lined up in front of mine, and he stayed in place. "Is that what you think?" A tremble rolled through me at the hush in his tone. His hand cupped my chin. "Look at me, Kendahl." I shook my head as I felt a tear gather at the corner of my eye. "I want to look into your eyes when I tell you that you're everything to me. You've crawled your way under my skin and into my heart, and I don't fucking know what to do with that."

Tears rolled down my cheeks mixing with the salty raindrops, and I brought my trembling hand to my cheeks to wipe them away, ignoring his hand at my jaw. "You don't mean that. You made it clear in there when you bragged about your trip and all the women." I hated how insecure I sounded. This wasn't me. After Ben, I was done letting myself cry over a man.

I gave in and let him tilt my face up to meet his eyes as another gust had me stumbling backward. He grasped my shoulders, firm but soft. I studied his face in the darkness. Those eyes looked almost black under his knitted brows, and his jaw was clenched tight.

"My father died."

I choked on a breath. "What?"

"That's why I left. I had to bury my father." His words from the previous night swirled around my mind. His father, the abusive alcoholic who made Coby's childhood a living hell. Why would he keep that from me? From any of us? He slipped his hands off my shoulders, and I instantly missed the warmth of his touch.

"I'm so sorry." I chewed my lip. Anything I wanted to say seemed pointless compared to the bomb he'd dropped. "Why didn't you say something earlier?"

He paced again and his boots scraped against a rough board. "That life is in my past. There's no space for any of it here and now," he said in a flat voice. "I wanted you to know to put an end to all the rumor bullshit."

"Coby, you can't cut an entire part of your life away like that. There's only one of you. Not a past version and a present version but a whole man standing in front of me."

A sardonic laugh filled the air. "What if I don't want that part of me? Goddamn." I watched him stop and rub the back of his neck. "It was easy before I met you. No one gave a shit about where I came from or who I was so long as I was providing them with laughs. And the women... Fuck. They cared even less about me and what was in here," he balled up his fist and thumped his chest, making me jump, "as long as they were coming, they were happy. And you know what? I thought I was too."

I leaned against the wet wall blinking the tears out of my eyes. "But you weren't?"

He stayed quiet for so long that I wasn't sure he heard me.

"I didn't know happiness until I met you. Jesus, Kendahl. You make me feel. So. Many. Things. Feelings I hadn't thought I could feel. I've spent so long hiding behind a mask that I built like an iron cage around my heart. If I never took anything too seriously, then I'd never get hurt again. I won't say I haven't been a bastard because I have. I hurt you. And knowing that I caused you pain kills me every day. All I want is to see you smile, hear you laugh, and see you bite your bottom lip as you think about the next insult you're going to throw at me."

Slowly, like he thought I might run, he stepped toward me. His eyes burned with intensity in the jet-black night. My heart was pounding against my ribcage making me dizzier the closer he got.

"I regretted sending that text the moment I did it. I don't know if it was my fucked up version of grieving, but I couldn't let you see me like that. I couldn't let you in. But, baby, the whole time I was away from you, every fucking day, you were the only thing keeping me going. I'd stare at your picture, and it gave me a reason to smile through it all."

My breaths escaped in shallow pants as he brought his body flush against mine. My head told me to push him away and tell him to fuck off. I didn't need him or any man. He brushed his palm against my cheek, sweeping it down the curve of my neck and my heart took over. "What are you saying?"

He reached around and gripped the back of my head angling my face so we were eye to eye. "I'm saying this is real. Fuck the rules. You may be the most infuriating woman I've ever met, but I can't get enough of you."

His lips crashed into mine, matching the energy of the storm around us. Demanding and hungry like he either wanted to take me over his knee or suck the life force right out of me. I opened for him, and he slid his tongue inside, teasing my mouth until every inch of me ached for more. I gripped onto his rain-slicked shoulders as he worked his way down my neck, nipping and sucking the drops of water from my pebbled skin.

I moaned and threw my head against the wall. "I'm addicted to the sounds you make." His voice held a rough edge like he was a string about to snap. I moaned again, louder over the gusting wind. "Fuckkk."

He gripped my ass and lifted me until I was flush against his thick cock. I wrapped my legs around him and pushed back against the textured wall, letting the painful scratch add to the friction from his body. Need squeezed my insides tightly, and I had to feel more. Using the wall for leverage, I ground against his cock. His hard bulge hit me right where I ached as he nipped and sucked my neck. Coby pulled back slightly as I tried to grind on him again and murmured in my ear. "Look at you, so used to having to take what you want." He hoisted me up higher while wrapping his palms around the outside of my thighs. I was a ball of knots, so close to release. A whimper escaped my lips, and I bit my tongue to keep myself from crying out in frustration.

Something rattled in the distance as another gust of sandy wind pelted my exposed skin. Coby kept his gaze trained on me with such tenderness that I thought I would cry again. Every feeling overwhelmed me. My hammering heart, the throbbing between my legs, the painful sting against my sensitive skin, and his heated look that said I was the most precious thing he'd ever seen.

"Coby..." I whimpered.

"I'm memorizing the way you look right now. So needy and so fucking beautiful." He tightened his hold on me. "You don't have to take anymore, baby, because I'm going to give you everything. Whatever you want, whatever you need. I'd bleed for you if that's what you wanted."

I wrapped my arms around his neck and captured his lips, dragging my tongue across his bottom lip before sucking it into my mouth.

"What I want is you."

He deepened the kiss, and I swore I could feel him trembling as he held me tight. "Hold on, baby." Without a moment of hesitation, he pulled the door open and carried me upstairs.

Chapter 28

Kendahl

HE DIDN'T LET ME go until we were in the quiet of our room. I lit a candle and watched the flame cast Coby's dark shadow against the wall. He'd gone contemplative again as he leaned against the edge of the bed, and for a moment, I wondered if something had changed. I didn't want to let myself think too hard. I only wanted to feel.

When his husky voice broke the silence, my knees trembled. "Come here." My heart hammered with each step, and I rolled my teeth over my bottom lip. "Good girl. Now lift up your arms." I did as he asked, lifting my arms up and feeling my ribcage expand. He curled his fingers on the hem of my shirt and peeled the sopping wet material off me before tossing it to the side. His eyes grew molten as he took in my bare breasts. I couldn't tear my gaze from the look of pure reverence on his face.

"Your tits are fucking perfection, baby." His praise rolled over me, soaking into my skin. I knew my panties were as drenched as my shirt, and I found myself wanting to hear what he was going to say when he reached them. I started to unbutton my shorts, but he put a hand out to stop me. "Let me. I don't want you to lift a finger. I'm going to worship at your feet. Now, don't move unless I tell you to."

I was shaking with anticipation. No man had ever let me turn my brain off. If he didn't touch me soon, I might die.

Slowly, he trailed his palms across my collarbones dipping lower when he reached my sternum. He cupped my breasts, letting them fill his palms and brushed his thumbs across my sensitive nipples. "Coby," I moaned. "Please."

"Shh, patience, baby. We have all night, and I've been waiting to take my time with you like this." My knees buckled as he pinched my nipples between his thumb and index finger, and I pushed my thighs together to keep from moving. "Yes, stay nice and still for me."

"Fuck you," I gasped, not meaning it at all. He chuckled, an infuriating sound that vibrated through his entire body.

"I will soon, baby." I squeezed my thighs together again, a small enough movement that he didn't notice. He trailed his palms lower, grazing the side of my waist and the soft skin of my stomach. So damn slow. I reached out to hook my hands under his wet shirt, wanting to feel the warmth of his skin. "Nuh-uh," he clicked his tongue. "Don't move. Remember?" But seeing what I wanted, he pulled his own shirt off and let it drop to the floor.

His body was perfection, all tan and lean muscle. He had a fine dusting of dark chest hair that led down his corded abdomen. I'd seen him shirtless before, but it felt different in the candlelight of our room. I was getting frustrated. He was taking so damn long, and I knew what I wanted. I was used to initiating, leading, taking, then making my partner feel good even if I was left wanting. But this? This slow edging torture was testing every ounce of patience I possessed.

Coby chuckled again like he could read my mind. "You wear every thought on your face, baby girl. Did you know that?"

I huffed. "I've been told."

He reached out, unbuttoned my shorts, and pulled them down my hips. I didn't move to step out of them even though I wanted to kick their heavy wetness across the room. Coby kneeled and peppered warm kisses down my legs until he reached my feet. He lifted them, one at a time, and pushed my shorts to the side until I was standing before him in nothing but my damp black thong. I squeezed my fists until my nails cut into my palms, feeling so incredibly vulnerable.

He took my hands in his, peeling my tight fists open and planting a kiss to the center of each palm. "I'll get on my knees for you every single day, pray to you, worship you, and kiss you from head to toe until I've worked my way into every cell of your body. Now bend over the bed like a good girl and let me fuck you with my tongue."

Holy shit.

He crawled to the edge of the bed and pulled me down so I was bracing myself on my forearms. I ground against the edge of the bed, needing to feel friction against my throbbing clit. It wasn't enough. I buried my face in the comforter to stifle my moan. I needed more. My nipples scraped against the fabric in an almost painful pleasure.

He was behind me, his warm breath touched my sensitive skin. He palmed my ass with a hand on each cheek before he yanked my thong down my legs, spreading me wide. I'd never felt so open or so on display.

I lifted my ass higher, needing...wanting. As he slid a thick finger into my slit, I swore I heard him utter a prayer.

"So wet and ready for me, aren't you?" he moaned.

Yes.

The rough stubble of his beard teased my skin as he dipped his face against me. He held me open, giving him all the access he needed. And like he'd promised the other night after I'd told him about Bcn, he feasted. He dipped his tongue into my slit, dragging it through my opening and up until her reached my clit. I pushed against his mouth, arching my back and lifting my face for air. "Please, Coby," I begged.

He steadied me with one hand on my back and held me still. "You never have to beg, baby." Then he took my clit between his lips, sucking hard and moving in rhythm as he slid a finger into me and curled it until I was screaming my release. I bucked against him and let the waves of pleasure roll through me. When I couldn't take another second, I squirmed, and he released me with one last suck.

I collapsed onto the bed, trembling all over, as aftershocks of my orgasm rolled through me. The bed shifted, and I turned my head to see Coby laying back on his forearms, face glistening in the candlelight. He grinned, putting those dimples on display. "I knew you'd be delicious."

I reached for him, wanting to feel his skin touch mine and taste myself on his lips. He met me, capturing my lips in slow, lavish kisses. With a shaky hand, I reached for his shorts to make it known what I wanted. He stopped me by holding my wrist and looked into my eyes with intensity. "Is this real for you?"

My chest rose and fell rapidly against the soft mattress as I took in air. I sat up and pulled his palm toward me, kissing it. I'd never forget the look on his face as he waited for me to answer—hopeful but terrified. I was sure I looked the same way.

"Yes." I could barely get the word out before he hoisted me up the bed and onto my back. I collapsed into a heap on top of the pillows, and he hovered above me like a god. I reached for his shorts again, but he'd beaten me to it as he released the button and slid them down along with his boxer briefs. His cock bobbed, thick and hard and mouthwatering. The things I wanted to do to him... I rolled my bottom lip between my teeth and bit down.

"I hope you're ready because once I'm inside you, I'm never going to leave." He dipped down to suck a sensitive nipple into his mouth, making my insides tighten again. I reached for his cock and finally took him into my palm and squeezed.

"Fuckkk," he groaned, releasing my nipple with a wet pop. He was so thick that I could barely wrap my hand around him. We tangled our tongues together, and I worked his cock with my hand, spreading his drops of pre-cum down his shaft. So smooth and dripping perfectly. "You're going to make me come if you keep doing that."

He rolled over and reached for the side table. I heard him fumble around in the drawer until he came back with a condom. I chuckled. "Someone came prepared."

"Wishful thinking." He grinned and his intense gaze lit up my nerve endings with need. I took the condom from him, and he let me roll it down his cock with two hands. He hovered over me and rubbed himself over my wet slit. "I want to hear you scream, baby. Don't hold it in."

Before I could answer, he slammed into me, not giving me time to adjust to his size. I cried out in a mix of painful pleasure. He was so big, so much bigger than any man I'd ever been with. He slid all the way out before driving into me again, stretching my pussy to fit him.

"You take me so well." He pounded into me before throwing my legs over his shoulders so he was hitting me deep.

"Yes...Oh my God!" I screamed as I felt myself climbing that peak again. He groaned and his movement became harder, rougher. I grabbed his ass, sinking my fingernails into his skin and pushing him deeper.

"Come for me," he said through gritted teeth. His words drove me over the edge, and I wrapped my legs around him and squeezed tightly, so there wasn't an inch between us. I shuddered as I rode the waves of my release again. "Good girl. Milk my cock."

"Shittt!" My vision was dotted with spots as the waves kept coming. He adjusted my leg and pressed his thumb against my clit, circling until I screamed his name.

"That's right." He pounded on. "Scream my name. It's the only name that'll ever be on your lips again." He pushed into me with another jerky thrust, once, twice, until he spilled into me with my name on his lips like a prayer.

We stayed like that for a long time while I panted and exhaustion melted my limbs. "You're fucking incredible." He trailed his hands over my belly and across my waist. "Such a good girl, the way you come around me." He pulled out, and I instantly missed the sweet fullness of him.

But my eyelids were drooping as my body came down from the whiplash of the night. I barely noticed when Coby left the bed only to come back with a damp washcloth. Gently, he wiped my sensitive core, murmuring words of praise. The last thing I remember, before sleep took me, was him walking to the dresser and extinguishing the single candle.

Chapter 29

Coby

KENDAHL'S HONEY SCENT ENVELOPED me as I woke the next morning with her head in the crook of my shoulder. A sliver of sunlight illuminated her golden hair. She was so damn beautiful that my chest ached and dick throbbed when I looked at her. I lifted my head an inch as realization hit me.

There was sunlight peeking through the window. The storm must have passed. I shifted on the bed, adjusting my morning wood so I wasn't poking her in the thigh.

She turned, angling her front so not only was my boner touching her, but it was pressed against her core. I sprang to attention. Goddamn. I'd waited so long to be this close to her. Skin on skin. She murmured something unintelligible before blinking up at me.

"Hi." Her cheeks raised in a wide grin. There was the pang again. I'd need to clear my schedule for a week to accomplish all I wanted to do to this woman, and even then, I wouldn't get my fill. Her hand trailed up my side, letting her nails scratch my skin in the most delicious way. "Looks like you woke up... happy." She ran her fingertips back down my torso, then gently tangled them into my pubic hair.

"Five," I said aloud. She raised a brow but inched her hand lower. "Four," my voice was gravelly with sleep and lust.

"Why are you counting down?" She hovered right against the base of my cock, teasing me with those nails. I breathed deeply. Fuck, she smelled amazing.

"I'm giving you a few seconds to stop me from devouring your sweet pussy and fucking you so hard you won't be able to walk all day." Her eyes glazed over, and she rolled her bottom lip between her teeth. "Three."

She squeezed my cock, bringing her hand up to glide along the tip. I hissed, needing to be deep inside her. "Two."

"One," she finished my countdown, and I flipped her over onto her back and yanked the bunched up covers to the side.

"Mmm, breakfast. Spread for me, baby." There was no hesitation on her end. I let loose a small sigh of relief at knowing that last night wasn't a pity fuck. She was dripping already—all for me. She wanted me as much as I wanted her.

A small moan brought me back from my thoughts as she writhed on the bed, desperate for my tongue. "Please."

"What did I tell you?" I sucked and licked my way down her tight stomach to the sharp angles of her hips, lifting my head when I reached her center. "You never have to beg for me."

She writhed again, whimpering. I'd played enough. "Tell me you want to come." With a palm on each smooth thigh, I spread her wider. I needed to explore every bit of her pussy.

"Yes, yes. I need to come," she said, her voice thick from sleep.

I inhaled deeply before sinking into her, then flattened my tongue and slowly licked up her slit. Last night was quick and desperate. I'd waited so long to have her like this. I wanted to take my time now that she was mine.

Slowly, I lapped at her, dragging my tongue up to her clit, I flicked and pressed until she was bucking against me chasing her release. Her pussy quivered, she was so close. Lifting up, I braced myself on my forearms. She moaned. "Don't stop."

"You want to fuck my face, baby?"

Her flushed face shined golden in the morning light. My question hung in the air. As I was about to slide my tongue back into her, she nodded. "Yes. I've just...," she hesitated, "...never done that."

My chest swelled knowing that she'd be this open for me and only me. Her dumb fucking ex didn't know what he was missing. I climbed up the bed to lie against the wooden head-board, meeting her plump lips and kissing her until her chest was heaving. "I'm the luckiest man in the world. Hold onto the headboard and fuck my face, Kendahl." I licked my lips, ready to feel her coming on them.

She scrambled onto her knees and climbed over me, her thighs trembling. I helped her the rest of the way by palming her ass and lifting her in place. Heaven, pure fucking heaven. If I died right here and now, I'd be fulfilled.

She rocked against my stiff tongue, rubbing her dripping seam rhythmically. She moved so her swollen clit was right over the tip of my tongue. I watched her unable to tear my eyes away for a second. Her beautiful tits bounced with each movement. I reached out to pinch and flick her hard peaks as I let a moan slip loose. I'd never been this hard before. I thought that same thing the night I'd watched Kendahl bring herself to orgasm and again last night. But I was wrong. My cock was leaking, I was so hard.

She arched her back and lifted enough for me to slip two fingers into her tight pussy.

"Oh God."

That's right, baby. Her noises were driving me wild.

She rolled her hips, grinding her cunt onto my lips as I drove into her with my fingers. She was close. Her walls were beginning to clamp down on my fingers, squeezing them like a vise. The headboard knocked into the wall. Hell, the whole bed could collapse, and I wouldn't give a shit.

"God, Coby." One more rough grind and she screamed with her release. She was so wet I could feel her soaking my facial hair and dripping down my neck. I'd never felt anything hotter. I was feral for this woman. Gripping her hips, I lifted her off me like she weighed nothing and positioned her over my cock.

"Baby, are you on birth control?" Panting, she nodded. "Good because I need to fuck you raw."

I drove into her, letting my cock fill her inch by inch. "You feel..." she murmured, her voice raspy.

"Tell me. How do I feel?" With my hands firmly grasping her hips, I helped her rock against me. She felt fucking incredible. Her tight pussy gripped me with each roll of her hips.

"So full... Mmm..."

She angled herself forward so her slick clit was grinding against me giving me perfect access to her tits. I took one nipple into my mouth at a time and lavished them with attention, sucking and swirling my tongue around the peaks.

"Coby," she moaned into my ear. "I'm going to come again."

She moved against me, changing her angle so she was lying on top of my chest, skin to skin. I pistoned my hips up as she thrusted more and more, harder and deeper. Fuck, I was so close.

"God, Ken." My breathing was erratic, but I guided her rocking motion. She took my earlobe between her teeth and sucked hard.

"Fill mc up, Coby."

Her muscles clenched, squeezing my cock as I drove in, shooting my cum inside her.

"Yes!" She writhed, rolling her hips to ride out her release. She collapsed on top of me as our chests heaved.

Nuzzling into her neck, I whispered, "I think being inside you is my new favorite place."

"Oh yeah?" she asked with a husky laugh.

Running my hands over the warm expanse of her back, I was certain. My new favorite place was wherever she was. "Yeah."

"I don't know how you two pulled this off," I said to Mia and Kendahl.

We'd watched Mike and Jill recite their vows in front of their closest family and friends. The ceremony turned out better than I think anyone expected. Couches and tables were moved, in favor of folding chairs decorated with ribbons and faux flowers. Dozens of candles cast soft light into the dim room, and somehow, they'd even found a classical music cassette tape, so Jill could walk down the aisle they'd created.

"We had a lot of help," Kendahl said and sipped a mimosa.

"Yeah, it was a group effort. I have to say, I wasn't expecting any of the evacuees to stay once the storm passed this morning, but a bunch of them saw us scrambling around and offered to help out. Turns out, one of the women was a hairdresser and was able to make Jill feel as gorgeous as she deserved..." Mia chattered on about all the small details they'd put into the ceremony, but I couldn't take my eyes off the most beautiful woman in the room.

Kendahl wore a gauzy blush pink dress that stopped at the middle of her thigh. It was backless, showing off her soft skin, dotted with freckles, and tied with a bow. As soon as I had the chance, I wanted to untie that bow and unwrap her like a present. Her long hair framed her face in soft waves, and she wore a touch of makeup. Her skin glowed in the warm light. I liked to think maybe I had something to do with that glow as well.

She peeked up at me as she sipped, noticing that I was drinking her in. Instead of scowling in that adorable way of hers and telling me to fuck off, she smiled so bright that her eyes lit up. My heart beat harder and faster the longer I took her in. A cadence, a rhythmic melody, each pump thrumming a tune. *Her, her, her.* The feeling was something entirely new but instinctual. Kendahl was as much a part of me as the organ in my chest keeping me alive.

The realization hit me. I was falling for her and it scared the hell out of me.

Chapter 30

Kendahl

I WAS IN AWE with how we were able to set up the restaurant next door into a beautiful reception space. Yeah, some of the nautical décor was basically plastered to the walls, but with how open and inviting the rest of the area was, I hardly noticed it.

Jill was glowing with her simple curve-hugging sheath dress and dark hair styled in an ornate updo. I couldn't help but smile watching her and Mike dance on the makeshift dance floor to terrible party music.

With the storm subsided and the power back on, the chefs were back in the kitchen cooking mouthwatering food for us. I sat back in my chair, glass of wine in hand, taking in the perfection of the moment. Coby stood at the bar getting us a drink while eyeing me every few seconds like he was hungry and I was his meal. I raised a brow flirtatiously and felt more wanted than I ever had.

The music changed from "The Cha Cha Slide" to "Dreams". My song. I started to involuntarily sway in my seat and hum the tune.

"Dance with me." Coby reached his hand out to pull me up. I let him lead the way, joining the rest of our friends. He pulled me flush against his warm chest, and I sunk my head onto his shoulder.

"I can't believe they're playing Fleetwood Mac. Every other song tonight has been nothing like this."

Coby nuzzled his chin against the top of my head. "I might have had something to do with that." His dimples were on full display.

"That's so sweet. I can't believe you remembered." Twisting a piece of his hair around my finger, I watched his expression turn thoughtful.

"When I saw you again the other night dancing to this song, you looked...I don't even know how to describe it. Peaceful and full of energy all at once. Like you were being transported somewhere else, somewhere special. I'll never forget that look."

I pushed up on my tiptoes and kissed him, not because we were in front of all our friends and not because I knew Aiden was recording us. I kissed him because I'd never wanted to kiss someone as badly as I did in that moment. It started out sweet and slow, but within seconds, my hands were tangled in his hair, pulling him closer against me. His hand rested on my low back but drifted lower until his fingers were curling against my hemline.

"Aww, look at you two." Tipsy Mia's voice was unmistakable. Coby moved his hand and broke away from my lips. She was slow dancing with Shawn, or attempting to, with how stiff he looked. "Bestie, they're playing your song," she crooned.

"They are." I laughed, noticing that Shawn was essentially holding Mia upright. "Looks like you're having fun, Mi."

"Shawn, I never knew you were such a good dancer," Coby teased. Shawn smirked and gave Coby a slow middle finger in response. I shook my head at the two of them.

"Let's go attack the buffet, Mi." I winked at Coby and gave his firm booty a pinch before taking hold of my bestie and starting toward the food. "I think I saw a cheesy pasta that looked incredible."

Mia hung onto my shoulders. "Oooh cheese. Let's go."

Coby and Shawn both chuckled following closely behind.

"I'm in a cheese coma," Mia groaned while pushing her plate toward the center of the table.

"Same. But I regret nothing." The food was mouthwatering. Chicken in a garlicky mushroom sauce, some kind of white fish lightly breaded and drizzled with lemon butter, crisp veggies roasted with herbs, and of course, cheesy penne in a rich red sauce. They'd be setting out dessert soon, and there was no way I had room for anything else.

Coby stretched out and patted his stomach. "Definitely beats the sandwiches we've been eating all weekend."

"That's for sure," Shawn added pushing his plate aside as well.

"There you lovebirds are." I turned to find Aiden taking a seat across from us, camera out. "I didn't realize you had left the dance floor."

I took a large sip of wine, groaning internally because even drinks were stretching my too full stomach. "It's your aunt's wedding, Aiden. Maybe you can, oh, I don't know...focus on her instead of trying to film for your channel. Plus, we're not all that interesting."

A flash of annoyance crossed his face. "Honestly, you're right." What? I nearly fell backward. "You two need to get more interesting. Let's think of some drama to reel in the viewers."

I groaned this time out loud. "Seriously. That's what you got out of what I said?"

"Listen, man. What happened the other night, isn't going to happen again. There's no drama here." Coby slung his arm around my shoulders and gave me a warm grin. "We're just two regular people. We started out rocky, but now..." He paused and I turned to see his eyes blazing. His tongue darted out to moisten his lips, and he swallowed, his Adam's apple bobbing. "Now we're two people in love."

Love?

The word echoed in my mind like he'd shouted it from a mountaintop. Holy shit. Did he really love me? Or was this all an act for the camera?

"Kendahl? Hello? I asked you a question." Aiden leaned with his forearms on the table to get as close as he could to us. "Oh, there she is. Welcome back to earth."

I cleared my throat, avoiding Coby's intense gaze. "Sorry, what did you ask?"

"I sense trouble brewing." He messed with something on his camera, most likely to zoom in on us. "Coby said 'you're two people in love', but then you looked like you went into cardiac arrest. Do you feel differently?"

I reached for my wineglass and sipped the last drop. My mouth felt like it was glued together. I couldn't look at Coby. Shit. Why did he have to spring this on me now of all times? And in front of a camera.

"Hey man, is that one of the Kardashian's over there by the bar?" Shawn said, breaking the tension of the moment. Aiden's neck practically snapped with how fast he whipped around.

"Where?" he whined. "I only see my great-aunt, Marjorie."

"Why don't you guys go find somewhere private to talk. I got him," Shawn said in a hushed tone. Coby nodded, pulling himself to a stand. I finally looked up at him and instantly wished I hadn't.

His shoulders drooped, and he wouldn't meet my eyes. "Come on, let's go upstairs."

Standing and adjusting my dress, I gave Shawn and Mia a quick nod and forced smile before following Coby outside.

Chapter 31

Coby

I ROYALLY FUCKED UP. We'd been back in our room for ten minutes already and neither of us has said much of anything. *Why, Coby?* Why do you always say and do things and then want to punch yourself in the mouth five seconds later?

The thing was, I meant what I said. Or at least my end of it. I did love Kendahl. I knew that before this trip, but the past few days had only cemented my feelings. I was scared shitless.

"I'm sorry." Kendahl's soft voice broke through the silence of the room. Why the hell was she sorry? I was the one who messed up.

"You have nothing to be sorry for. Once again, I jumped the gun." Pacing in front of the bed, I rubbed my chin for concentration. "I shouldn't have said what I said."

When she didn't respond, I looked up, forcing myself to stop studying a small pull in the carpet instead of looking straight at her. She was cross-legged on the bed, rolling her bottom lip between her teeth, and twisting a piece of hair around her finger. The silence grew between us like grains of sand filling an hourglass. Each second that neither of us spoke got me closer and closer to breaking down.

"Do you mean that?" she asked.

I stopped pacing and kneeled on the bed in front of her.

"Mean what?"

"That you shouldn't have said that you love me?" Her voice cracked on the last word.

Fuck. I'd hurt her. Again.

"Kendahl." I moved closer and tipped her chin up so we were eye to eye. "I meant that I shouldn't have said that the way I did." I forced a breath in through my nose and channeled a bit of the old Coby. The Coby who actually had confidence with women and wasn't a scared pussy.

"So how should you have said it?" Her blue eyes pierced mine, and I dropped that shitty persona immediately. She saw through my crap in a heartbeat.

I licked my lips and raked a hand through my hair, never breaking eye contact. "I should have told Aiden to go away. I should have taken you by your hand and led you up here, to our bed. I should have held you in my arms and kissed every inch of your gorgeous body. And I should have looked you in the eyes like I'm doing right now and told you that I'm in love with you.

That I have been since the moment I saw your smile. That I'm scared to death because I know I'm no good at this. But I want to be good, for you."

Quiet fell between us again. I couldn't get a read on what she was thinking and it terrified me.

"I," she hesitated and my pulse pounded so hard I thought I might pass out. "I love you too, Coby."

The sweetest smile spread across her lips, and she looked up at me through her dark lashes. I gathered her onto my lap and held her face gently, rubbing my thumb over her cheek. "This is real?" I asked, sounding more desperate than I'd ever sounded in my life.

She brushed her lips over mine. "Yes," she breathed. A shiver made its way from my spine through my muscles before I claimed her lips.

I started slowly, tracing her lips one at a time with my tongue. She opened for me and breathed a moan into my mouth. Her sounds had all my blood rushing to my cock. Our mouths moved in a slow rhythm as she rocked on my lap. Every dip of my tongue teased sounds from her lips. Every whimper and moan set me more on fire for this woman.

"Lie back for me, love," I said as I lifted her off my lap. A pink flush traveled up her chest toward her cheeks. I loved all the ways I could tell that she wanted me as badly as I wanted her. I hovered above her, kissing the curve of her neck down the base of her throat.

"I've been waiting all night to pull this tiny dress up and devour you."

Propped up on her forearms, she raised a brow. "Well, what are you waiting for?"

Good point baby.

When she came with my name on her lips, every fiber of my being knew I'd never want to hear my name out of another woman's mouth for as long as I lived.

I rolled over in bed, but my hand landed on a cold pillow instead of Kendahl's waist. "Babe?"

I sat up and rubbed the sleep out of my eyes. Darkness still cast the room in shadows except for a faint glow coming from the opposite side of the room.

"Sorry, did I wake you?"

Sitting in the armchair, her knee bounced a mile a minute, making the light from her open phone seem to vibrate.

I reached for my water bottle on the side table and took a sip. "Not at all. I just rolled over and found a pillow instead of you. Everything okay?"

"Yeah." Grabbing a hair tie from her wrist, she twisted her hair into a bun. "No." She hesitated and pulled her hair down. "I don't know."

I pulled the blankets down and patted the spot in front of my lap. "Come here, baby."

With her phone held tightly in her hand, she nodded and came to sit. I pulled her back into me so I could wrap her up in my arms. "Is it the interview?" She nodded again letting her loose hair tickle my chest. I gathered it in my hands and pulled it back for her, then kneaded her tight shoulders.

"Mmm, that's nice." Her head lolled back onto my shoulder, and I felt her body relax.

"Good girl. What's bothering you?" I murmured against her cheek.

"I don't know if I'm making the right decision. It's a lot." She nuzzled into the crook of my neck. "When I sent my resume, I never thought I'd actually get a call. Stratestar is huge, Coby. Like A-list celebrities huge. The CEO had a reality TV show for a season…like that big."

Massaging the base of her neck, I said, "Of course they'd want you. You're incredible. You're a force, and they'd be lucky to have you."

"Yeah?"

"Of course. And so what if they're famous or whatever, they're human like the rest of us. Be yourself, and I'm sure they'll love you."

"Mmm, thank you." She turned and planted a sweet kiss on my lips. "I kinda like sweet boyfriend Coby."

"Sweet? Hmm, it seems my reputation might be in jeopardy here." I laughed.

"Oh, it definitely is. Just wait until I tell everyone at the gym how much of a sweetheart you are." She nipped at my nose, then my chin.

"Okay, you're in trouble now." I pulled her across my lap and gave her tight ass a playful smack. "I think I need to show you how not sweet I can be." She screeched and giggled, trying to escape my grasp.

Chapter 32

Kendahl

WAKING UP IN COBY'S arms to bright sunshine streaming in through the window gave me a renewed feeling of confidence. I wanted to cringe at my vulnerability the night before, but somehow, he had made it easy to reveal that side of myself. We'd slept in until well past eleven and woke in a tangle of limbs with the blanket somehow lying on the floor.

As Coby went downstairs to get us some coffees and something to eat, I sat watching the time tick down on my phone. I'd gotten myself as presentable as I could with what I had packed by curling my hair to frame my face and applying a full face of makeup. Comfy road trip clothes were all that was still clean in my bag, but I'd fished out my cardigan to hide the faded blue T-shirt I wore.

After finally being able to charge my phone properly last night, I was inundated with more messages than I'd thought. I had texts from Claudia and Lee, DMs from every one of my social media accounts, and missed calls from unknown numbers. I scrolled the notifications and saw that my mother had called me at some point during the storm.

In all the chaos, I'd forgotten to check in with her. With only a few minutes to spare before the interview, I clicked her name on my screen. My chest tightened with each ring until finally, as it was about to go to voicemail, she answered.

"You had me worried sick," she said in place of a greeting. Her raspy voice was a whole octave higher than usual. That was laughable.

"Mom, I'm okay. There was a storm and the power got knocked out. It's back on and everything's fine."

She puffed her cigarette, and I heard her murmur something under her breath.

"What did you say?"

"Nothing, I was just telling Richard that you're alright. He knows I was worried sick. I barely even ate last night." Richard's deep timbre came through from the background.

"Did you make it to your meetings all weekend?" I needed to get down to the nitty gritty. The clock was ticking, and I couldn't be late to this interview.

"Yeah, don't worry. Richard brought me. They served us stale cookies last night. Can you believe that?" She sounded as if stale cookies were the absolute worst thing she had going for her.

"The audacity. Anyway, Mom, I gotta go. Glad you're doing good." I bit my lip, hesitating. "And uh, tell Richard I said hello."

"Richard, my doll face says hi, and she can't wait to meet you," she hollered far too loudly for my pre-coffee ears. "Thanks for calling, Doll."

I cleared my throat. "Of course. Love you, Mom."

"You too. Now get home safe."

I clicked end and sat back in the lounge chair. Since when did my mother worry about me or thank me for calling? There's no way forty-eight hours of me not checking in on her made that much of an impact. It was almost as if she was acting, *motherly*. I chewed my lip again, silently cursing my nervous habit when I realized I was smearing my lipstick.

After checking myself in the mirror and smoothing out my hair for the tenth time, I went back to the chair by the window and opened up my messages to the email from Victor's assistant.

It's now or never.

I clicked the connect call button and inhaled deeply.

"Oh my God," Mia squealed, wrapping me in a hug. "My best friend is going to LA to meet with Victor Moss in a week!"

A big grin spread across my face. I had Mia on one side of me and Coby on the other as we waited in the lobby for the rest of our group to come downstairs.

"She was amazing." Coby beamed. "I have to say the way you did that thing to your voice. It um," he laughed. "It really did it for me."

I hip bumped him. "What thing?"

"I know what you're talking about," Mia added. "She does her 'PR voice.'"

I shook my head and sipped some water with a shaky hand. My adrenaline was still on high alert from the interview.

"Fine, I know I do a voice. But to be fair, everyone does. It's a thing."

Shawn joined us, lugging two suitcases that looked stuffed to the brim. "What are we laughing about?"

"How Kendahl does her PR voice." Mia kissed Shawn on the cheek and nuzzled close to him.

"You mean the voice that sounds exactly like *your* accountant voice?" Shawn smirked.

"See! We all do it!" I said.

Mia laughed it off, and Coby shrugged in defeat. "So tell us how it went. What did they ask you?"

Coby had walked into the room halfway through the conversation, so he knew some of the answers to Mia's question. A muscle ticked in his jaw. I knew he was happy for me, but I didn't think he was crazy about the questions that had been asked. Mr. Moss's assistant didn't come across as a particularly warm person, but this was business. And, on the plus side, there was no mention of the video.

"Oh, you know, the normal job interview stuff. Where I saw myself in five years. Why was I thinking about relocating. That sort of thing." I shrugged, feigning a casual posture.

"As much as I'm sad for me, I know this is something you've wanted for a long time so I can't wait to see how it goes." Mia hugged me again as Avery joined the group hand in hand with Bethany and all smiles. We waved and greeted them.

"Where's your bag?" Shawn asked while tapping his foot. Knowing Shawn, he was very much ready to get back home to Remy and his woodshop.

"I'm going to spend a few more days here." Avery's grin lit up her face, and I watched the subtle shift in her body language as she moved in closer to Bethany. "Beth wants to show me around the island now that the storm has passed."

"You two are so sweet," Mia cooed. Avery blushed from her neck up to her forehead.

"I'm happy for you, girl," I said. A few days ago I probably would have excused myself to go wait outside at the first adorable sign of them holding hands. But now, looking at Coby leaning against the wall, one hand in his pocket, and one rubbing protective circles across my low back, I couldn't feel anything other than joy for them. We said our goodbyes to Mike and Jill who were also staying a few more days to enjoy the island.

"Bethany, I hope you can come visit Palm Cove soon," I said before realizing that even if she did, I wouldn't be there. No one noticed my mistake. They all chimed in that she'd have to try a level one class at the gym and that Mia had to bring her to Taco Bout It for burritos. It looked like my little family would keep growing after I was gone.

I forced a smile and squeezed Coby's hand. "Ready to go?"

"Yeah, I'll get our stuff."

Chapter 33

Kendahl

"YOU THINK YOU CAN take me down? Think again." I pounded the target pad with a low punch, then planted my foot along the bottom edge in a powerful stomp kick. Sweat beaded along my brow line, but I wiped it away and continued my advance. We'd been back home for a few days and Coby couldn't wait to get back to the gym.

Electronica pumped through the speakers of Krav Maga on Main spurring on my adrenaline. I loved it when we got to do these types of drills in class where we stacked different combative moves together. I looked at Coby who was my partner for the night since Olivia was stuck working late. He had the most infuriating grin on his face, which only made me punch harder.

"What's with the grin?" I scowled and stepped back as I wiped my brow.

"You remind me of a caffeinated squirrel." His grin widened and that jerk started to laugh at me, letting the pad slip as I reared back and punched. Lucky for him, I could aim. But I had considered going a bit lower for the money shot.

"A caffeinated squirrel? That's oddly specific."

Punch, kick.

"I saw one in a movie once. It's the way you're moving." He chuckled. "It's adorable."

Punch.

"Adorable?" I scowled again. "I'm supposed to be menacing." I sidestepped around him, trying to catch him off guard. "If I'm a squirrel, then you look like a donkey."

He leaned forward, trying to catch his breath from laughing so hard. "Seriously? How so?"

Crap. I didn't know why I said donkey. I had to think fast.

"Because when you kick you look like a donkey. Or a mule, maybe. Or a Clydesdale." I had stopped pacing, too deep in thought, which gave Coby the advantage. Before I knew what was happening, he had me slung over his shoulder.

"That's not very nice, babe. At least a squirrel is cute. But a mule? My feelings are hurt."

I smacked at his firm ass even though I knew he'd laugh and punish me later. By punish, I meant he'd make me come multiple times until my voice was hoarse from screaming his name. So really a reward.

He slung me down onto the padded mats pinning me to the ground in a straddle position. Pairs of my fellow level one students continued to work on the other side of the room with our instructor Mark watching from the corner. I gave Coby a playful push on his shoulder.

"Everyone is going to see us. Let me up," I said.

His dimples popped out as he grinned down at me. "Let them look. I'm showing my partner proper rolling technique. That's all. Now, apologize for calling me a mule." His eyes blazed, waiting on my response.

I decided to use another tactic and hooked my leg around his. I gave my sweetest wide-eyed expression. "I'm sorry, baby. You're not a mule. My baby is one hundred percent stallion."

His brows raised, and he lowered his head to my ear. "That's right. And since I'm a stallion, then that means you're going to have to ride me later."

I bit my lip and moaned low in the way that drove him wild.

"Too bad all these people are here. You looked so fucking hot practicing before and now you're whimpering. I bet you're so wet—"

I didn't let him finish his sentence. Quick as a damn caffeinated squirrel, I bucked my hips—hard and sent him off balance. Then I gripped him tight with my leg already hooked in position and threw all my strength into rolling him over.

"What the—" he said.

My chest heaved as I straddled him with my smuggest grin. I watched his stunned look and pressed into his hard length, gyrating my hips for good measure.

"Looks like the squirrel beats the mule today."

Planting a wet kiss on his lips, I climbed off him and left him lying on the ground to watch my ass as I walked away.

"That's what you get for underestimating me." I chuckled. I couldn't wait to tell Mia later.

"I never understood the appeal of this movie." I shoved a handful of popcorn in my face. Coby laughed and popped a few pieces that landed on my lap into his mouth.

"I can't believe what I'm hearing. It's a classic example of love conquers all," he said.

I pressed stop on the remote to banish the image of swans flying over a lake. What a dumb ending.

"I get that. Noah is definitely the hot, mysterious type. The way he looked at Allie...swoon. But is it really the great love story people make it out to be? Like the house, for example, yeah, it was cute that he painted it the way she wanted, but it was his dream to buy it."

Coby rubbed his chin. "Okay, you have a point. What about the letters though? That was romantic as hell."

I scoffed. "Or creepy as hell. Move on with your life man. You dated this girl for a summer, fought constantly, and made it seem like her lifestyle was wrong. I could go on and on."

He sat back, deep in thought. "You're kind of right. Fuck. Why do I feel like my entire life has been turned upside down?"

"I'd say I'm sorry, but I'm not." I wiped my hands on a napkin and put the nearly empty bowl aside. It wasn't lost on me that my relationship with Coby hasn't been all that different from that of Noah and Allie. A summer romance that ended before it really began due to a lack of communication.

"Okay, now that I know you're practically a one-woman Rotten Tomatoes, what's your favorite romance movie?"

"Easy. The Addam's Family." I grinned as I watched his face morph with confusion.

"You've got to be kidding me." He shook his head, chuckling lightly.

"Gomez and Morticia, baby. They are one hundred percent the embodiment of a healthy relationship. He adores her, worships the ground she walks on, and isn't afraid to show it to anyone, anywhere. In turn, she does the same for him. They take care of their family, are pillars in their community, and aren't afraid to let their freak flags fly."

The man who had a comeback for everything was stunned silent.

"Holy shit." He pulled me into his lap, which made some of my fallen popcorn kernels spill to the floor. "So you're saying I should be less Noah and more Gomez?"

"Oh yes. Gomez always."

He lifted my arm out to the side and peppered kisses up and down while making the loudest, most obnoxious smooching noises. Once my arm was good and wet from kisses, he went for the curve of my neck. I laughed so hard, I almost peed. And we were definitely not at the point in our relationship where peeing in his lap would be something I could laugh off.

"Oh my God, I'm going to pee my pants if you don't stop."

He lifted his head, his gray eyes like molten metal. "Okay, okay. Gomez would always listen to Morticia's commands. Plus I'm not into any pee kinks."

I scooted aside and went to use the bathroom, wondering how I ended up with this goofball. When I came back into the living room, he had poured me a glass of wine, set out my favorite cheese and crackers, and had The Addam's Family queued up on the TV.

"Ooh, I'm very much liking what you're thinking."

I plopped next to him. He picked up my legs, put them on his lap covering them with a blanket and rubbed one of my feet. Damn, he was good at massage. No wonder his clients love him. He's told me that his favorite thing to do in his practice is to stretch and work his client's muscles manually.

"Feel good, baby?"

"Uh-huh," I hummed. I was practically drooling. He pressed play on the remote and went right back to kneading.

The entire time the movie played, I couldn't stop glancing at him. He knocked out halfway through, leaning on a pillow with both hands holding my thighs. A piece of his dark hair fell over his forehead, and his face looked so soft and peaceful.

I'd fallen—hard. There was no doubt about it in my mind. We'd both avoided the 600-pound gorilla in the room since

Monday. My potential move. And it was wearing on me. I wanted to talk about it, but I didn't want to jinx anything.

Maybe I was waiting to see if any of this was worth the time and energy of a conversation. I didn't have a job offer yet. The trip was a trial run. A meet and greet. The chances I got the job and would be moving were slim. We'd talk if and when the time came. Until then, I'd enjoy my time with Coby. Even if a little voice in the back of my head kept telling me it was only a matter of time until he left again.

Yawning, I sat up to grab the remote from Coby's side of the couch. I would be joining him in dreamland soon if I didn't make myself get up and get ready for bed. Both of us sleeping on my two person sofa would not make for a good nights sleep. He mumbled something while I climbed over him, still asleep. As I was about to grab the remote I noticed his phone vibrating with texts.

I tried not to look. Really tried. But the messages were right there in my face, plain as day.

Bartender at Dockside: *Hey handsome. It's been a while. I get off at 12, let's catch up. Meet me at my place?*

Wow. He didn't even save her name in his contacts. I left his phone where it was and pushed to a stand, looking down at the man I loved. Jealousy bubbled close to the surface, ideas simmering of what I could say or do. I could wake him up and start a fight. I could text this woman back and claim what's mine. That thought had me laughing out loud. Yes, I'd been hurt before but that wasn't who I was.

Coby stirred, opening his eyes. He blinked and stretched his arms above his head. "Damn, I missed the ending. Sorry, Krav must have kicked my ass."

"It's okay, we can finish it another night." I switched the TV off and turned toward my bedroom. "By the way, your phone went off before."

I kept my voice even, shutting down my insecurities.

"Oh, I thought I put it on silent for the movies," he said, his voice gravelly with sleep. I watched him open the screen, glance at the message, then back at me. The entire thing took all of two seconds but my stomach twisted up wondering how he'd respond. "Did you see this?"

I rolled my teeth between my lips, before answering. "I did."

"I'm sorry, baby. She's nobody important. Just someone from my past. Honestly I can't even remember her name." He stood, pulling his hand through his messy hair.

"It's fine, Coby. I knew you weren't exactly a virgin when we started dating." I tried to make my voice sound playful. "Really. It's no big deal. I do have a question though."

"Ask me anything. Well, except her name. That I couldn't tell you."

"Does this kind of thing happen a lot? The hook-up texts?" God, I hoped I didn't sound needy and pathetic. But the thought of me being in LA and him getting calls and texts from women was too much to handle.

He made his way over to where I stood, tilting my chin up to meet his gaze. "It'll never happen again. First thing tomorrow, I'm changing my number."

"What? You don't have to do that. It's too much of a hassle," I argued.

"Nothing is too much of a hassle when it comes to you. Your number is the only one I'll ever need again." He brushed his lips against mine, soft and sweet. My body melted against his. "I don't want you to worry about any of that, okay. It's only you for me."

I nodded against his chest and he wrapped his hands around me, hoisting me up. "Let's get you to bed. If I remember correctly, I didn't get to finish Gomez kissing all the spots I wanted to."

Laughing as he kissed his way from my shoulder to my neck, I let myself revel in the pure happiness that was being in Coby's arms.

Chapter 34

Coby

"I GOT THE JOB!"

Of course she got the job. They'd be idiots not to hire her. It took less time than I'd thought for them to make the offer, she'd only arrived the previous day. I shoved down my initial reaction, which was to panic about us. She didn't need that shit. If this is what she wanted, then I'd be happy for her. I'd support whatever decision she made, and we could figure out the rest together.

"That's amazing." I pulled on the back of my neck. "I knew they'd love you. How's LA?"

I tapped my PT assistant on the shoulder and signaled to my office door. I had a few minutes to chat with Kendahl in between my patients.

"It's interesting so far. I've only been here for two days, so I haven't seen much outside of the office."

She sounded less enthused than I thought she would be. "Maybe you can sightsee a little? Check out Hollywood?"

"Maybe."

Thinking about her alone in a city that size made the coffee I drank on an empty stomach churn in my gut. Even though I knew she was learning Krav, I still didn't like it.

"How's your new boss?"

A chair squeaked in the background and she sighed. "He's, how should I say it... interesting."

"Soo, everyone and everything is...," I hesitated, "interesting?"

She laughed. "Sorry, I'm exhausted, and it's only lunchtime. My vocabulary is lacking. Victor reminds me of Kronk physically with the personality of Yzma."

"Yzma and Kronk? Like from the Disney movie?"

"Yes of course, *The Emperor's New Groove*. I can't help where my brain takes me, keep up."

"I shall try. But I've never seen that movie."

"What? It's only the most underrated Disney movie of all time. We will have to fix that. Anyway, he has this whole, I'll take over the empire thing going for him. I've never met someone with such an eagle eye for everything that goes on in the media. This man must have spies all over the country. And I've only been here for two days!"

Laughing, I added, "On the plus side, you can learn a lot from him."

"That's my hope. I can't wait to get some clients and get my hands dirty. Show him how much I can take."

Now that she sounded uplifted, that familiar spunk to her voice. "You can take a lot. I should know." I dropped my voice an octave. "You like to get your hands dirty too."

I knew she was shaking her head and scowling. "Always bringing the conversation back to sexy talk."

She laughed again, the sound brought a grin to my face. I'm glad I could cheer her up.

"I miss you. And before you go there, not for *that* reason," she said.

"I miss you too, baby. It's only a few days until you're in my arms again." A few days and then she'd be packing to move across the country. I forced a smile. I didn't want her to hear any disappointment in my voice. "I gotta go. My favorite crotchety old patient is coming in any second. I love you. And congratulations, you deserve the world."

"I love you too. Talk later."

For the rest of the day, I let my mind stay focused on my patients. Doling out exercises, massaging scar tissue, and stretching limbs kept me from focusing on how I was feeling. Which was like shit. I just got her back, and now, I'd be losing her again. I knew this was what she wanted and more than anything, she deserved to be happy.

I loved her. But I knew firsthand that love wasn't always enough. I was still scared as hell of taking things to the next level. Could I see myself moving to California again? Palm Cove was my home, even if it already felt empty without her. There was nothing left to do but to wait and see.

I finished up what felt like the longest work week ever, although it was only Wednesday. I'd be picking Kendahl up the following evening from the airport and couldn't wait to wrap my arms around her. For now, I'd take what I could get even if it was just a FaceTime movie date.

She was due to call me soon, so I changed from my work polo and khakis into comfortable sweats. I opened my shirt drawer, then closed it again, deciding that it wouldn't hurt to be a tease and show off what she was missing.

Her gorgeous face lit up my phone and I swiped to answer purposely angling the lens so half my chest was in view.

"Hey—Oh damn, I was not prepared for your naked chest." She narrowed her eyes. "You did that on purpose, didn't you?"

"Maybe." I shrugged, raising one brow. "Or maybe, you caught me while I was getting dressed. What do you think shirt or no shirt?"

"No shirt obviously," she said. "Even though it's mean to taunt me, I wish I was there already. Tomorrow is too far away." Her lip jutted out in an exaggerated pout.

"I know, baby. Trust me, I feel the same way."

I watched her get settled onto her hotel bed and open up her laptop. Her golden hair swung into her face, and I itched to feel those soft strands wrapped around my fingers.

"I'm thinking I need a comfort movie tonight," she said with her eyes focused on her computer screen.

"Okay..." I said. With Kendahl that could mean the most twisted horror movie or the extreme opposite, a Disney classic. "And what would that be tonight?" I tried to keep my voice level but hoped she wasn't about to say *The Texas Chainsaw Massacre* or some shit. That was not my thing.

Her eyes lit up as she landed on her intended pick. She held her phone up and flipped the screen so I was looking at her laptop.

"*The Emperor's New Groove*?" I laughed.

"You said you'd never saw it and that needs to be remedied immediately." The way she sounded so matter of fact had me cracking up. "Open up your Disney+ app, Barnes. It's time for you to 'beware the groove.'"

"I have no clue what you're talking about, but your wish is my command, oh movie goddess."

I giggled like a lovesick teenager as I watched Kendahl recite almost every line in the movie. The way her face lit up had me physically aching to be near her and kiss those full lips to draw a moan from them. As the credits rolled, she shifted in bed and placed her head on her forearm.

"So what did you think? Good, right?"

I scratched my beard, making a show of being deep in thought to get her fired up. It worked. She scrunched her nose and narrowed her eyes making me chuckle.

"You were right, extremely underrated. Kronk and Yzma...epic duo. Also, I now have a sudden craving for spinach puffs."

Those blue eyes sparkled as quickly as they'd narrowed, and she laughed. "I'm so glad you liked it. I didn't want to have to dump you for your taste in movies," she teased.

"Damn, I'm hurt that you'd drop me so quickly. After all we've been through." I let my voice deepen to a playfully hurt tone.

"What can I say? I need a man with good taste."

She grinned and flopped back on her pillows. Her sassy attitude shone through in the way she tilted her head, egging me on.

"I'm pretty sure I have the best taste. I picked you, didn't I?"

"This is true. You make a good point." Nuzzling her head into the pillow, she yawned. I glanced at the time, it was midnight here, which meant it was nine there.

"Hey, technically I get to see you today. It's twelve here."

"Ooh damn. I'm sorry for keeping you up so late. You want to go?"

"Nah, I'm good. I took tomorrow off, so I can sleep in if I need to," I said. "How about I help you get to sleep?"

She brought the phone closer to her face. "What did you have in mind?"

What didn't I have in mind? I wanted everything. I ached to taste her and feel her body clench beneath me as she cried out her release. My mind came back to the night at the inn when I walked in on her making herself come. Goddamn, she was so hot writing on the bed pleasuring herself while I watched. She knew what I meant, but she loved to hear me say it.

"Did you bring a toy?" God, I hoped she did.

She shook her head. "No, I was so nervous. I forgot to."

"That's okay, baby. You don't need one." She nodded, slowly releasing a breath. "Prop the phone up somewhere so you can have your hands free."

Without hesitation, she turned and set her phone aside leaving me with a side view of her body from the torso up. I didn't need to see all of her, just her gorgeous face as she made herself come.

"Now what?" she asked with her eyes closed and chest already heaving.

"Pull off your shirt, nice and slow."

Her slender fingers trailed across her collarbone, agonizingly slow. She reached lower, tracing the peak of each nipple through the thin fabric of her pajama top.

"I'm hard as a rock watching you, baby. You're so damn hot." I widened my thighs to give my cock some much-needed space. She pulled the hem of her shirt up and over her head, then tossed it aside. Those pink peaks stood taut just waiting to be pinched. I'd give anything to nibble them until she was rolling her hips against me. "Pinch your nipple and pretend it's my teeth," I groaned.

"God—I'm already turned on." Flushed cheeks and sharp breaths meant she had to be soaked and ready. I watched her rub her hard nipples one at a time, biting her lips until she started to drift one hand lower.

"Did I say you could touch your pussy?"

Her hand stopped and splayed against her stomach. She opened her blazing eyes. So needy and ready.

"Slide your underwear off," I said, watching her follow my instructions. "Grab your phone. I want to see how soaked you are."

She picked the phone up and propped it against something so I had a perfect view of her spread legs. Christ, I thought I was prepared, but seeing her so deliciously wet on screen did things to me. Her bare pink pussy, glistening and open, and her perfect little clit was begging for relief. My cock strained against my sweats, painfully hard.

"Fuck, Kendahl. You have the prettiest pussy I've ever seen. Be a good girl and show me how you fuck yourself," I growled. "Circle your clit until you're shaking, baby."

"Yesss," she hissed, reaching her palm all the way down to her core. "You too. Let me see your cock."

I was waiting for her to ask, thank God she had because I was about to burst. I pulled my dick out and angled my phone so she could see.

"Look what you do to me, Kendahl. Fuck, I'm going to come from watching you."

"Let's come together," she gasped. "God, I miss you."

She plunged a finger into her slit, then spread her wetness and started strumming her clit, by drawing circles as she bucked her hips. I loved how she wasn't timid or embarrassed with me. She chased her pleasure with reckless abandon, and I loved every single second of it.

"That's right, baby, fuck your fingers."

I spit into my palm and wrapped my warm fist around my cock, imagining it was Kendahl's hand not mine. I did exactly what she would do. Her soft hand would grasp me and squeeze me, softly at first, then she'd slide her palm from base to tip.

"Feels so good," I murmured, listening to her soft moans as she climbed higher.

I matched her rhythm, gliding my fist faster and rougher and rubbing my thumb over the sensitive head of my cock. The room blurred around me and everything melted away except us, our moans, her fingertips working her clit in clumsy circles as she lost control, and my fist pumping in rough, jerky thrusts. I forced my eyes to stay open, watching my girl shudder and shake with her release and my name on her lips.

"Baby, I'm coming," I groaned as I pumped my cock one last time. My balls tightened and white spots dotted my field of vision.

"Let me watch," she said.

I shifted the phone in time for her to see my cock erupt with hot streams of cum.

Breathless and spent, I dropped the phone against my chest while I came back into my body and cleaned up.

"That was so hot," Kendahl said. Her soft voice floated over me bringing me back to life.

"Everything you do is hot, but that...damn. Watching you fuck yourself will be engrained in my head for as long as I live." I brought my phone back toward my face and saw Kendahl stifle a yawn. "You should get some rest for your last day there."

"You're right." She leaned over to switch off the lamp, casting herself in darkness. "Can't wait to see you tomorrow. This has been hard."

"You'll be in my arms before you know it," I said. "Goodnight, beautiful, sweet dreams."

She murmured a sleepy I love you and hit end. I padded into my bedroom, exhausted but still turned on. I didn't think I could ever get enough of Kendahl Edwards.

Chapter 35

Kendahl

As soon as my plane touched down at Orlando International airport the muscles in my shoulders relaxed. I hadn't even realized how tense I'd been the entire flight home until that moment. A small part of me was already missing the hustle and bustle, and looked forward to getting back and digging in.

The past few days in LA had been all kinds of stressful. Not all bad stress though, most of it was nerves about learning the ropes in a new office and a new city. I was decent at reading people, and even though Victor's personality was a lot at first, by the time I left this morning, he'd given me a thumb's up. His eyes never left his phone when he did it, but I took what I could get. I'd gotten along well with the other PR specialists that I'd be working alongside. They mostly seemed to keep to themselves, or maybe they were swamped with work and had little time to chat.

Through the sea of people making their way out of the terminal, I saw Coby holding a huge homemade sign over his head that read Congrats Kendahl! Balloons in varying shades of pink and purple danced around it. Heat rose to my cheeks and I laughed at his ridiculousness.

I picked up my pace and tossed my bags to the ground as soon as I was within hugging distance. He dropped the sign and let the balloons float up as he wrapped me in his arms. I kissed him, letting my lips linger as we both breathed in each other's scents. "I love the sign. Is that glitter?"

"Yeah, let's not talk about the glitter. Hearing the word might make my eye start twitching." I laughed and kissed him again. God, I missed this man.

"We should probably get going," I said. "I think I saw some teenager recording us over there by the window."

"Probably because the hottest woman he's ever seen just walked in front of him. I'd record you too. In fact, you've given me an idea for later."

I smacked his arm and smooched his cheek. "You're bad. Come on, let's get home."

"I actually had other plans, if you're up for it?" Those slate gray eyes stared down at me with intensity.

"I'm intrigued." I reached for my bags, but he beat me to it. "If I say yes, am I going to regret it?" I never knew with him.

He chuckled, deep and rich. "Never. You're with me, remember?" And he flashed a beaming grin with his dimples on full display.

"That's what I'm worried about." I laughed.

"Oh my God. Disney World?" I screeched as Coby presented me with adorable pumpkin themed Mickey ears. We'd grabbed sushi at a decent place near the airport after he picked me up and instead of driving back toward Palm Cove, Coby drove to a hotel. We spent the night tangled in each other. I was exhausted. But we stopped for pumpkin spiced lattes and bagels, and I felt as giddy as a little kid.

I'd never been to Disney before. We never had the money growing up, and once I became a Florida resident, I told myself I'd go but kept putting it off. As we parked in the garage, I could barely contain my excitement.

"Look at mine." He pulled out a pair of green Grogu ears from the bag in his backseat. "Badass, huh? I found them at the airport when I was waiting for you and knew we had to come today."

I kissed his cheek. "You've never looked sexier than you do right now."

"Nah, it's not me. It's the Grogu effect. Makes everyone seem sexy as hell. That's why the entire world is obsessed with that Mandalorian guy."

"You mean Pedro Pascal?" My face heated. "Do you think the Mandalorian will be here to take pictures with?"

His brows scrunched together. "No. I'm keeping you far away from him."

Laughing, I added, "What? You're the one who brought him up."

"You're right. I want pictures with him too," he grinned. I shook my head as tears reached the corner of my eye from laughing. "Galaxy's Edge first then?"

"Duh. Let's get our space on."

"Take a bite of my churro." I shoved my cinnamon covered delicacy into Coby's mouth. "It'll help you feel better."

"I can't believe I'm this lame." He chewed slowly and swallowed a small bite. "I've never had motion sickness in my life."

Passing him the cold water we were sharing, I hugged his side. "It happens. At least you didn't barf on Space Mountain." I didn't add that it was a combination of spinning and dark ride anxiety that got him.

"The only upside of that experience," he groaned.

"Hey, you got to snuggle me the whole time. That has to be a plus." I knew my teasing would help him perk up.

"Of course it is." He finished off the rest of the churro and stood up, stretching his arm so that a sliver of his tanned abs peeked out from under his shirt. I couldn't help staring. He was too freaking sexy. "Now I need to find a way to get rid of that incriminating picture you have from the ride."

Impersonating the evil queen, I let out my best villain cackle. "Never. This pic will be all mine *forever*."

In a smooth voice, he said, "I guess I'll have to show everyone at the gym the picture of you spilling blue milk all over your chest when you saw Mando, which by the way, I'm still salty about the way he flirted with you."

"There was a rock on the ground and I tripped, you big butthead. I did not spill blue milk because I happened to cross paths with the hottest man in the entire Star Wars universe."

"Right..." he teased and scrolled his phone to pull up the picture in question. "And this picture of your jaw touching the floor didn't have anything to do with said spill? I'll let Mia be the judge."

"Oh, go stuff this churro somewhere inappropriate."

Immediately, he gave me that look, and I knew what was about to come out of his mouth.

"Only if you help."

Day turned to night too quickly and crowds of people settled all along Main Street to get seats for the light show and fireworks. Autumn here was everything I hoped it would be especially since I loved the villains best.

We'd had to squeeze in on a bench and as the area got more packed with people, I slid onto Coby's lap to make room for others. The light show started with spooky music and dancing characters. Kronk and Yzma tossed candy out to the crowd, and

I had a fangirl moment. I wanted to memorize everything from the way my body felt against the warmth of Coby's chest to his arms wrapped around me tight, plus the smell of cinnamon and cool air mixed with his fresh scent. Finally, I wanted to memorize the sound of his husky voice as he whispered I love you into my ear after I screamed "Oh my God," as Darth Vader walked by us. It was the most perfect day.

I found a real appreciation for how comfortable my office chair was because I was so close to never sitting my butt in it again. And an appreciation for Lee, man I would miss them. I could say with certainty that there would not be another person like Lee at Stratestar. I never knew what they were going to say and they always made me laugh even when they made the most facepalm inducing mistakes. I was even appreciating the fine citizens of Palm Cove such as Mrs. Mullins from Berry's Vineyards who kept me on the phone for an hour this morning talking about all the different wines available for tasting at her event. I actually found myself craving her citrus wine, and that shit made cough medicine seem tasty.

After my amazing weekend with Coby, reality set in. This was my last week living in Palm Cove, and I had so much to do. I'd already done the hardest parts like breaking the news to almost everyone close to me. Mia was prepped, so when I called her and told her I'd gotten the job, she screeched at a pitch so high that Remy howled.

Breaking the news to Claudia was tough. I'd looked up to her as a boss and a friend for so long that my nerves ate away at me the entire time I was in LA. I hadn't lied to her about my reason for needing more time off, but I wasn't up front with where I was in the interview process either. I had figured why rock the boat when it wasn't a done deal.

When I sat across from her in her office on my first day back to work, she took one look at me and said, "You got the job," as a statement. She always read me like a book. Maybe it was the fact that I'd chewed what little fingernails I had down to the skin, or that I was biting the crap out of my lip that gave me away. Either way, she came across her desk, crouched down, looked me in the eyes, and she said, "You show them what you're made of," then she kissed my cheek, gave my shoulders a squeeze, and went back to work like nothing had changed.

I was a mess for the rest of the day.

I spent the rest of the week saying my goodbyes to everyone at the gym. I promised Dina and Mark that I'd find a Krav gym in LA so I could continue bettering my skills. Before I'd gotten home that evening, Mark had texted me a list of five different gyms he'd found online. He had added that none would be nearly as awesome as their gym, and he was probably right.

The hardest part of the entire week was going to be breaking the news to my mom. I decided to take her out to dinner to buffer what I knew would be a difficult conversation. I'd wanted it to be just me and her, but she insisted that her "new man," her words not mine, join us. Since Richard was coming, I invited Coby too. I'd wanted him to meet my mom anyway. That felt like a true test of our relationship. Could he deal with her crazy? Or would he escape out the men's room window?

Coby and I arrived fifteen minutes early at Enzo's, a quaint family-owned Italian restaurant in the heart of town.

"We need to get a table in the back, far away from the other diners. That way when she starts to freak out, it won't cause a scene." He held the door open for me, which let the scent of herbs and garlic waft through the door.

"How bad of a scene are you anticipating? I thought you prepped her?" Coby followed behind me as I made my way to the hostess stand.

I bit my lip. "I told her I had news."

"News? So she has no idea you're moving across the country in a few days?"

My mouth went as dry as sand, and I nodded. He cursed under his breath, then laughed low. "Well, from what you've told me about your mother, this should be interesting."

A family of four was ahead of us at the hostess stand, so I took a moment to breathe. *This is fine*, I told myself. Sconces with warm light emanated a calming glow and that mixed with the divine smells coming from the kitchen, I calmed slightly.

"Good evening. Do you have a reservation?" The young hostess greeted us, smiling broadly.

"Yes, it's under Edwards." Her eyes shifted to the iPad screen in front of her before she glanced back up at me.

"Edwards party. Your guests have already arrived. You'll find them in the dining area. Would you like me to lead you there?"

I needed wine, but I couldn't drink in front of my mother. Maybe I could make a mad dash for the bar area and down a quick glass. We're early, so no one would know. I made eyes at Coby, but he was already scanning the crowded dining area.

I saw the exact moment he found my mother because his eyes widened, then he glanced back at me for confirmation. I was hoping she'd have at least dressed appropriately, but I knew from Coby's face that that wasn't the case.

Pink. So much pink. And those were sequins. Where did she even get a dress in a shade so offensive? My mother dressed for attention. It was one of the things I'd hated my entire childhood. But I couldn't recall a time where she went this hardcore on one color.

But then there was her hair. It had always been light like mine though she'd been bleaching it platinum since I was in college, so between the hot pink outfit and the platinum hair, she was like a beacon in the dimly lit room.

"Yup, that's my mother." I said in a hush. "We will be having words about that dress."

Coby chuckled and followed me to the table.

Chapter 36

Kendahl

"My daughter didn't tell me she was dating a male model." My mother blurted as she gaped at Coby.

"Mom, keep it together," I groaned as Coby laughed and then being the charmer that he was, he took her hand and kissed it before he shook Richard's hand, formally introducing himself.

"I was starting to think you weren't coming," she said. "Right, Richard? Didn't I say that." He nodded but kept his eyes glued to the menu.

"Mom, we're early." I scanned the menu also even though I already knew I wanted the chicken parm.

"You're late. You told me six. I know it was six because I was on the phone with Sally. She's chewed my ear off going on and on about some show she started watching. That's when I heard the sound you set up on my phone, and you told me in the message six o'clock."

Absolutely no part of that story was necessary. I definitely said six thirty, but there was no use in arguing. I looked at my fork and contemplated staging some sort of fork accident that would get me out of this dinner.

"Okay, Mom. Sorry we were late," I said. Coby chuckled beside me as the server came to our table to take drink orders. I wanted a glass of wine. A jumbo glass. But I ordered a seltzer with lime instead.

"So what's the news?" I should have known she'd waste no time. "Are the two of you getting married? I could see it on my Doll's face. You make her happy, handsome. Watch out though, she can be a tough one to live with. Has to have what she calls her 'personal space.' God forbid you ever invade that space, you'll have to deal with her attitude for days."

"Mom for the love of—" I inhaled a deep breath. Come on garlic and herb aromatherapy send calming vibes into my brain cells. "We're not getting married. We only got back together recently."

"Then what is it? Don't get my hopes up. I told Richard earlier that I was hoping you were engaged. Right, Richard?"

She patted Richard on the forearm, and he responded, "Uh-huh."

I sipped my seltzer, unable to form words. Why was she the way that she was? And where the hell did this woman come from? My mother hated marriage. She never dated a man for more than a few months.

"I won't speak for Kendahl, but I know I love her more than anything and what we have is the real deal. We're not rushing anything though, right babe?"

Way to save the moment Coby. "Right." I cleared my throat. "Sorry to bring this up in front of Richard, but who are you and what have you done with my mother?"

She cackled loud enough that a few diners turned to stare. That fork accident was looking better and better. I forced a smile through gritted teeth at our onlookers.

"Maybe I'm getting sentimental as I get older." She glanced at Richard. "Not that I'm a day over forty."

Right.

"Or maybe, I can tell that my Doll is happy. Really happy. That's all I've ever wanted for you." She reached across the table and gave my hand a squeeze. My throat clogged with emotion. "I know about the job."

"What? How?" I swiped at the corner of my eye where a tear formed.

"Did you forget I'm on Instabook? Or Facegram? Whatever they're called. I saw your post the other day."

Coby gave my thigh a reassuring squeeze under the table, anchoring me. If he hadn't I might have forked myself for real because surely this was a dream. A bizarre dream where my mother was replaced with a pod person who still had the same hideous fashion sense and the same taste in boring men.

"Why didn't you say anything?"

Shrugging and taking a sip of her Diet Coke, she said, "I wanted to see when you'd tell me. I said to Richard the other day, I wonder when my dearest first-born child will tell me that she's leaving me to go off to Hollywood with the movie stars. Right, Richard, didn't I say that?"

First-born child? Try only child. Here's the mother I knew so well.

"Yup," Richard grunted, eyes still on the menu. What was he reading? The menu was two pages long.

"I'm sorry you found out that way. It's been a busy week, and I wanted to tell you in person."

She dabbed at her eyes with the cloth napkin before the server interrupted us again to take our orders. It was funny how as soon as he reached us, she dropped the napkin and started to flirt with the poor guy. We ordered our meals and even Richard managed to break his eyes away from the menu. Instead he moved on to gazing intently at the tea light candle on his side of the table.

"Are you going to meet Brad Pitt? I told Richard—"

I couldn't take hearing another "I told Richard..."

"Maybe. I don't think he's a client of the company I'm working for, but we'll see. I think I heard someone mention one of the Baldwin brothers the other day. You like them, right?"

She huffed. "Eh, they're alright. Who I adore these days is that superhero man who lives in the ocean. What's his name Richard? I told you I saw him on a clip on *The Today Show*."

Richard shrugged. "Don't remember."

Yeah, because according to her, she tells Richard something every five seconds. It probably flies in one ear and out the other at this point.

"Jason Momoa?" Coby suggested.

"That's it!" she yelled causing the same people to stare again. "What a hunk. What I wouldn't give for an hour alone with him. Right, Richard? Didn't I say that?"

I got a visual I very much did not need and never asked for.

"If I ever see him, I'll make sure to get a picture." She grinned like a little kid and continued telling us what else she saw on *The Today Show* until our entrees came to put me out of my misery.

Two hours later, after Richard insisted on paying the check, my mother pulled me into the lady's room so we could "freshen up." She promptly lit a cigarette and leaned against the counter.

"Mom, you can't smoke in here." I waved my hand around trying to help the haze dissipate.

"Eh, what are they going to do, kick us out? We're finished anyway." She had a point, but still, gross. "I wanted to tell you in private that I'm proud of you. And I don't want you to worry about me. Richard may be more reserved than me, but he can be very commanding in other ways." Her eyes burned as she puffed her cigarette. Once again, a very uncomfortable visual flashed through my mind. "He takes care of me and makes sure I don't do anything stupid."

I would have breathed a sigh of relief if not for her cloud of smoke. "I'm happy to hear that, Mom. Not that I needed to know that he's commanding. Ew."

"I needed to find a man who knew how to use his dick for once. Trust me when I say, a good dicking can go a long way."

My dinner threatened to leave my system.

"Mom! I'm leaving now." I turned to leave, but she grabbed my forearm and pulled me into a hug.

"I love you, Doll. Don't ever forget it."

"I love you too." I squeezed tight. As much as she irked me with her ridiculousness, I was going to miss her. "But Mom, please remove the term 'a good dicking' from your vocabulary. No one needs to hear that, ever."

She cackled and pulled away to run her cigarette under the tap. "I'll save those conversations for Sally."

"When you and your mom went in the bathroom, I actually got a few words out of Richard. Seems like a nice dude."

I stripped off my black dress from dinner. I somehow found sequins in my bra from our hug.

I laughed. "He probably had to wait for my mother to leave the room so he could get a word in. What did you guys talk about?"

I dressed in my favorite shorts and tank top pajama set, and then I hopped onto the couch, edging closer to Coby's warm body. We switched on season one of *The Mandalorian* for background noise.

"Not much. He told me his son lives in LA, and he hopes you like it there." Coby rubbed circles on my thigh, making a shiver run down my body. "And he said to tell you that he was taking care of you mom and not to worry."

I leaned my head against his shoulder and played with the stubble on his chin. "My mom said something similar in the bathroom. It's a relief to hear. I was worried about leaving her. She's always needed me you know?"

He moved his hand to rest on my stomach, splaying his palm so his fingers rested on the curve of my breast. "I know what you mean. I felt the same way when I left my mother. I still feel guilty. I almost wish she had a Richard to take care of her."

"Well if you heard what Richard and my mom were up to in their private time you might feel differently."

Chuckling, he slid his palm higher so he was cupping my breast with one hand, while the other inched higher on my thigh. "I don't think I want to know. But if I had to guess, does Good Ol' Dick have a good dick?"

"You hit the nail on the head." I laughed, only the sound came out husky and needy. Coby rubbed circles around my nipple drawing closer and closer to the hard tip. So much so that I arched my chest forward, needing more.

"On the dick head?" he grinned, clearly pleased with himself.

I cupped his chin and brought his face closer to mine. "No more talk of Dick's dick. Not while you're touching me like this." His gaze was lit with fire as he chuckled and slid his fingertips under the hem of my shorts. My tongue darted out to wet my lips while I waited for him to touch me where I needed it. I shifted closer as he dragged a finger along the outer edge of my pussy. He was toying with me, but I could do that too.

Closing the distance, I brought my lips to his. Demanding and needy, I drove my tongue inside, and his intensity changed. He explored my mouth right back, matching my fervor.

We groaned into each other's mouths as he finally pinched my nipples. Our combined sounds were so hot I could've melted into the couch. I gripped his stiff cock beneath his shorts and slid my hand along the thick shaft up to his sensitive head.

"Fuck, Ken..."

He kissed me deeper, stroking my tongue with his. My entire body was on fire. I straddled him and pulled my tank top off, giving him more access to my tits. His eyes widened and he directed his tongue to my nipples, sucking one at a time until I was shaking with need. I rocked against him, wanting there to be nothing between us. My shorts were absolutely drenched and useless anyway.

I pushed up to stand, using his chest for leverage and slid my shorts down my legs, leaving me bare. I'd never felt so beautiful, so sexy.

"You're the most gorgeous woman I've ever seen, baby. My chest hurts just looking at you."

I bent down and pulled his shorts and boxer briefs off in one tug. "Thank you, babe. You're not so hard on the eyes either."

I got on my knees in front of him, which gave me a better look at his mouthwatering cock. It was perfect. I took him into my mouth and gently licked the pre-cum off his head.

"Mmm, you taste so good." I lapped at his head some more, slowly sliding my tongue along the seam.

"Your mouth is going to kill me." He groaned and gripped a fistful of my hair. He didn't tug instead he held me in place. I looked up at him through my lashes, wanting to see the lust in his eyes as I took him deep into the back of my throat. "Fuck..."

I loved watching him like this. His eyes rolled into the back of his head each time I sucked hard. With a hand at the base of his cock, I worked him up and down, dripping saliva so he was good and wet. He gripped my hair harder, and it drove me wild.

He bucked his hips, then stilled. "Fuck, I don't want to choke you. But your mouth... You're going to make me come."

I pulled off him with a pop and slowly circled my tongue along his head. "Choke me. Fuck my mouth until you come."

"Christ, Kendahl." He pulled a hand through his hair and stood up. I stayed on my knees, loving that I was still in control even like this. "Tap my thigh if it gets to be too much."

I nodded and brought myself higher on my knees. "Grab my hair and pull."

Coby released a feral growl. He loved when I talked dirty.

He gripped the back of my head and wrapped both hands around my hair, twisting his fists. The tugging sensation felt so damn good. "Yes," I moaned and arched my neck.

I parted my lips for his cock, and reached out to grip his hips. He pushed into me slowly, letting me adjust until he hit the back of my throat. I gagged, so he slowly pulled back, but I grabbed his ass and pulled him in again, harder and deeper.

My cheeks hollowed out, and I sucked hard.

"Baby, you're taking me so well." I murmured a response and he bit his lip to hold back a groan.

He tensed as he pounded into me, harder and faster. Tears streaked down my face and he smoothed his thumb across them.

"I'm close." Desperate, he pumped into me using my hair to keep his knees from buckling. "Are you ready for my cum?" I nodded and let loose a needy moan as his cock pulsed inside me. "Ken, Baby...don't stop." I cupped his balls, sliding my fingertip along them. He lost control, quickening his pace until I was choking on him.

"F-fuck!" Every ounce of tension in his body snapped as he spilled myself down my throat. I was so wet and needy feeling him come apart for me.

His knees gave out, and he collapsed onto the couch. I stood up and climbed onto his lap giving him a lazy smile.

"You destroyed me, you know. Nothing will ever feel as good as being inside you."

"I know." He pulled me closer and slid his tongue against my lips, tasting himself.

"Your turn," he said. With a groan, he pushed me onto my back against the couch and opened my legs. "I don't know how

I'll live without making you come every day. The noises you make when you're close to falling over the edge. The way your hips arch seeking your pleasure. Your taste, better than anything on earth." He kissed his way down my stomach to the apex of my thighs.

I pushed those thoughts aside and focused all my energy on the here and now. Taking every moment in while I still could.

Chapter 37

Coby

My phone beeped and I smiled, looking at the new message from Kendahl.

Kendahl: *By the time I figure out these light switches, it'll be time for me to move out. I just did it again.*

Me: *You hit the switch connected to the kitchen appliances again, didn't you?*

Kendahl: *Ugh! I don't understand the wiring in this place. I was trying to turn on the light and ended up turning off the refrigerator.*

I hit the FaceTime button on my phone. I needed to see her annoyed scowl in real time. She answered, and there it was.

"I'm ordering you labels," I said.

She plopped down onto the red sofa in her temporary apartment and softened her scowl.

"I wish I'd thought of that." She sighed and took a sip of a clear beverage. "I'm glad I realized my mistake before all my groceries went bad."

I took in her flushed face. Her makeup was a bit smudged, probably from her rough day at work, and her hair was pulled into a messy bun on her head. It had only been a week since she left, but seeing her face on the screen made it feel like it had been months. So damn gorgeous. I wished I could reach in and pull her into my arms.

"What did you end up getting at the store yesterday?"

"Let me preface this by saying Foodietown in Palm Cove is far superior to Whole Foods near my new place," she answered, chewing her lip.

I chuckled, she was about to start another tirade.

"Foodietown has my favorite chips, which I've never been able to find anywhere else. So I have to agree," I said.

"Exactly my point!" She sighed and shifted on the couch, bringing a gray throw pillow onto her lap.

"So, what did you end up buying?"

"Umm, okay, but don't laugh. I was overwhelmed!" Her already flushed face grew even more red.

I held my hand up in a scout's honor pose. "I promise I won't laugh."

"I spent like ninety-five dollars, and I left with one bag. I got lettuce and carrots. But I also got pumpkin spice hand soap, organic cotton swabs, barbeque sauce, and a bag of cashews." She fell back on the couch and covered her face with the pillow.

"At least there's something edible in that haul."

"I'm so done with that store. The smell was intoxicating. I was in a cloud of lavender floating toward the artisanal soaps. I barely knew what was happening when I handed the cashier my debit card."

God, I missed her.

"I'm sure there's a regular supermarket nearby. Something more Palm Cove's speed."

"I hope so. And another thing, what is this town's obsession with green juice? I swear I haven't seen one person eat actual solid food all week. Coby promise me if you see me drinking something green that isn't a margarita, you will come here immediately and stage an intervention."

I covered my mouth with my hand to hide my laughter.

"I swear I won't let you turn to the green side. However, I happen to like green juice. I make it before class sometimes."

"Of course you do," she said.

She laughed and settled into the couch. It'd been like this all week, random texts and calls and talking about thoughts that popped into our heads. I told her how much everyone misses her already, true story, and she told me how her new job has been going.

So far neither of us has said anything about moving to be together. The thought scares the hell out of me. Every fiber of my being aches to be near her, to hold her, and to kiss her every damn day. We needed to have a conversation about the future but it could wait until she was more settled.

"Check your email really quick," I said.

Her brow arched, "Okay?"

I watched her swipe out of our screen and open up her mail app. While we were chatting, I'd gone online and ordered her a bunch of stuff.

"Babe! That was so sweet. And my favorite cookies!" Her voice went up an octave or two.

"And the trail mix you love. Gotta make sure you're eating enough protein." Her face came back into view with a wide smile on her lips.

"I love you."

"I love you too."

Sweat dripped down my neck as I rolled Shawn off me and pushed to a stand. We'd been practicing our guard techniques for our upcoming level five test, and he wasn't taking it easy on me. I didn't want him to. If I couldn't get these techniques down, then I didn't deserve to level up.

We reset our position with Shawn hovering over me on the ground. Within two seconds, I had him in a headlock position, held tightly to my chest. As I was about to push out of position and onto my feet, he gained the upper hand, broke free of my hold, and jumped back where he was free to kick me right in the groin had this been a real-life situation.

"Your head is not in this, man. I don't blame you. Hell, I didn't even come to class when Mia and I broke things off." He leaned against the wall, wiping his brow.

We had the gym to ourselves since we decided to come in outside of class to practice. Dina sat in the office doing paperwork and checking in on us every so often.

"We didn't break anything off." I rolled up to a sitting position and wiped my sweaty palms against my shirt. "We're doing the long-distance thing for a while."

He lifted his hands in surrender. "Sorry, I kind of thought that given how I know you feel about relationships that you guys would have taken a break or moved on to someone new."

I ground my teeth together, thinking of a reply that didn't come off douchey. "People change. You should know that."

He sat next to me on the floor and suddenly this felt like it was turning into some kind of emotional sharing circle. I hadn't signed up for this shit.

"You're right. Sorry, man. I hope things work out for you guys. I may not have started out in your corner, but I can tell you're good for Kendahl. Plus, Mia would kick your ass if you ever hurt her best friend. So since she isn't planning an attack yet, you're still in the clear." He chuckled and the sound lightened the mood.

"I wouldn't do anything to hurt her. I already fucked up once, I won't do it again," I said through gritted teeth.

Shawn pulled his knees up to his chest. "All I have to say is, if you're not going to go after her, someone else will. She's special.

A woman like that, single in a city like LA... I don't envy you, man." He stood up and pulled me up to a stand. "Ready to get your ass beat again?"

Fucking dick.

He had a point though. My idea of surprising Kendahl over the weekend had just become a full blown plan. I sighed and got back into position. "Bring it on."

"You've got to be kidding me," I said. The TSA agent in front of me shook his head and gestured to the small room off to the side. I knew not to put up a fight when it came to this kind of thing, but fuck. I was already running late for my flight and the next one was a red-eye. "Can you tell me why? Is it something I said?" I asked him, knowing it was a pointless question.

"It's random, sir." He lowered his voice, "If I could, I'd let you through but I'm being audited today."

"It's fine," I huffed, even though it really wasn't.

Two more agents followed us into their screening room, one held my luggage and the other held the bin containing my phone, wallet and keys. God sure did enjoy fucking with me lately. All that was missing from this shitshow was another hurricane. My phone vibrated against the plastic bin and I almost reached out to grab it, but thought better of it when the second, much less friendly agent, glared at me.

I watched the second hand tick on the clock hanging from the wall. *Tick, tick, tick.* Each one took away precious time that I could have been spending with Kendahl. The agents had gone through my bag, examining every item, including the new Bluetooth vibrator I'd bought for Kendahl. The looks they gave me when they pulled that out were something I'd laugh about later when I wasn't so pissed off.

I sat idly watching the supervisor walk the agents through their protocol, using me as some sort of test subject for training. When the clock showed that I'd missed my boarding call, I bit my tongue to keep myself from blowing up.

They finished with me over an hour later. Exhausted, I dragged my suitcase to customer service and changed my flight. I wasn't usually a complainer, but in this case, I unloaded on the poor worker. He placated me with an upgrade and use of the VIP lounge until I'd board my red-eye flight into LA.

Seated in a plush recliner, with a much needed beer in my hand, I finally checked my phone.

"Shit," I said, causing a snooty looking businessman to look my way and scoff. I'd missed a call from Kendahl. Hopefully she was okay. It was almost better that I wasn't able to pick up. I was such a shitty liar that she may have noticed something up with me. The last thing I wanted to do was give away my surprise visit. I hadn't told anyone from the gym about coming either. I couldn't trust that Mia and Shawn would keep quiet. With my luck she'd hear a boarding announcement and ask questions about where I was.

It was too late to call her back anyway. My whole plan of meeting her at her apartment after work was ruined. Fucking TSA. I'd have to surprise her at her office now. While I waited for my new flight, I looked up the addresses I'd need and cemented my plans for the morning.

Of course my rental car would get a flat in the middle of a four lane LA highway. And of course, the shitty rental company didn't have a jack or a spare.

I stood up, staying as close to the right side of the shoulder as I could, and yanked my hand through my hair. Cars sped past, not giving me a second look. If I were in Palm Cove at least three people would have pulled over to help me by now.

The combination of morning heat and car exhaust fumes gave this nightmare a fun little added bonus. I coughed and wiped a bead of sweat from my brow. Cities were the fucking worst.

It was already past eight o'clock and Kendahl was likely either at work or on her way in. I really didn't want to call her and ruin the surprise, especially if it pulled her from important work meetings.

Back inside the car, I looked up a tow company and called them. Thinking about seeing Kendahl's face soon was the only thing keeping me going.

It took all day for the tow to pick me up, get me to a shop, and for the shop to change the fucking flat. They were all moving so slow, that at one point I wanted to rip the wrench from the mechanic's hand and do it myself.

I was finally on my way to Kendahl's office. Once she was in my arms, none of the bullshit from the past twenty four hours would matter. I turned up the radio, drumming the beat of a *Metallica* song on the steering wheel. My chest felt lighter with each mile that brought me closer to her. When I made it to the parking lot of her office building I was so giddy I could float.

I peeked at myself in the visor mirror, cursing under my breath at how disheveled I looked. What else could I expect after the ordeal I went through. I changed my shirt and did my best to fix my hair, thinking, it was now or never.

As I made my way into her building, I was hyper aware of all the sensations around me. The overly bright waiting area that smelled of expensive perfume, the chattering of too many voices, the clicking of keyboards coming from offices down the hall, the frigid air blasting from overhead vents.

This was where Kendahl spent her days. Nothing about this place carried the same warmth that she gave off. Maybe I'd expected something else, something more comfortable. It didn't matter, she was here, so it was already the only place I wanted to be.

I approached the receptionist, a guy who looked to be in his midtwenties with coifed hair. "I'm here to see Kendahl Edwards. She's a PR specialist."

He looked me over and turned his lips down. "Do you have an appointment?"

"No, it's a surprise visit." I shifted from one foot to the other, cursing myself for telling him the truth instead of making up a bullshit story. He silently clicked away on his mouse, while I stood there feeling like an awkward outsider. After a full minute when he still hadn't looked up I cleared my throat. "So...can you point me in the right direction?"

"I'm waiting for clearance from my boss. Visitors without an appointment aren't allowed inside." He cast his gaze back down, apparently done with me.

"Nevermind," I said, pushing away from the desk. I was done with all the bullshit. I'd call Kendahl and get her to come out here.

Stepping aside, I pulled out my phone and called her. It rang multiple times, before sending me to voicemail. *Of course.* I tried again while pacing the gleaming white tile floor. No answer.

She had to come out at some point. I'd wait. Maybe seeing me sit there taking up valuable lobby space would get the receptionist to bend the rules for me.

An hour went by, and still Kendahl hadn't called me back. My chest tightened thinking something was wrong. This was the longest amount of time we'd gone without talking since her move.

Movement from outside the window caught my eye. A black Rolls Royce pulled in front of the doors. At first I ogled the car, it was classy as hell. Until I shifted my gaze to the person getting out of the backseat. Kendahl. She looked gorgeous, in a form fitting navy dress. Her hair was pulled back, showing off her sloping neck and delicate collarbones. And those legs looked a mile long in her heels. I stood, readying myself to go to her, to finally feel her against me.

But I stopped as someone followed her out of the car. A tall, handsome guy in a suit that looked like it cost more than my entire wardrobe. He reached out and placed a palm on Kendahl's bare upper arm. Every one of my nerve endings were on high alert. I shifted my gaze to her face. Surely, she'd look bothered by the contact. She'd shrug him off, right?

He trailed his hand down her arm and grasped her hand in his and she laughed at something he said. She fucking smiled, a bright, genuine smile.

I saw red. It took everything in me to not storm through the door and yank that fucker away from her.

He pulled her in for a hug. *A hug.* My chest tightened as I struggled to suck in a breath. This wasn't happening again. I couldn't lose her the way I lost Amy. I bent over, rubbing my palms over my knees.

"Sir?" the receptionist called to me sounding like he was far away. "Sir?"

"Coby?" Kendahl questioned. "Oh my God, you're here!"

She came to me, pulled me close. I was smelling her honey scent, and feeling her soft skin but nothing was registering.

"Coby, are you okay?" She stepped back and reached up to take my face in her hands.

I backed away and watched her clutch her hands to her side. I wouldn't look at her, I couldn't.

"Who was that?" I asked through gritted teeth. She started to explain, but I went on, raising my voice. "Who the fuck was touching you, Kendahl?"

"Coby, what the hell? Let's go outside and talk." I flexed my fingers, tightening them into a fist. Every muscle in my body tensed but the sound of her voice pulled me back. "Coby? Come on, let's go outside." I raised my face to meet hers and she looked devastated. Fuck. What had I done?

Chapter 38

Kendahl

I STOOD STOCK STILL, completely mortified as Coby stalked out the door. What in the world was that all about and when did he get here?

Noticing the receptionist was watching me closely, I stepped to his desk. "How long was he here?"

"A while." He rolled his eyes and went back to his screen. Okay then.

I took a deep inhale and followed Coby outside. He waited for me along the side of the building, pacing between a palm tree and an empty parking space. While his head was down, I watched him. It looked like he'd had a rough day. His shorts were dirty and wrinkled, his hair stood on end more so than normal, and he had sweat beading on the back of his neck. Another deep breath made its way to my belly while I gave myself an inner pep talk. We were two grown adults who had already worked through a lot of bullshit together. Communication is all we needed. Even if I wanted to knee him in the balls for talking to me the way he did, I'd give him a moment to explain himself.

He noticed me coming his way and his face fell. Five minutes ago his nostrils were flared and eyes were wide, and now he looked devastated.

"Baby, I'm sorry I lost it in there." He scrubbed his palm over his face. "I saw that guy's hands on you and I-I got so jealous." As I approached him, he squeezed his eyes shut. "I'd understand if you wanted to end it."

I grabbed his hands and pulled him to me. "Coby. Of course I don't want to end things. Just-will you come here? Hold me."

The sunlight bounced against his watering gray eyes making them shine. Without a word, he took me into his arms and held me tight. All my anger melted away. He was there, in LA. God, I missed him. Finally, our lips met and it had been like no time passed. His kiss was searching, demanding, and I drank him in. When we pulled apart my breaths came in quick pants.

He nuzzled his face in my hair and laughed. "Surprise."

I ended up giving him the key to my apartment so he could go shower and get some rest. He said he'd make it up to me later, to which I replied, "it better be good." Even though just having him here was enough for me. I scrambled back inside before the receptionist had a chance to spread rumors about me and Coby. Judging by the looks I got on the way to my desk, that ship had sailed.

Incredible scents of rich tomato sauce and herbs led me up the stairs to my short term rental apartment. I hoped he'd ordered take-out because he was clearly exhausted and needed to rest, not cook a whole meal. I went inside and found Coby in low slung sweatpants and a cut off T-shirt bent over to check something in the oven.

"I'm enjoying the view," I said with a whistle. He turned, giving me that gorgeous smile of his. The one that made both his dimples pop. A rush of warmth filled me from head to toe. "Whatever you made smells amazing."

"Oh, it came highly recommended. A recipe from Shawn, he chuckled saying I couldn't go wrong with his lasagna recipe. It better be good with the way he gushed about it." I laughed, remembering the lasagna story from Mia and Shawn's first real date. Coby quirked a brow. "Maybe I don't want to ask?"

"Yeah, it's probably for the best."

He ushered me into the dining area, where he'd set the table with candles and fresh flowers. This was a side of Coby I hadn't seen and I'd be lying if I said I wasn't loving it.

"Maybe we can skip dinner and get straight to dessert," I called into the kitchen. It had been too long, although with Coby, a few hours was too long for me. It was hard to believe after my terrible luck with men, that I was this happy.

"No Ma'am. I know you've been living on trail mix and take-out." He came into the room holding two plates, set them down, and went back in for a bowl of salad and a bottle of wine. "Let's eat and talk. I've missed looking at your gorgeous face."

Heat made its way up my neck and I'm sure he noticed. "I've missed your face too, especially when you're being sweet." That drew a smirk out of him. He poured me some wine and I took my first bite. "Oh my God, Shawn wasn't kidding," I said as I finished chewing.

"This is damn good. Glad I took his advice." Coby swallowed a bite and took a sip of wine. "I know I said it earlier, but I'm so fucking sorry, baby. I acted like a complete asshole. It's like sometimes, I can feel this small part of my father trying to creep its way out of me, you know?"

"I actually understand perfectly. There's times where I catch myself being way too Melanie Edwards, and I mentally check myself before correcting whatever it was that I was doing." It was true, sometimes, even though we fought those parts of ourselves, they could creep out if we didn't catch them. "I'm sorry my friendly interaction with my client triggered you, but don't ever raise your voice at me again, okay?"

"I won't. I never, ever want to be like him." He reached out for my hand, tracing circles with his thumb. "When I saw that guy touching you, it reminded me of Amy. We haven't talked about her much. But I know I've mentioned her when we first met."

"Amy, yeah. You're ex-wife?" He hadn't said much about her other than they split almost ten years ago.

"That's her." I squeezed his palm, urging him to go on. "She left me for some rich guy, didn't even wait for the annulment to go through. It was right after I brought her home to Wyoming to meet my family. It," he hesitated, "it didn't go well. Let's just say my father and Clyde weren't on their best behavior. After that visit, I hadn't been back until recently."

He sat back in his chair and sipped his wine. He hadn't seen his family in almost ten years. As much as my mother drove me crazy, I couldn't imagine not seeing her in years.

"I'm not Amy, you know that right? Like I said back at the inn, you're not two separate people, past and present you are the same and I love all of you."

His smile reached his eyes, "I wouldn't say I'm the same, but I'm trying. I want to be good enough for you. This is hard, the distance most of all but also trying to be a better person, be someone you deserve."

"Coby," I started, before he leaned across the table and planted a kiss to my lips. "Are you going to kiss me every time I try to argue with you?" I laughed, once we broke apart.

"I read that kissing helps couples communicate better. Some psychology blog." His thick brows wiggled and I knew he was full of crap.

"Oh really? I may need to check your sources." Between the wine and him being here my head was dizzy with giddiness. I stood, gesturing toward my bedroom. "Right now."

"Thank God." He pushed up and lifted me into his arms, kissing me until I was breathless. "I'm an open book, check any source you want."

We spent the rest of the weekend working on our communication. Thoroughly. It may have been the most *communication* I'd gotten in years. But the time passed too quickly and I could sense the dread he had at having to leave me again.

"I don't want to go, baby," he said wrapping me in a hug. We stood by my apartment door, where we'd been dragging out our goodbyes for the past twenty minutes. The lights were dim and already the place carried an empty feeling and he hadn't stepped outside yet.

I let his scent seep into my clothes, knowing it would be weeks or more until I'd be comforted by his smell again. "I wish you didn't have to."

Something like a spark flashed in his eyes and he tipped my chin up for a light kiss, keeping his palm there. "I'll move here. If you want me to?"

"You'd move for me? Leave Palm Cove? What about your practice and the gym?" I wanted to pinch myself to see if I was dreaming.

"I'd do anything for you." He wet his lips and continued in a quiet voice. "They don't matter to me as much as you do. Nothing does."

Pushing up on my tiptoes, I planted a kiss on his chin, then his dimples, before brushing my lips against his. "I love you so much. Let's talk about this when you get back, okay?"

He nodded and pressed his lips to mine again, before opening the door. "I'll call you once I'm through security."

"Good luck. Let's hope this time around is a better experience." I laughed to lighten the mood even though I wanted to curl up in a ball on my bed.

Shutting the door, I faced my empty apartment. It had felt like home for a few days with Coby there but now it was back to feeling devoid of life. Would he really move here? He made it clear that he was choosing me. Finally the man I loved was putting me above all else. I could hardly believe his words. I'd have to decide if LA was really it for me, before he uprooted his entire life.

Chapter 39

Kendahl

CRAP!

My favorite button down decided to pop a button at the worst possible time. I needed to leave to meet my client at a photoshoot in ten minutes. Coby's surprise trip the other day still had my mind reeling which made me more flustered than usual. I scrambled around my office for a safety pin so that I wasn't relabeled all over TikTok as "wardrobe malfunction lady" instead of "puking karaoke lady."

In the process of rummaging through my purse, three different people popped into my door to ask unimportant questions, and my phone went off a dozen times. Why did my shirt have to betray me this way?

Ah-ha! I stood up to my full height and spotted a cardigan I kept on a hook on the wall. They always kept this place like a walk-in freezer, so I made sure to leave an extra sweater here in case I needed it. I shrugged it on and buttoned it up to my collarbones. It wasn't a perfect match with my olive green high-waisted pants, but it would do. No one would be looking at me at a Carina photoshoot anyway.

"Miss Edwards?" Victor's assistant peeked into my doorway. "The driver is ready for you."

I nodded and grabbed my purse.

The black Rolls Royce rolled up to my client's luxury apartment building and the driver, Albert, waited outside to open the car door. Having a driver was still something I was getting used to. Victor insisted on us using the driver to pick up our high-profile clients for media functions.

My palms were clammy despite the air conditioning blasting through the vents. This would be my first time going to a photoshoot with my own client.

Zoey Tejada signed on with Stratestar a few day ago after one of her Instagram posts went viral. She became the most requested model in LA with every top designer vying to book her. She was gorgeous, of course, with glowing tan skin, big green eyes, and curves that I certainly didn't have when I was only seventeen.

We'd only chatted on the phone, so seeing her in person, as she left her apartment, had me a bit speechless. She had an aura about her, something you couldn't put a finger on, but I could see why she was so sought after.

She hugged me as soon as she got in the car, and we chatted like old friends. She was nervous about her first real shoot too. By the time we reached the studio, which looked like a large warehouse from the outside, both of our nerves had calmed.

"I'm here to support you in any way you need," I reminded her. "Your agent may also stop by, so let us know if you need a break."

"I will," she said beaming. Her whole demeanor changed as we pulled up. She radiated confidence, and I channeled some of her energy as we walked inside.

We were immediately greeted by the stylist and her assistant who pulled Zoey away to hair and makeup leaving me alone to check out the space.

The studio was a large open room with gray walls. They'd put together a bedroom set in the middle of the space and more stylists were busy setting up finishing touches and adjusting lights.

I found a seat, away from the chaos, and pulled out my phone to text Coby.

Me: *Guess where I am?*

He answered right away.

Coby: *Starbucks?*

Me: *I don't think that would warrant a text. I'm there every day lol*

Coby: *That's why it was my first guess.*

Me: *You have a point.*

I snapped a picture of the studio and hit send.

Me: *I'm at my first photoshoot!*

Coby: *That's amazing! It looks huge in there.*

Me: *It is! Zoey is so sweet. This is her first professional shoot, so I came along to make sure everything runs smoothly.*

I saw someone walk by with a coffee cup and got up to find out if there was a craft service table, a perk of the job.

Coby: *I'm sure she's glad to have you there.*

In front of me was a whole spread of untouched pastries, fruit, expensive bottled waters, and carafes of coffee. I helped myself to a piping hot coffee and made my way back to the shoot area.

Me: *She's in hair and makeup now. Actually...I think she just came out. I'll let you know how it goes later.*

Me: *Kiss!*

I almost dropped my phone when I looked at the scene in front of me. Zoey was in barely-there lingerie and was being directed to sit in a provocative pose on the bed. I'm no prude and I'd never shame another woman for posing nearly nude or even fully nude, but Zoey was only seventeen. It gave me all sorts of icky feelings. In between shots, she waved at me with a sort of grimace on her face before being directed to bite her lip.

What the hell? I had no idea this was the type of shoot she'd been booked for. Did Victor know? I paced the edge of the space wondering if I should call him or Zoey's agent, Shelby, who hadn't arrived yet. Was it legal to shoot a seventeen-year-old in this manner?

They called for a break and gave Zoey a sheer robe. I pulled her aside.

"Are you doing okay?" I asked trying to keep my voice steady.

"I think so. I didn't realize the shoot was for lingerie, but Joseph and his team are making me as comfortable as possible."

I could see the worry in her eyes. She was so young and so new to the ways of the world. I hated that they were sexualizing her. I breathed deeply.

"Do you want me to call Shelby? See what kind of contract you have with them?"

Her eyes bounced between me and the set before she shook her head. "No, it's fine. This is the business I'm in. May as well get used to it."

They called her back to change and get touched up. While I had a moment I called Victor. His assistant had given me his personal cell number in case of an emergency, and to me, this warranted using it. I could see this as a PR nightmare; "Underage Girl Bares It All For Photoshoot." On top of that, I'd put my clients' needs and feelings first.

"Victor Moss," he answered in lieu of a greeting.

I cleared my throat. "Victor, it's Kendahl Edwards. I'm at the Carina photoshoot with Zoey—"

"I know where you are, and what you're doing," he cut in. "Is there a problem?"

I stammered at his abrupt tone. "Y-Yes, actually, I wanted to find out her contract details because this shoot could destroy her image, therefore, creating problems for us."

If I kept my thoughts strictly PR related, maybe he would soften and listen to me.

"In what way?"

"Nudity. I don't know if you're aware but she's underage," I added.

"I'm aware of every one of our client's personal information, Ms. Edwards. And frankly, I don't see an issue here. This is a problem for her agent, not us."

"But I—" He hung up on me.

Nobody had hung up on me since I was in high school. I ground my teeth together and paced. Another stylist led Zoey back onto set and every muscle in my body seized. They had her in a leather mini skirt and literal nipple tassels.

What. The. Fuck.

I rushed the set like a mama bear in protection mode.

"This is unacceptable." My hands flew out in front of me of their own accord. "What kind of shoot is this? She's underage!"

Zoey grabbed her robe and slid it on, and a frown lined her lips. Joseph stepped up to me so close that our bodies were almost touching.

"Who are you?" He gestured at one of his assistants. "I want this woman off my set."

He towered over me, but I was too enraged to care. "Apparently, I'm the only person here with a conscience. I'm taking my client home."

I turned to Zoey who looked like she was about to cry. "Come on, Zoey. Let's get you dressed and out of here."

"No." Zoey pulled me to the side. "Kendahl, I'm fine. I want to finish the shoot."

I searched her gaze. She looked conflicted. "Are you sure? You don't have to do this."

With a soft nod she said, "I'm sure. But maybe you should go." She turned to Joseph who was pacing in front of a light tower as he cursed under his breath. "It would be for the best."

I waited before nodding and turning to leave. I couldn't stay to witness this anyway. I reached the exit with my fists clenched at my side, but before I left, I turned one more time. They were positioning Zoey on the bed again. Before I changed my mind and went into a full rage, I forced myself out and to the car.

I had Albert drop me at my apartment. There was no way I could go back to the office in the state I was in. After shedding my work clothes and getting into leggings and a sports bra I googled Krav Maga gyms in my area. I needed to release my pent-up anger in a healthy way otherwise I'd find the nearest bar and down a bunch of drinks. That had always been my mother's stress reliever of choice, so I went for the opposite option.

I was in luck. Not only was there a gym, but it was only a fifteen-minute drive from my place. I called them to confirm my trial class, ordered an Uber, and before I knew it, I was enveloped by the familiar sounds of fists striking pads.

Mark and Dina's gym could have fit inside of Krav Maga LA three times. The amount of space was intimidating. Not one person greeted me or even looked my way, and I didn't know if

I should be happy about that because I wasn't in the mood for small talk or sad at how being here made me ache for my friends.

I found a place in the back of the room as the level one class started warming up with shadowboxing. With each stretch of muscle and small movement the peace I'd found when I first started Krav coursed through me.

The instructor was a guy so tall that I'd have to crane my neck back to look him in the eye. He called to a student in the front of the room to help him demo. I found myself searching for Coby in every man I saw even when I knew damn well he wasn't there.

My mind wandered back to the first time Coby partnered with me in class. We had only been talking for a few weeks and had been on a date or two. I liked him but could sense he wasn't ready for anything serious. Mark and Shawn had demonstrated how to do a roundhouse kick and made the move look effortless. For me, it was a nightmare. My hips wouldn't cooperate. At one point, I got so twisted up that I fell on my ass but instead of being embarrassed or resigned, I was pissed. I needed to perfect that kick. I was so focused on getting my starting form right that I didn't realize Coby was behind me until his hands were around my hips.

I whipped my head around, about to cuss someone out, when I was met by eyes the color of steel and a smile so perfect my breath caught in my throat. "Coby...you made me jump. I was about to cuss you out."

"Need some help?"

Mia was holding the pad for me and piped in. "She does." I did, but it would be weird for Coby to help me. I glared at Mia but she shrugged.

Coby's warm voice murmured directions into my ear as he adjusted my hips. With his chest pressed against my back, he guided me through the movement. The sound of his breathing being so close to my ear mixed with being held against his strong body had me feeling more at ease than I had since I started classes there. I remembered being turned on almost immediately, but I more so remembered the feeling of being safe and cared for, and that's what I was missing in LA.

I thought joining a new gym would help me feel better. I had released some of my adrenaline from my shitty day, but I ended up leaving there feeling more alone than I had in weeks. How could I ask Coby to leave Mark and Dina's gym for a place like this?

Chapter 40

Kendahl

WHEN I CAME INTO work the next day, word had gotten around about the photoshoot. Every person I passed made themselves look busy as I walked by. Ever since I'd started, I'd get bombarded with messages and phone calls from the moment I walked in, but not today.

I let myself get settled in, stowing my purse and jacket and checking for any important emails. One had come in from Victor's assistant early this morning.

To: KEdwards@Stratestar.com
From: LBarr@Stratestar.com
Date: Tuesday, Nov 15 at 7:02 AM
Subject: Meeting with Mr. Moss

Ms. Edwards,

I've scheduled you for a meeting in Mr. Moss's office for 4:00 pm. Any appointments on your schedule for today have been shifted to other representatives.

Best,

Lindsay Barr

Personal Assistant

Stratestar Agency

A meeting at the end of the day was never a good thing, and neither was moving my appointments to other representatives.

It would be fine. I had expected some backlash for how I reacted, so instead of letting my mind spiral out of control, I kept myself busy clearing my personal inbox and checking in with Coby.

Me: *Please tell me your day is going better than mine.*

I scrolled Instagram while waiting on him to respond. It looked like Lee was keeping up with the posting schedule for all our clients. *Their clients*, I corrected myself. The sweetest picture of a fluffy lab mix puppy curled up next to a black kitten caught my attention. The caption read: Spoiled to the Bone Grand Opening and Adoption Event. Come Meet Your New Best Friend!

My heart sank. That was *my* event. I'd started the preliminary planning before I moved. I pitched it that right before the holidays would be a great time to run it. Tears formed in the corner of my eyes even though I was so proud of Lee or whoever Claudia had hired to fill my position.

A text from Coby popped up.

Coby: *Three of my patients canceled because of the stomach flu that's going around. Sooo...I'm currently misting myself with rubbing alcohol.*

Why could I see him doing that? I wiped the moisture from my eyes. Everything in me wanted to tell him about the shoot yesterday. I wasn't sure what held me back.

Coby: *What's wrong and how can I make it better?*

Me: *Just work stuff. Nothing to worry about.*

Me: *I'll call you later.*

I set my phone on my desk and sat back in my chair. It vibrated, letting me know I had a new text. Picking it up and reading it would mean I'd end up starting a conversation with Coby that I wasn't ready for. Especially since he was already updating his resume looking for physical therapy practices nearby. Now wasn't the time to tell him how miserable I was at this place. I left my phone where it was deciding to figure everything out after the meeting.

With my stomach in knots, I knocked on Victor's frosted-glass door at exactly four. The sound of my fist against the thick material reverberated through my bones. His assistant opened the door with a grim look on her normally neutral face.

"Edwards, come have a seat," Victor called.

Of the three times I'd been inside his office, I'd always been equally intrigued and weirded out by the collection of items he kept on display. Each time, I discovered something new to focus on. The first time had been a sculpture of sorts on a pedestal in the corner. I was about to comment on how I also loved Oogie Boogie from *The Nightmare Before Christmas* but luckily, looked closer and realized it wasn't Oogie Boogie but a human-looking face on a large sack-like body. I shivered and kept my mouth shut. The second time, I'd realized the pattern on his lamp shade was eyes of varying colors. It gave me the creeps.

Today, when I very much needed to focus on what he was saying to me, my eyes fixed on a painting I hadn't noticed before. How I hadn't noticed it was beyond me because this piece of art depicted multiple human-like figures engaging in various sexual acts. It was oddly horrifying and mesmerizing.

"I'm not happy." Victor steepled his fingers and brought them in front of his face. "I'm sure you've surmised that though."

I pulled my gaze away from the creepy painting. "Yes."

"After your little outburst, I had to deal with a pissed off photographer and agent yesterday. We almost lost our hottest client because of you." His voice was cold as he enunciated every syllable.

Heat crept up my chest to my face. I steeled myself, formulating my response.

"There is one thing every single person who represents this agency needs to remember. But maybe I didn't make it clear to you." He leaned forward placing each forearm onto his expensive wooden desk. "My word is law."

My eyes tried to wander away from his cold glare, but I forced them to keep contact. This was something I wouldn't back down from. Willing air into my lungs, I began to speak, but before I could get a word out, he cut me off by standing and walking to his office door. He opened it and gestured for me to leave. My tongue was heavy with what I wanted to say. I swallowed hard and went to the door.

"You'll be on errand duty for the rest of the week. That should teach you a lesson. Remember, Kendahl, you may think you're something special because of your little five minutes of fame, but deliberately disobey me again and you won't be able to work PR for a lemonade stand." He spoke with such severity that I stepped out of his office without a word, grabbed my belongings, and hurried directly to my car.

I drove around for an hour letting Victor's words replay in my mind over and over again. Instead of seeing the glitz and glam of what I wanted Hollywood to be, darkness came through. Graffiti covered overpasses, stand still traffic, and barricaded alleyways stood out among the palm lined streets. Every turn led to another street that looked the same as the one before it, too large yet too suffocating. I wanted to breathe and to see something real. I pulled off the road and parked alongside a few tourist shops, resting my face against the steering wheel.

The reality of what he said hit me at once. He'd known about my video, probably for the whole time. Years of talent, hard work, strong morals, and building relationships with my clients may have had no bearing on him hiring me. My face stung like I'd been slapped. Being condescended to the way I was and then relegated to a gopher was worse than a physical slap to the face.

Going back to my apartment didn't even offer the comfort I needed. The furniture was not mine, and I was only able to bring what personal items I could pack into my suitcase on the plane. The service that delivered my car to me wouldn't let me pack anything in it due to liability issues. The place felt cold and empty like a ghost town.

I longed for my worn in zebra striped duvet I'd had since college and my old bathroom door that never fully shut because the hinges were rusty. I missed staring out my big front window watching gray clouds roll in as afternoon thunderstorms ripped through town. I missed the smell of orange blossoms that permeated the walls each spring. Hell, I even missed cranky Mr. Fry banging on his ceiling with his broom handle whenever I'd walk around with my heels on.

I crawled into my cold bed and pulled the scratchy white duvet up to my neck. Admitting defeat and crawling back home would be like forcing myself into clothes that were too small. How could I admit that I'd failed or that I wasn't good enough to make it in a city like Hollywood. My phone rang from my purse by the door where I'd dropped it, and I made no move to get it. What was I going to do?

I pried my eyes open and rubbed dried mascara from my lids. Judging by the pitch blackness of my apartment, I'd fallen asleep. It could have been any time from nine o'clock at night to three o'clock in the morning with how groggy I was. Sitting up, the reality of the day hit me again, and I fought the urge to let my bed swallow me into the bliss of sleep, but my bladder needed emptying and my bra was digging into my armpit.

I dragged myself to take care of business and grabbed my phone from my bag once I was ready to get back into bed. I hadn't responded to Coby all day and had missed my daily check in with my mother. The glow of the screen lit up the darkened room, and I squinted until my eyes adjusted to the light. It was just past eleven, which meant I'd slept for at least three hours. There were two missed calls from Coby and one from my mother. It was too late there to call, so I opened my texts instead and noticed an unread message that Coby had sent in between his calls.

Coby: *My mama took a fall at assisted living. Have to go out to Salt Lake City. Will update you when I get a chance. Love you.*

I sat upright, twisting at a strand of hair.

Me: *I'm so sorry! Do you know anything yet? What can I do to help?*

My stomach churned knowing what he'd just gone through with his father passing and how he was already worried about his mom. I had to be there for him.

Without thinking about any repercussions, I pulled up the airline app on my phone and booked the next flight into Salt Lake City as I said a silent prayer for Coby's mom to pull through this.

Ten hours, two coffees, and a lot of phone calls later I rushed through the hospital doors and followed signs on the second floor toward Mrs. Barnes's room. I had no idea what I'd be walking in to. I knocked lightly with trembling hands and bleary eyes before cracking the door and peeking inside.

Mrs. Barnes lay in the bed, her eyes closed and bony arms at her side. Various tubes and wires connected her to IVs and monitoring machines. The hospital bed swallowed her frail frame. Coby sat on a chair in the back of the room with his head against the wall and his eyes scrunched closed. His chest rose and fell in soft waves and I took him in. Tears welled in my eyes. God, I missed him. I closed the door behind me and the small click caused Coby's eyes to jerk open. My heart cracked at seeing them red rimmed and lined with shadows.

"Baby, you came."

"Of course I did."

I wiped my eyes and buried myself in his chest. He rested his head against my hair and wrapped his arms around me. We stayed quietly soaking up the comfort from each other.

"Let's go out in the hall," he said against my ear.

After checking that his mom was still sleeping soundly, we slipped into the brightly lit hallway. He reached out to cup my chin and our eyes met. I saw how exhausted he looked. I brushed my lips over his and rubbed my cheek against the soft stubble of his beard.

"You don't know how much I've missed these lips," he said.

"I think I do," I said, leaning my face against his. "How is she?"

He stroked his beard. "It's still iffy. She hit her head pretty bad when she fell, so they're worried about a brain bleed. No breaks or fractures thankfully. She seems pretty out of it, doesn't remember slipping."

"Shit. I'm sorry. So what's the plan?" I swallowed down the lump in my throat, taking in his pained expression.

"They did most of the tests last night and started her on some meds. The hope is that she'll be able to avoid surgery." He let loose a long sigh. "I'm hoping for an update from the doctors after lunch."

I wrapped my arms around him. "It'll be okay. You're taking care of her."

"She has to be okay. After everything she went through with him," he hesitated, swallowing hard. "She's only just begun to live again."

"She's a fighter, I can tell." Rubbing circles over his back, I got on my tiptoes and kissed his chin. "Just like you."

He took my face in his hands again and planted a gentle kiss on my lips. Breathing deeply, he pulled back to study my features. "Babe, your job? How are you here?"

I leaned against the wall and stared at the scuffed white floor. Anything to keep him from seeing the hurt in my eyes. He didn't need to hear about my issues with work, not while his mother was lying in a hospital bed.

"It's fine. Victor approved me taking off." As the lie left my lips, my stomach twisted. Slowly, I lifted my eyes to meet his and willed myself to keep my emotions in check.

Do not cry.

It was no use. He didn't have to say a word, his face did the talking for him. His brows lifted and his eyes blazed as he stared right through me. A tear rolled down my cheek, then another, and before I knew it, a heaving sob expelled from deep inside me.

"Come here," he pulled me into his chest and held me until the sobs subsided. "Let's go find a place to talk."

We found a small seating area where he made me a cup of coffee from the Keurig in the corner before he sat next to me, close enough that we touched. I needed that contact more than he knew.

"I knew something was wrong. You've been distant since the other day. You know you can tell me anything, right?" The little space between his brows creased, and I hated that I was adding more stress to his already full plate. But he was right, I couldn't keep this from him. Especially when I was pretty sure I was unemployed now.

"I know. I should have told you right away. I needed time to process, time to figure out what I wanted. And you've been busy looking into moving, I didn't want to bother you." I swallowed a sip of coffee and winced.

"Sorry. There was only that powdered creamer." A genuine smile lifted his lips, the first one I'd seen all day.

"It's fine." I sipped again but let most of it dribble back into the cup. He took it from my hands and tried it.

"That's awful, and you're a terrible liar." Laughing, he tossed the cup in the nearest trash and came to sit beside me. "Okay, no more distracting coffee. What happened?"

Everything that happened at Zoey's photoshoot, how Victor handled it, and the way I'd been feeling about living in LA came pouring out of me like a flood. The more I spoke the firmer my resolve became. I needed out. Palm Cove was my home. His features changed between anger and concern, but he never interrupted just listened until I sat back utterly spent.

"I'm proud of you. You're so fucking strong baby. Never back down from your values." His palm encircled mine, and he squeezed reassuringly. "I'll support whatever decision you make."

"Thank you. I—"

"There you fucking are. I've been looking for you for ten minutes now."

A man, a bit shorter and thinner than Coby but with the same dark hair and gray eyes stomped into the seating area. He wore dirty coveralls and a thermal shirt. His hair was long in the back and had the same wave that Coby's hair had on top. He crossed his arms in front of his chest and leaned against the wall. Coby froze as stiff as a statue.

"My big brother being all cozy with a woman while our mama lies half dead. It's just like you to chase tail instead of taking care of your own."

Damn.

This was Coby's brother.

Chapter 41

Coby

"CLYDE," I SAID THROUGH gritted teeth. "You didn't tell me you were going to show up."

I glanced at Kendahl who was looking between the two of us, her eyes wide.

"Course I came. Daisy called me up as soon as she hung up with you. Interesting that you'd call my wife and not your own brother. Maybe you're too famous to care about anyone in Verdant. Got yourself a sweet piece of ass and fancy interviews and suddenly, you're too good to call your family." It took every ounce of restraint I had to not wring his neck right there in front of the coffee machine and packets of sugar.

"Don't you fucking talk about her like that." I stepped to him so we were inches apart. "You have no clue what you're talking about."

"Really? You've always been too good for us ever since you up and left for your fancy school and your first bitch. Where is she now? Left your ass, didn't she?"

"I'll go check on your mom," Kendahl said as she came up beside me.

I nodded too pissed to say anything. As soon as she was out of view, anger poured out of me. "You have no right to talk about my life. You're acting all high and mighty like you were the good son who took care of mama. You're a joke. Nothing but a piece of shit drunk who beats on his wife. The whole month I was there all you did was show up wasted and pass out. Thank God I moved mama out of there."

Clyde's nostrils flared and he snarled, "At least I know how to keep my woman in line." He glanced in the direction that Kendahl went. "You should take a lesson from me before that one finds another dick to ride like the last one did."

I bared my teeth, my breaths coming out in puffs. I knew what he wanted. He was waiting for me to throw the first punch, so he could claim I attacked him. Coward. I stepped back, clenching my fists so hard my nails dug into my skin.

"We're not family, you understand? The same blood may run through our veins, but that doesn't mean shit to me. I want nothing to do with you or Verdant, and mama doesn't need you here either."

"I'll let mama decide that for herself. I'm not the one who shoved her in some home so I could feel better about myself." Flecks of spittle left his mouth, and my stomach churned. I fisted my hand through my hair. I was done. Nothing good would come from arguing with him here while mama's life hung in the balance.

Kendahl was probably booking the next flight out of here, far away from this shit show.

"Whatever you say, Clyde. I'm done listening to you." I pushed my anger down deep and left him red-faced and cursing under his breath.

Through the small glass window on mama's door, I could see Kendahl sitting close to her. Kendahl's lips were moving, but being on the other side, I couldn't hear her words. The sight calmed my breathing.

She hadn't left. Not yet at least.

My chest tightened as she looked up at me with her ocean eyes and offered a tentative smile. I made my way to her side.

"She opened her eyes before and was talking to me," Kendahl said.

Thank God. I released a breath. Kendahl wrapped her small hand around mine and squeezed.

"Son, is that you?" My mama's voice came out in a whisper, and she began to stir.

"I'll go to the nurses' station. I'm sure they'll want to know," Kendahl said.

"Thank you."

Her lips brushed over my cheek so fucking sweetly that I nearly cried.

"Mama, it's Coby. I'm right here." I cupped her cheek and she rested her face against my hand. "You took a fall and scared the heck out of everyone. Are you in any pain?"

She shook her head gently. "Just a headache is all." Blinking awake, her hazel eyes met mine. They looked browner in the dim light. "She's lovely. Is this the one you told me about?"

"Kendahl," I said through the lump in my throat.

"Beautiful. She loves you. I can tell. I'm glad you took my advice." Her fragile hand reached out and held mine. "Do you love her?"

"Mama, we can talk about it later. Let's get you better."

Her eyes blazed, and for a moment, I saw a spark of who she used to be before my father beat her down. She raised a brow, challenging me.

"Yes. I love her very much."

"Then don't let her go," she said.

Clyde ruined our moment a few minutes later by barreling into the room and getting combative with the doctor. Mama's test results were in. She would be okay. They didn't see any brain bleeds just a slight concussion and some bruising on her knees. They'd keep her another day for observation and then she'd be free to go back to her place.

The doctor had barely left the room before Clyde said, "Mama, I think you should come home with me. Daisy can take care of you, and you'll have the whole town behind you." He glared at me with his arms crossed.

"The town that turned a blind eye to your father's problem, you mean?" She spoke with such clarity that I was taken aback. "No. I'll be going back to my new home. Your brother will see to it."

"Of course," I said. Kendahl smiled up at me with pride in her eyes.

"You should go home, Clyde," Mama said.

"You sure he'll have time for you? Looks like he's too busy with his new whore," Clyde spit.

My mother gasped.

"Don't speak about me or Coby that way. I think you need to leave. Now. Before I really get mad." Kendahl said as she stood up and stared daggers at my brother.

"Why should I listen to you? You're nothing but a little—"

In a split second Kendahl slammed Clyde in the balls so hard that he slid to the floor moaning like a wounded animal.

"Listen to your mother. Get out or I'll call security." She came to my side and squeezed my hand.

Clyde looked up with his eyes narrowed and slowly got to his feet. He looked from my mama and back to me.

"Fine. Don't ask me for shit. I'm done with you all."

He left, still doubled over.

"What a dick," Kendahl sighed. "Sorry for my language, Mrs. Barnes."

"It's fine, sadly he became just like his father." Her head drooped. "Maybe he'll come around one day. I only hope him and Daisy don't have children though, no child needs to go through what my boys went through."

"Rest, mama. You're taken care of and safe," I said as I adjusted her blanket.

"Thank you. You're a good boy." Her eyes closed and her lips tipped up in a serene smile. "No wonder why she loves you so much."

With Kendahl against my shoulder, solid and unwavering, it finally felt real. She loved me even after seeing where I came from and who I'm related to. I cupped her face wanting so badly to lift her in my arms and take her somewhere, anywhere we could be alone.

"Have I told you how incredible you are? Because if I did, it hasn't been enough. I love you so much, baby," I said.

"I did just knock a grown man to the ground. I am kind of incredible, aren't I?" she whispered, nuzzling my ear. "I love you too. And I'm coming home."

"Home? You mean back to Palm Cove?" My heart pounded.

"Back to Palm Cove."

"I don't understand how it's possible to have as many shoes as you have." I hauled another bin full of shoes into my bedroom closet. I should say *our* bedroom closet. With how quickly Kendahl wanted out of LA, there wasn't much time for her to find a place, which gave me the perfect opening to ask her to move in with me.

She had stubbornly argued that it was too soon, and she didn't want to invade my personal space. But I made it clear that I wanted her in every inch of my space, every single day. I should have considered the amount of stuff she'd be bringing in from her storage unit. The closet space I had very much thought would be enough was apparently not.

"Shoes are life's greatest gifts, and I will not apologize for my collection. They're my children," she said as she stacked pair after pair on any available shelf space. Her bending over each time she grabbed a new pair made me salivate. It should be illegal for her to wear those leggings with that ass.

"Greatest gifts? I thought I was life's greatest gift." I slid in behind her to wrap my arms around her. She turned to face me, lifting up on her tiptoes.

"I should be nice to you considering I'm taking 90 percent of your closet space," she said. "But you're sorely mistaken. The order of gifts is shoes, Riesling, all cheeses, chocolate, Disney movies or wait maybe horror movies I can't choose," she stopped and chewed her bottom lip before adding, "then you." With a peck to my cheek and a flip of her ponytail, she got back to unpacking.

I had other plans.

"I bet I can make you change your mind," I murmured low into her ear.

Without waiting for her to respond, I caged her against the wall of shelves with my arms from behind.

"Doubtful," she quipped, but I could read the change in her voice. I could read every one of her tiny responses. The husky undertone, the way her chest rose and fell, and the way her thighs pressed together. I nipped her earlobe, then bit my way down the side of her neck. She pushed her ass against me. I was already hard, but the friction with her thin leggings had me throbbing.

"I think you want this cock." I paid extra attention to her earlobe while I brought my hand up to cup her throat gently. The hottest little moan slid out of her. "Don't you?"

She squirmed against my grasp while whimpering needy moans. I yanked her leggings down with one hand, running my palm up her soft inner thigh and stopping right alongside her wet pussy.

"Fuck, baby, you weren't wearing any panties in these things?"

"No, they look better without them."

I slid a finger up into her seam. "If I had it my way, you'd never wear panties again."

"Mmm," she moaned.

With my palm, I pressed her low back, bending her against the shelves. Her ass was on display for me, and her drenched pussy was waiting to get fucked. I circled her clit finding the rhythm she loved.

"But then I'd have to kill every man who stared at your sweet ass, and I don't think you'd like that, would you?"

Her legs trembled, and I used my other arm to hold her hips up while she grabbed on to the shelf for support.

"Yes," she said in a breathy moan.

Need filled every part of my being, a need to feel her coming around my palm, a need to be so deep inside her, and a need to brand her with my cum.

I circled her clit faster. She was so close. I could feel her pussy starting to pulse. I let go of her hips and yanked my gym shorts down, desperate to be inside her.

"Come for me, Kendahl." I slammed my cock inside her, sliding all the way in, then spanked her perfect round cheek.

"God, Coby."

She tightened around me, riding out her release. I soothed her cheek with my palm while pulling almost all the way out of her and thrusting back in.

"Fuck... So good," I groaned.

I spread her cheeks to watch my cock spear into her gorgeous pussy. Shoes fell from the shelves, and her head thumped into the wall, but we didn't give a shit.

"Yes," she groaned. "Harder." She changed her angle and pushed her ass into me. I gave her what she wanted, what I needed. Sweat beaded on my forehead as our skin slapped together with each thrust. Everything about her was intoxicating. Her neck arched, and I watched her bite down on her lip as her eyes opened, peering straight into my soul.

With her eyes on me, my muscles tightened and my cock swelled. "I'm going to paint you in my cum, baby." I pushed into her one more time and pulled out slowly as my cock spasmed and cum spurted all over her sweet ass.

"Fuck," I groaned. "You're incredible."

We panted, trying to catch our breaths. I grabbed my shorts from the floor and used them to wipe her down.

"You're not so bad yourself," she said, laughing.

"Are you saying I secured your spot as the greatest gift to humankind?" I pulled her to me, kissing her sweet lips and breathing in her scent.

"Hmm..." She made a show of scratching her head. "I don't know."

"Do you need another spanking?" I teased and swatted her bare ass.

"I think I might."

I picked her up and hauled her over my shoulder while she squealed and tried to reach down to pinch my ass. Plopping her on our bed, I growled, "You're in for it now."

Epilogue

Kendahl

NEARLY EVERY OUTFIT I owned was scattered across our bed by the time I finished packing my suitcase. I'd made sure to include the ugly Christmas sweaters I got for us even though Coby tried to hide his in the back of his dresser. Nothing said Christmas like a flashy sweater that read Jingle My Bells adorned with actual bells. So what if there also happened to be an image of a naked man? At least his bits were covered by said bells.

I'd wear my sweater proudly. Mine, however, was covered in fuzzy kitties wearing Santa hats. Honestly, I wish mine had some bells on it too or at least a kitty pun filled with innuendo. But I'd settled for being adorably G rated.

"Babe, did you get the rest of Grogu's stuff together?" I yelled loud enough to reach Coby in the living room.

His aggravated plodding started toward me while I held in a giggle because I knew exactly what he was about to say.

"Why did we adopt that creature again? And why the hell does a cat need a whole suitcase of stuff to go to a pet sitter's house?"

He leaned against the doorframe with his arms crossed. The sleeves of his shirt were rolled up just enough to get me distracted by the muscle of his forearm flexing. Before I could get any ideas, the "creature" in question ran sideways through the hallway making a sound I'd come to call his cat bark. He stopped right in front of our doorframe to rub against Coby's leg.

"Every time he makes that sound, I swear he's summoning an army of beasts from whatever circle of hell he came from." Coby bent down and scooped the scraggly little guy into his arms and plopped him on the bed. Grogu arched his back and his gray striped fur poofed out before he trotted back to Coby's feet.

"Look how much he loves you. You may be a grump, but I saw you go out of your way to put him in your lap last night," I teased.

"You saw no such thing."

"Make sure you pack his special mouse toy. And his bag of treats. I don't know if Lee has any at their place. I'm almost done here." I zipped up my luggage and headed into our bathroom to grab the last of my toiletries.

We were going to spend Christmas at the Marin Inn. It was Coby's idea. I made sure to check the weather forecast thoroughly before he booked the room. We didn't need a repeat of our first visit. We even convinced Mia and Shawn to join us. I never thought those two homebodies would want to travel for the holiday but maybe they wanted to enjoy the island this time.

I'd miss my fuzzy little gremlin cat though. When I moved back to Palm Cove, I had asked Claudia if I could help at the adoption event. It was coming up the following week and my heart was breaking to not be a part of it. She did me one better and offered me a promotion at the office. I was now a partner with equal pay and responsibilities as her. It took every effort in my body not to break down and cry when she made me the offer. I was filled with so much joy to be back.

Grogu was the last cat standing at the end of the day. When he was brought into the shelter as a stray, he'd had such a bad infection in one of his eyes that they couldn't save it. But his floppy gray ears stood out to me more than his one eye. They were the largest, pointiest ears I'd ever seen on a cat. He had patches of missing fur from his time on the streets and needed some TLC badly.

I'd had my eye on him the whole day, watching person after person pass him by. As we were packing up, I picked him up and brought him to Coby who was busy loading folding tables into the back of a van. Grogu immediately chirped when he saw Coby and purred so loud with the crackliest purr I'd ever heard.

Needless to say, we brought him home and the little guy had come out of his shell. He especially loved to knock Coby's stuff off his side table, chew up charging cables, and scatter his kibble all over the floor. Coby wasn't amused, but I loved to watch his heart grow for the little guy.

The setting sun reflected shades of burnt orange and deep purple onto the rippling waves as we drove along town toward the inn. I rolled down the windows and pulled briny ocean air deep into my lungs, listening to the caw of seabirds. I looked over at Coby. He'd been uncharacteristically quiet the whole car ride. He'd kept a hand on my thigh the entire time, rubbing circles and nodding along to the holiday station on the radio. It was nice that we could be so comfortable enjoying each other's company without constant conversation.

We passed beautifully decorated storefronts and a huge tree on Main Street where families stopped to snap photos. The inn was all decked out in white lights and faux pine. It felt surreal. Like we'd been there years ago instead of only four months ago. So much had changed since that first night there.

Ginger greeted us with a hug and a freshly baked cookie.

"Did we die and come back as characters in a Hallmark movie?" I whispered in Coby's ear.

He kissed my cheek and rubbed his beard against me. Nope, this was real life.

I found Mia and Shawn sitting by the lit fireplace sipping something out of mugs and ran to my best friend. We'd both had such busy weeks leading up to the trip that we hadn't seen each other in too long.

"Ken Dolly, you're here!" she squeezed me tight. "I didn't think this place could get any cuter but Ginger outdid herself." She pointed to a large tree set up in the corner, and I laughed.

"How'd I know she'd go nautical with the Christmas décor too."

"Right? After seeing those bins of decorations last time, I'd say this was the way to go. I love the conch shell ornaments, so original," Mia said.

I spotted Coby and Shawn chatting quietly a few feet away and grinned. Seeing their friendship grow was so sweet.

"I think they missed each other," I said to Mia, nudging her to peek over at them.

"Aww, give them a day or two and I bet they'll find somewhere to spar though. I'd put money on it." She pulled me by the arm to show me some other changes Ginger had made to the lobby since our last visit.

"How's Alex doing? I haven't talked to Olivia in a few weeks." I picked up a pine scented candle and brought it to my nose.

"He's okay, recovering well and ready to be running around again. I offered to stay for the holiday and help her out, but she insisted she had everything under control." Mia raised a brow. "Something's fishy with her. Between you and me, I think it has to do with a guy, but her lips have been sealed."

"Interesting," I said. "Best friend detective work when we get back?"

"You read my mind," Mia laughed.

After unpacking in our urchin room and reacquainting our-selves with the bed and shower, we got ready to meet Mia and Shawn next door for dinner. Coby had been insatiable from the moment we stepped foot into the room, fucking me like it was the first time he'd felt my body.

I was starving from our marathon. My mouth watered think-ing about all the delicious options on the menu that I'd been dying to try.

Coby and I walked hand in hand to the restaurant while the cool breeze tickled my skin. His warm presence filled me with a sense of calm and joy that I didn't know was possible. How had I gotten so lucky?

He tilted his head toward mine and a small smile played on his lips. Opening the familiar door to the restaurant he asked, "You ready?"

"Of course, I'm starving," I answered, confused.

"After you," he held the door and followed me inside with a palm on my low back.

"W-What..." I stuttered. "Babe, what's going on?"

The tables were all pushed to the side with the exception of one right in front of the stage area. White twinkle lights were the only light in the space, casting a glow. Mia and Shawn were nowhere to be seen. In fact, the whole place was eerily quiet. I looked up at Coby, a silent question in my eyes.

"Come sit down," he said, guiding me to one of the chairs and pulling it out for me. He took a deep breath in through his nose and adjusted the neckline of his shirt. Butterflies flapped against the walls of my stomach and the sensitive skin on my arms prickled with goosebumps.

He hopped up onto the stage and nodded. Then it started "Dreams" my song. The opening beat I'd know anywhere played from a speaker somewhere in the room.

Tears welled in my eyes. Coby smiled. A sweet lopsided smile that made his dimples pop, and I thought my heart might burst through my chest. He began to sing, no microphone and no fanfare like last time. Just him and I and this song that's grown to mean so much more than what it did during my childhood.

He reached the chorus and crooked his finger for me to join him. On shaky legs, I stood up, kicked off my heels, and climbed the step to him. Up close I could see the blush of his cheeks and a glint in his steel eyes. He gathered me into his arms with the most intense look on his face.

The music changed to another upbeat song, but the volume lowered.

"Coby?" I asked, biting my lip.

I knew this song. Oh my God.

"Marry You" by Bruno Mars. Tears streamed down my face as Coby crouched down on one knee.

"Kendahl Elizabeth Edwards," his voice shook. "I knew from the first moment I saw you that you were special. You were the most gorgeous woman I'd ever seen. Then I got to know you, your beautiful heart, your quirks, and even your stubborn side...I never stood a chance. You've had my heart from day one.

It took me pulling my head out of my ass to see that. I'd fight the world for you, burn down cities if you asked me."

I trembled all over, trying to keep it together, to take his words in and hold them against my heart.

"I want to spend forever with you if you'll have me." He reached into his back pocket and pulled out a ring. "Marry me, baby? Be my wife?"

I collapsed to my knees and he gathered me in his arms. "Yes," I breathed. "I love you so much."

"Fuck," he stammered and released a deep breath. "Come here."

He slid the ring on my finger, a gorgeous band unlike anything I'd ever seen. White gold with clusters of different colored blue stones framing a diamond so sparkly it shimmered in the dim lighting.

Our mouths collided, tongues tangled and tears streamed down both of our faces.

Suddenly, the lights came on and people were around us clapping and hollering congratulations. I pulled back and looked around the room at everyone I loved. Not only had he invited Mia and Shawn, but my mother was there, with Richard, Mike and Jill, Mark and Dina, Avery and Bethany, and even Claudia. Champagne bottles popped all around us and everyone pulled us in for hugs.

We ate and drank until the early morning hours, singing songs at the top of our lungs and dancing barefoot on the stage.

My mother pulled me aside. "If this is the engagement, I can only imagine how the wedding will be," she cackled, her face glowing with happiness. She kissed my cheek. "I'm proud of you, Doll."

Coby joined us, a smile spread wide across his face. "What are the two most beautiful women in the room talking about?"

"Uh oh, Doll. You better watch out with this one." She smooched his cheek and gave it a quick pinch. "I'll leave you two lovebirds to enjoy the rest of your night." Waggling her brows, she added, "If you know what I mean."

"Mom...seriously?" I laughed. She walked back to Richard where he sat waiting with eyes only for her. They waved to us and headed for the inn.

"I think your mom has a point. We should go enjoy the rest of the night." He checked his watch. "There's about three hours until dawn, and I have an idea on how we can spend them."

Wrapping my arms around his neck, I brushed my lips against his. "Okay, but should we set some ground rules first? I mean I am your fiancée now, things might get weird."

He chuckled, low and husky. "What did I say a few months ago? Rules were meant to be broken." He scooped me into his arms and carried me out into the breezy December night.

Acknowledgements

Where do I begin? Fight For Her has been a blast to write but it wouldn't have been possible without the support of so many amazing people.

To my readers, my lovebugs, I appreciate you all so much! Without you, my dream of being an author would still be out of reach. Every post you share or kind word you send my way fuels this passion of mine. I'm eternally grateful.

To Bobby, you've been my biggest cheerleader and supporter, pushing me to keep going even when things get hard. I love you so much and appreciate everything you do for our family.

To my Earpers, from the very first idea until the last typed word, you've been there supporting me and cheering me on. So much of what I write comes from our friendships and all the amazing times we've had. Love you ladies more than words can say!

Leah, Crosby, and Branden, you've come into my life when it was pure chaos and helped me feel like a real author. You've supported me so much during the creation of this book and I honestly don't know how I would have done it without you. Hugs!

Brittany, I'm leaning as I write this. Thank you again for being the best editor in the world. I'm so grateful for the relationship we've formed this year! Enni, thank you for another beautiful cover. You're the best!

Skyler, Lucas, Riley and Robbie- you've embraced this new norm in the rhythm and flow of our daily life better than most grown adults would. Thank you for being the reason I chase my dreams. I love you.

About Author

Lauren lives in Phoenix, Arizona with her full chaotic family. When she's not crafting her next happily ever after, you can find her playing taxi to her teenagers, being pulled by her two large dogs, and when she's lucky reading with a cup of coffee.

Also by Lauren

Fight For It-Palm Cove Book 1

instagram.com/laurengreenebooks

Made in the USA
Middletown, DE
28 October 2023

41451211R10231